Alessandra —

Thanks for your help and assistance with the "Factory Tour"

Ferrari have the nicest people — "fortunate to have you"

Welcome to my Millcreek — "enjoy"

James

James Zardo

Review jameszardo@gmail.com

Meet Me At Millcreek

James H. Zardo

Noble House
Baltimore, Maryland

Meet Me At Millcreek

Copyright © 2003 James H. Zardo

All rights reserved under International and Pan-American copyright conventions. No part of this book may be reproduced, stored in a retrieval system, or transmitted in any form, electronic, mechanical, or other means, now known or hereafter invented, without written permission of the publisher. Address all inquiries to the publisher.

Library of Congress
Cataloging-in-Publication Data
ISBN 1-56167-778-7

Library of Congress Card Catalog Number:
2002094843

Published by

8019 Belair Road, Suite 10
Baltimore, Maryland 21236

Manufactured in the United States of America

ACKNOWLEDGEMENTS

To my most loving, beautiful, and fictitious Laura, whose image put the thoughts of love in this novel. When I think of her, I think of her with a smile, for all the loving memories she left with me. Perhaps one day, maybe in another world, our paths will cross again, and she will Meet Me At Millcreek.

To the kids—

Don't be shocked. Always remember—the most interesting and exciting entities about me are the entities you don't know. Now, you know a little more.

To my wife Shirley—
"Eccentricity" comes with the territory.

To Deanna and Rob—
For the knowledge of "THE COMPUTER" and for printing my manuscript.

To Gail Smiler from Fitzroy Crossing "down under"—
GREAT input for translation—English and Urnintum (Aborigine).

To Ivana . . . "That's for sure."

The love that is displayed in this novel has been bottled up in me for years. If you have it, or find it, don't abuse it. Being with the people you love is the most gratifying, sacred, and closeness of love that you will ever reach on this planet. . .
I wrote it... my way

James

Contents

chapter I 1
chapter II 7
chapter III 13
chapter IV 24
chapter V 30
chapter VI 34
chapter VII 38
chapter VIII 42
chapter IX 48
chapter X 56
chapter XI 61
chapter XII 68
chapter XIII 76
chapter XIV 84
chapter XV 88
chapter XVI 96
chapter XVII 100
chapter XVIII 109
chapter XIX 120
chapter XX 128
chapter XXI 133
chapter XXII 142
chapter XXIII 146
chapter XXIV 151
chapter XXV 157
chapter XXVI 164
chapter XXVII 178
chapter XXVIII 182
chapter XXIX 190
chapter XXX 193
chapter XXXI 199

chapter XXXII 205
chapter XXXIII 210
chapter XXXIV 212
chapter XXXV 223
chapter XXXVI 243
chapter XXXVII 246
chapter XXXVIII 252
chapter XXXIX 257
chapter XL 263

Before me a mill on a river I see, in the long ago when my true love and me, in tenderness plighted our troth with good will, no listener to hear save the old Humber Mill.

Now sightless it stands, its life has departed, my love too, has gone, I'm left broken hearted, and roofless, but grand, yet dear to me still, even in its decay that old Humber Mill.

Year after year as the summer wheels round, love's pledges are made on that old lover's ground, the secrets it holds, how much could they fill, but never betrayed by that old Humber Mill.

And methinks when at length I meet her above, we oft will return to renew our old love, freed from sorrow and death and all other ill, by that time hallowed spot, the old Humber Mill.

—John Campbell "1909"

chapter 1

**FORT WAYNE, INDIANA
TUESDAY, NOVEMBER 14, 1995
10:00 A.M.**

The forecast called for snow flurries and the temperature was dropping to thirty-four degrees. The cold November winds were sweeping down from Lake Michigan. This was a good enough reason to leave Indiana for a warmer climate. It wasn't his reason for boarding an American Airline Boeing 757 at Smith's Airport in Fort Wayne, destined for Oakland, California.

Alone in his first class seat, staring unseeingly out the aircraft window, he wondered why for the second time in less than three years something so beautiful had been torn from him without rhyme or reason. He found himself again seeking shelter.

Philip Joseph Mariano was the son of an Italian immigrant. His late father came to America from a small provincial town in Northern Italy just before the Depression, and settled in Valleyfield, Indiana, thirty miles southwest of Fort Wayne.

Philip had light brown hair and soft blue eyes that reflected kindness and intelligence. He had an honest face, but was a very masculine, complex man who always had control of his emotions.

He kept his fifty-two year old, five foot eleven frame in good condition. He was a self made millionaire, owner and president of Stefaniacs, one of the largest import/export companies in America.

A few weeks ago they were passionately in love, and then,

because of an ugly rumor, she sent him away. "I've gone through all the emotions of losing her; what do I do now?" he thought.

His mind then wandered back to that unforgettable day in October 1993 at the Valley Hospital where his wife, Sarah, was terminally ill with cancer.

Philip had parked his car in the hospital parking lot. Walking to the entrance, he noticed the emergency helicopter resting on the landing pad. It had just brought in someone who had been seriously injured in a car accident on one of the main highways. Michael and Carol, their son and daughter, were in the lobby waiting for their father to arrive. When they saw him, they greeted him, and then they embraced.

Michael, the eldest, was twenty-seven. He worked with his father and was married to Diana. His sister, Carol, was twenty-five. She had fair hair and blue eyes like her father, but had the beauty and grace of her mother. Carol was married to Jack Dawson who also worked with Philip.

They proceeded to the elevator that took them to the third floor. At the nurse's station they were told that Sarah was now in room number 303. When they entered the room, Doctor Graham West, the hospital's chief surgeon, and also chief of staff, and Philip's closest friend, was there to meet them.

He had called Philip earlier to let him know that Sarah's condition had worsened although Philip had only left three hours earlier spending the night at her bedside.

"Tell me, Gray," Philip asked, "what's her condition? What do we do now?"

Gray took a deep breath, put his hand on his friend's shoulder and said, "The time is near. She's in a coma, could be anytime, her pulse is slow; she has no pain."

"Oh my God," was Philip's reply. "She seemed so well up until yesterday. We talked and she seemed to be in such good spirits."

"I know," Gray replied, "She was well sedated. That's how it is with this damn disease, one day you're feeling great, and then the worst hits you."

Michael and Carol were at their mother's bedside, holding her hand. Carol's eyes were filled with tears; she and her mother were like best friends. It was only three weeks ago they enjoyed lunch and shopping, and a serious talk about how Sarah was counting on Carol to watch over her father. She knew that he would have a hard time losing her because they were so much in love. She had said, "Carol, you will find a good friend, someone you will share time with, and in time, your father will too. I don't want him to be alone."

Philip came to the bedside. Michael said, "Dad, we'll leave you with Mother for a while." He always called her Mother, not Mom like Carol did. "We'll be in the coffee shop."

Graham also left saying, "I'll be right outside by the nurse's station if you need me."

Michael and Carol found Jack and Diana waiting for them.

Jack asked, "How is she?"

"Not good," Michael replied. "She's in a coma. Doctor West said it's just a matter of time."

Jack was holding Carol's hand and had an arm around Michael's neck. "I love that woman. She has been like a mother and a good friend to Diana and me."

Clutching Michael's arm, Diana agreed, "We will be at a loss… we could always depend on her to be there when we needed her advice."

Philip pulled up a chair as close as possible to Sarah's bed. He took her hand in his, kissed it, looked up at her and whispered, "I love you Sarah. You are my life." Then he leaned over and kissed her forehead.

Although she was in a coma, a smile seemed to come to her face, and Philip could feel a slight tension on his hand as she squeezed it. And then she took her last breath.

Heaven seemed to fill the room, as the angels reclaimed her soul.

When the kids returned, their father was sitting in the waiting room, with his head in his hands.

Carol and Michael rushed over to him, and Carol said, "Daddy?"

Her dad replied, "She's gone."

Carol broke down and hugged her father. The others did the same.

Jack said, "We now know where she is, and who she is with. And Philip, we're going to get through this together."

"Thanks Jack, I don't know if I could have handled this without you guys," Philip said. "I love you for being with us."

Graham came over to them and embraced them and said, "She was a wonderful woman. Betty and I are going to miss her terribly. So will the staff here at the hospital for all the volunteer work she did for us. I've called Betty. She is on her way to your house; I'll join her later. Philip, I'll look after everything here." He embraced him and said, "I normally wouldn't say this to anyone, but I've known you and Sarah for so long; I know how you feel right now."

When they had reached the main floor, Philip said that he would like to visit the chapel.

Michael said, "We'd like to join you, Dad."

The little chapel had three small pews, and a little pedestal with a bible opened on top of it. It was opened to Psalm 23.

The Lord is my shepherd; I shall not want,
He maketh me to lie down on green pastures;
He leadeth me beside the still waters.
He restoreth my soul: He leadeth me in the path
of righteousness for His name sake.
Yea, though I walk through the valley
of the shadow of death, I will fear no evil: for Thou art
with me, thy rod and thy staff they comfort me.
Thou preparest a table before me in the presence of
mine enemies: Thou anointest my head with oil: my
cup runneth over.

Surely, goodness and mercy shall follow me all the days of my life: and I will dwell in the house of the Lord forever.

There was also an array of candles, some lit, some not. Two nurses were leaving as Philip and the kids entered. They seated themselves in the first two pews, in silent prayer. Philip got up and went to where the candles were flickering. Michael and Carol joined him. He took one lit candle and lit another from it. He then handed the candle to Carol, and she also lit one from hers, and handed it to Michael who did the same, as he passed it to Jack and Diana. They all knelt and bowed their heads. After a short time they blessed themselves, got up and left. Needless to say there wasn't a dry eye amongst them.

As they were leaving the chapel, there were two ladies walking down the hallway towards the exit. There was an orderly with them pushing a wheelchair, with a little boy in it. When they approached the chapel, Philip accidentally bumped into one of the ladies and right away he apologized by saying,

"Oh! I'm terribly sorry. Are you all right? It was very clumsy of me."

The lady looked at him with a smile and then her smile turned to sadness as she said, "I'm fine. I'm really all right, it was nothing."

As the ladies walked on, the one that was bumped said to the other with a worried look, "Gosh, he really must have been sorry, did you see him; he was crying."

The orderly cut in and said, "That was Mr. Mariano. His wife died about an hour ago; she had cancer."

The lady said, "The poor man, he must have really loved her," as she kept that thought with her.

Suddenly, he could he hear someone calling his name. "Mr. Mariano, are you all right?"

As he turned he noticed a flight attendant standing by him. "Yes, I'm fine. Just dozed off I guess."

She said smiling, "Oh, that's okay, but I'd like you to buckle up. We're about to take off."

He could hear the closing of the luggage doors, and as he looked out the window he could see the loading ramp being receded to the terminal finger. A few minutes later they were airborne.

After the plane had leveled off, the flight attendant came by to see if Philip needed anything, a drink, a snack, or a cushion. He refused the first two, but said that she could bring him a cushion, and also told her that he wouldn't be having lunch, as he had a snack at the airport.

She left, and a minute later came over with a cushion. He thanked her and said smiling, "See you in Oakland."

Beside him in the aisle seat was a Japanese gentleman. Philip introduced himself, as he did to Philip. He was fiddling around with a laptop computer, so Philip presumed he wanted to be alone with his work. All the better because Philip wasn't too fussy on carrying a conversation with anyone at this time. He put his seat back, and decided to relax the three-hour flight.

Relax is what he couldn't do. His mind took him back thirty-three years ago…

chapter II

VALLEYFIELD, INDIANA
SPRING of 1962

Philip met Sarah in 1962 when he was nineteen years old. He was in his second year in a business college in Fort Wayne, taking a course in business and finance, while at the same time working part-time at an import/export company owned by Ernie Stefaniac, who founded it right after the big war in forty-nine.

One Saturday night, Philip and his two good friends, Graham West and Willy Jackson, decided to drive to Fort Wayne, thirty-five miles away, to check out the local bars for dancing and meeting girls. After a couple of hours, half a dozen bars, and no luck, they decided to head home.

As they entered the outskirts of the city, Willy yelled, "Hold it! Hold it, turn around."

Gray said, "What? What did you see?"

"There's a roller rink back there. There's always girls at roller rinks," Willy said.

"Hey, you're right," Gray said.

Philip made a U turn with his sixty Chevy and headed for the action, saying, "I guess we might as well. There's sure as hell nothing to do in Valleyfield."

There were probably seventy-five to one hundred people skating and sitting having a snack, mostly girls. They rented skates, and out on the rink they went. After a while, Philip decided to sit down and have a Pepsi. He noticed a couple that went to the same college as he, so he sat with them. Gray and Willy were still out skating. They had met two girls who came by themselves, so they were skating and chatting looking like they were enjoying themselves. The couple that Philip was talking to got up for another skate, just as Gray and Willy came to Philip's table. Their two friends decided to leave.

As Willy put it, "They deserted us."

While sitting there trying to decide whether to leave or stay, Philip noticed a beautiful young lady having a problem controlling her skating.

He said to his friends, "Excuse me gentlemen but I must rescue the woman that I'm going to spend the rest of my life with, the woman who will bear my children, the woman that I shall marry."

They laughed and Willy said, "Go get her, tiger."

He was true to his word. That was the beginning of Philip and Sarah.

Sarah Miller was eighteen when she and Philip met. She was from Irish ancestry, with dark hair, and eyes that would capture the attraction of most any man, but they were only for Philip. Sarah was in her first year of a three year course in marketing and would graduate in the spring of sixty-four.

By the end of his third year, Philip left to work full time at Stefaniac's import/export company. He was very smart and alert; he picked up the business well. Ernie had him doing a lot of traveling, and meeting many people in the business. In a few months Philip was running the company, while Ernie, getting along in years, took it easy. Within a year, Ernie retired and sold the business to Philip, and gave him as long as he needed to pay for it.

Over the next two years business boomed. He had major clients all over the world, Spain, Portugal, Italy, Canada, and Mexico. Wherever there was a market Philip would seek it out. He was also a good shopper and had an eye for bargains, choosing articles that appealed to others. Diligently he researched the market before selecting the merchandise, making sure that the items weren't already in the country where they would be sold.

Something else took place on that year of sixty-five. In September Philip and Sarah were married. Their honeymoon was blended with business on a ten-day trip to Spain. Two days were spent in Spain, having business dinners with clients. Then he and Sarah rented a car and traveled north to San Sebastian, and then took the coastal highway to Cantabria, and then to Castro Urdiales, a quaint seaside village on the north east tip of Cantabria, one of many seaboard villages that dot the two hundred kilometer cliff lined coasts. This is where the two lovers spent their romantic honeymoon.

One morning, as the late risers peered out their third story balcony window to greet the day (and the sun not knowing whether it wanted to shed its glow over the little village), they looked out into the crescent shaped harbor, to see it lined with brightly painted commercial fishing boats already back from their morning haul. Down the road an elderly lady was standing behind her fish cart slicing fresh eel.

After gazing for a few minutes, arm-in-arm, they decided to dress, have a late breakfast, and journey through the off-beaten track of the coastal area. All the sights to see and explore are not more than a few hours away from Cantabria, making the day trips easy.

Soon, the week ended and the two lovebirds left for home, but as he reminisces, their honeymoon was never over.

The next year Michael was born, and thirteen months later Sarah was pregnant with Carol, who was born in June of sixty-eight.

Sarah never went back to work at her original job with the electronics company. Instead she worked a couple of days a week with Philip, and spent a great deal of time organizing the volunteer work at the Valley hospital.

Now it's come to an end, Philip thought. What will I do without her? She was my life. When I wake, I reach over and she won't be there.

They left the hospital and headed for his house. Carol and Jack rode in Philip's car; Jack drove. Michael and Diana had their own vehicles. Before he left, Michael called Pedro and Juanita, who were at Philip's house in town, to inform them of his mother's passing.

Pedro and Juanita are a Mexican couple in their middle sixties who live in a two-bedroom house on Philip's mini farm, which is located in the Hills of Caledon.

When they reached the house, Pedro was at the door to greet them. Juanita was in the kitchen preparing food and coffee when Philip came in. Immediately they embraced each other, and Juanita said, in her Mexican accent, "Meester Philip," as she called him, "I will miss Meese Sarah so much. We had good times; we would laugh and talk like we were seesters. She always would say that I was her long lost friend that she was looking for, and I know that she was mine."

Philip answered her by saying, "I know, Juanita, she loved you like a friend, and she always looked forward to sharing your company. Now, you come and sit down. I don't want you working today," he continued.

Pedro spoke out and said, "She likes to keep busy, calms her mind."

At that moment Carol and Diana came in to give a hand.

As the day progressed, friends and colleagues dropped by the house to pay their respects, as they did the next day, and evening at the funeral home. The day of the funeral, two limousines were waiting in Philip's driveway to take them to the church, where the service would be held. Along with the family, Pedro, Juanita, and their son Alex, who is a doctor doing research at Chicago General Hospital, would join them.

The weather was sunny and warm; there was a slight breeze in the air. The flowers were still bright, beautiful, and tall. When you walked down the driveway, it was almost like they were greeting you. The leaves from the two rows of maples were breaking loose, and falling gently to the ground.

They arrived at the Church of St. Francis for a one-hour service. Needless to say the church was packed. Sarah had many friends and was well known for her charitable work that she took pride in. Philip's life long friend Willy and his wife Susan flew in from California to spend a few days, and many of Philip's business associates were also there. Plus there were many of Michael and Carol's friends.

After the funeral they gathered at Philip's house for a reception, where everyone was able to meet the family, people they hadn't seen in years. As time passed they started to leave, and before long there was no one there but the family.

Pedro and Juanita were cleaning up, washing dishes and putting things away with the help of Carol and Diana. Philip mentioned again that the cleaning could wait, but Juanita insisted, so Philip took her hand and said, "I understand. Sarah would be doing the same."

Michael and Jack left to go to the office, that had been closed for the past two days, to check out the fax machine from the foreign markets.

Philip was discussing with the two girls and Juanita, about getting Sarah's clothes together, not knowing that she had most of it done for a charitable organization. That's what she would have liked done with them.

When Jack and Michael arrived back home, they brought with them condolence cards and letters sent by e-mail from places where Philip did business, Spain, Italy, and one from his and Sarah's friends in Australia, Jim and Sylvia Cameron.

At that moment, Philip felt a slight touch on his shoulder. He turned to see the same flight attendant standing by him.

She smiled and said, "I'm sorry to startle you Mr. Mariano, but we're in our final flight path. We'll be landing in about twenty minutes. Can I get you a drink?"

"No, I'm fine," Philip said, "I was doing a bit of day dreaming."

She laughed and said, "We all do plenty of that, don't we?"

"Likely too much," was Philip's reply.

"I know just what you need, I'll be right back," the flight attendant said.

A minute later she came back with a hot wet towel for Philip to freshen up with, and also a dry one.

Philip said, "Thank you; that was great, you are very kind."

chapter III

**OAKLAND INTERNATIONAL AIRPORT
NOVEMBER 14, 1995
12:15 pm**

As the aircraft taxied up to the terminal, passengers were unbuckling their seat belts and retrieving their luggage from the upper compartments.

Philip arose from his seat and was met by the same flight attendant, with his carry-on.

He thanked her and also for her friendly service.

"Mr. Mariano, I should be thanking you for making my job so easy. You didn't demand drinks or even have your lunch," she said.

"I'll tell you what," Philip said jokingly, "the next time I'm on your flight, I'll eat twice."

They laughed, and she said, "Okay, I'll look forward to it."

"What's your name?" Philip asked.

"Helen." She replied.

"Really," he said, "my first girlfriend's name was Helen, and I have fond thoughts when I hear that name."

"I believe it signifies 'The god of love,' the beautiful wife of Menelaus, who was the king of Sparta. She was sadly abducted by Paris, which caused the Trojan War."

"You're really up on your Greek mythology." Helen said.

"No, not really," Philip replied. "It's that 'first love' thing, where you find out everything about her."

"Oh," she laughed, "so that's how it works."

He walked up the ramp and into the arrivals section where he spotted his good friend Willy Jackson waiting for him.

A smile came across his face. He hadn't seen Willy since he and his wife Susan were up for Sarah's funeral, two years ago; but it didn't matter if it was a hundred years, Willy's appearance never changes.

Willy is the same age as Philip, same height, but more muscular, a crew-cut that he's always had, and wears short pants almost continually, and smokes cigars, and that's exactly what he looked like today, except for the cigar, which isn't allowed in the terminal.

When he reached where Willy was standing, they shook hands and embraced. Philip broke away first, and Willy said, "That's okay, in this city there's a lot of that."

Willy was always a little rough around the edges. When they were kids, he was always known to be the tough guy, he liked to scrap, and he knew how. Most of the guys kept their distance from ever aggravating him or his friends.

"So, how have you been doing?" Willy asked.

"Pretty good," was Philip's lie. "I sold the house about a year and a half ago and moved up to Millcreek," he continued. "Pedro and I fixed up the old gristmill. It's kept me busy, and the place doesn't look too bad. It's liveable."

"How about the business?" Willy asked.

"Michael and Jack are running it. They do a pretty good job, most likely better than I. I'm doing most of the traveling. Keeps me out of trouble."

Philip had a skycap retrieve his luggage at the carousel and take it to the exit doors, while Willy went for his car in the meter parking area.

A few minutes later Willy drove up in a white Cadillac convertible. Philip's remark was, "What the hell is this? Since when did you lower yourself from a pickup truck?"

Willy laughed and said, "This is Susan's."

Willy never hurts for money, he owns an electrical contracting company, and has a couple of dozen electricians in his employ. He moved to Sacramento when he was twenty-four with an electrician's license and a sixty-one Pontiac. From then it was all up hill. He spends most of his time teaching water skiing and ski jumping, while his son Peter runs his company.

The skycap loaded Philip's luggage in the trunk, and Philip tipped him generously. He looked at the double-sawbuck in his hand and then to Philip and said, "Why, thank you sir, thank you very much, you sure come back again sometime." As he held the door, Philip smiled and gave him a short wave.

Philip will be spending a few days with Willy and Susan before leaving for Sydney, Australia, where he will spend an unlimited time living with some friends at their ranch. Possibly he will find the time to finish a novel that he had started writing a few years ago and for other reasons…

As they drove north on "880" and connected with the East Shore Parkway, chatting about the past and present, Willy turned to Philip and said, "Let's pull over for a beer."

"That's a good idea," Philip said. "I could use a sandwich too. I didn't bother with lunch on the flight down. I think I slept most of the trip."

There was a small restaurant on the east shore right by the water. They were sitting on the outer deck of the restaurant enjoying a "Bud" and a tuna-salad sandwich, temperature being high seventies and watching the boats come and go.

When they were finished, Willy lit up a cigar. Philip asked jokingly, "Are you still smoking those fifteen-cent White Owls?"

"No," Willy answered, "I've graduated to Monte Christos. I finished off that box of Cubans you gave me. Now that's a cigar."

"You should be a connoisseur on the subject. You've been smoking them since you were eleven, haven't you?" Philip remarked.

"I started swiping them from my dad when I was twelve, and you know, I always thought that he never knew; but a week before he died, we were in the hospital with him, and with a whisper, he said, 'Come closer,' so I moved up until my head was about six inches from his, and with his hand that didn't have the intravenous in, he whacked me on my head and whispered, 'That's for stealing my cigars. I forgive you.' Then he smiled."

"You know, Phil, that's probably the fondest moment that I had with my dad," Willy continued. "We worked together, fine, he taught me a hell of a lot, being a farmer, he also had to be every tradesman you could think of, plus an accountant. Enough about me." Willy said. "Tell me about her, who is she, and why are you running from her?"

Philip looked at him with eyebrows raised, and a half smile, and asked, "Does it show?"

"It's all over your face, and don't bullshit me Phil. It's me, Willy, like in Gray, Phil, and Willy. We've always shared our ups and downs with one another, plus Gray and Betty were here at the end of October for a couple of days. They're coming back down in January to spend a week with us. Gray had some kind of convention at the Civic Center, and he also filled us in on this lovely woman that you met, and now…. Well you tell me."

"Yes, I guess you're right." Philip said. "We've always talked to one another about things, and it will certainly make me feel better. I'm sure Gray will fill you in on more detail. I do want you to know about her. I never had a chance to show her off to you, and I know that you and Susan would have loved her," Philip said.

"Anyway," Philip continued, "I met Laura through Carol. Laura is a real-estate agent, she's been in Valleyfield about five years, came from Fort Wayne. Jack and Carol bought their house through her. They had been working with her for about four weeks, and when they decided on this certain house, Carol had me come and look at it, plus she was aching for me to meet Laura. Carol's been playing 'Miss Cupid' for some time now."

"That's my favorite girl," Willy said.

"We fell in love," Philip continued. "Right there and then, we both knew it. The crazy thing is, Willy, I accidentally bumped into her, literally, at the hospital the day that Sarah died. She, her friend Lucy, I'll tell you about her later, and Laura's son Nick were walking up the corridor towards the exit. The kids and I were leaving the chapel, I wasn't seeing too straight that day, and I practically knocked her down."

"We were inseparable. If we didn't see each other every day, we would talk on the phone and half the time we'd talk ourselves into meeting somewhere. There was no distance far enough to keep us apart. Every time we'd meet we always had a little romantic card for each other. Once we exchanged cards that were alike."

"The first gift I bought her was a 'Kit Kat' chocolate bar on our first date. It happened to be her favorite. Willy, we were like two kids giggling in church. Have you heard enough mushy stuff?"

"No, go on, she is part of your life, and you're a big part of mine," Willy answered.

"Then there's Nick, Laura's son. He captured my heart. He's eight years old, the little guy had a major kidney problem. He was born with only one functioning kidney, and it became diseased, but he's fine now. You know, it was like being young again, only being able to spend more time with him.

"When our kids were young, I was away a lot. Like you and Gray, we were building a business, but now I can make my own time. I just like having him around. He enjoys coming up to Millcreek. He loves to help out and work with Pedro, and he loves the horses. Last April the two of us flew up to Chicago to see a hockey game. Laura was busy with a house closing, so we left early in the afternoon, saw a few sights, had dinner, and went to the game. The Black Hawks were playing the Toronto Maple Leafs. The Leafs won. We got home about one in the morning. He thought that was a big deal."

"So, here I am spilling my guts out to you."

"That's what you're supposed to do, at least that's what you always say." Willy said.

"I miss them terribly," Philip said. "Whoever said, 'Absence makes the heart grow fonder,' has never been in love."

"You know Willy, I feel like a man whose house burnt down, I've nowhere to go."

"You always have 'here', you know that." Willy said

"I know." Philip answered.

"So, what happened, had to be something serious; another man?" Willy asked.

"No, nothing like that," Philip answered. Laura hasn't been with anyone since her divorce over two years ago. I could understand if that were the case, there's a difference of eighteen years in our ages."

"Older or younger." Willy joked

"Why don't you get us another beer and, I'll tell you what happened." Philip said. Willy went inside to the bar, and a minute later came out with a large jug of beer and two glasses. He filled one glass up for his friend, and then filled his own, and said, "Go ahead Phil." They both took a couple of swallows, and then Philip continued his story.

"Well, I was on business in Belgium closing a deal on some combines that we were importing. I was due back on a Friday. Flew into Chicago, and took the commuter to Fort Wayne. Laura was to meet me there. When I didn't see her I called her house, the phone rang a few times, then the answering machine clicked on. I left a message of where I was, and would wait a half hour in case she was on her way. Then I would take a cab, but I would call before I left."

"Nick wasn't well, in fact he had been very ill for the past few weeks, Gray had him on and off dialysis, so it was possible that she was at the hospital."

"After a drink, and a half hour later, I called her house again. It rang a couple of times, and then someone answered. It wasn't Laura. It was her friend Lucy Watson."

"Is this the same Lucy that you mentioned before?" Willy asked.

"Yes, Lucy is a very attractive woman. She's tall, about five feet nine, thirty-nine years old. Her figure is rich and firm, reddish brown hair, styled in a flared look. She has a lovely complexion, her skin is soft, and her eyes are dark. She is very intelligent, and unselfconscious about her beauty."

"Lucy is married. Her husband's name is Ryan, a great guy, Gray and I play golf with him every week. He's the manager, and part owner of a Ford dealership in Fort Wayne."

"They've been married for eighteen years, and still nuts over each other. No kids, but they adore Laura's little guy Nick, like he was their own.

"Willy, you would love her. Her beauty will hit you by surprise."

Willy cut in and said, "Hell, I'm already in love with her." They laughed, and Willy filled their glasses again, and Philip continued.

"After we exchanged how-do-you-dos, I asked her if Laura was there. Lucy said that she was detained, so I was a little worried and asked if Nick was all right. She said he hasn't been well, and added that she would drive up to get me. I told her that I'd grab a cab; it would be faster. She persisted, saying that she had to call by Ryan's dealership, and she'd see me in twenty minutes. I gave in and said okay."

"In less than twenty minutes she was at the arrival level, and Ryan was with her. They must have spotted me because the trunk lid went up as she stopped. It didn't occur to me why Ryan was there, because she would drive up quite often to have lunch with him, or take him shopping."

"I placed my luggage in the trunk, and got in the back seat. Ryan turned around and we shook hands. I said "hi" to Lucy and touched her shoulder. They didn't seem too pleasant, not the Ryan and Lucy I was used to. So I said, "Is something wrong? You guys aren't very talkative. Is it Laura, did something happen to her?"

"No, nothing happened to her." Lucy answered, as she drove out.

"Well what?" I asked.

Just then, Ryan suggested that we stop at a sandwich shop

that was just down the street. He said that he hadn't had lunch, and was hungry.

When we were settled in the shop, Lucy and I had a coffee, and Ryan had a sandwich, I said jokingly, "You guys aren't playing some kind of prank on me, are you?"

"No, Phil, I wish it was that easy," Ryan said.

This is when Lucy told me that Laura didn't want to see me any more.

I said, "I hope this is a joke, but I don't find it funny."

Then she told me what had happened at their office.

"I left on a Sunday night flight to Belgium. On Monday morning Laura and Lucy attended a board meeting at the Indy State Realty office, and you won't guess who works from the same office."

"Vince Tedesco, the sneak," Willy said.

"Right, how did you know?" Philip asked.

"When Gray was here we were going over assholes of the world, and his name just popped up. I guess he's now one of those tight assed jerks with the manicured nails, and the big mortgaged car. Who the fuck would buy anything from that clown?" Willy commented.

Philip smiled and thought to himself, same old Willy, never changes.

"Sorry Phil, go on," Willy said.

"Well, after the meeting some of the agents were sitting around chatting and having coffee. Lucy and a couple of the girls were teasing Laura about me. One of them asked my name. When Laura told her, she said, 'I think my husband has played golf with him at the Valleyfield Country Club. Doesn't he own an export company?'"

"Yes, he does," Laura answered.

"Then Vince, as Lucy put it, was sitting in the corner stuffing a donut in his mouth."

"That would be good old Vince," Willy cut in.

Philip continued, spoke out and said, "Of course you've heard his name. He was Headline News a few years ago."

Lucy, knowing that Vince was always good at running someone down, asked, "What do you mean?"

"I mean," Vince continued, "that you've got yourself a real catch, Laura. This guy has a few bucks, but we all know how he got it."

By this time Lucy was getting a little pissed off, just by the expression on his face.

Willy cut in again, and said, "I'm loving this girl more all the time."

Philip continued, "She said, 'What the hell are you talking about?'"

Laura was sitting in awe.

"Philip Mariano," Vince continued, "financed the biggest drug ring ever to hit these parts, up to Chicago, and across the border into Canada."

Lucy told him that he was full of shit, but that was all that Laura had to hear, as she rushed out of the room in tears.

Lucy followed her, but before she left she called Vince a lying, cruel, little bastard.

He just sat there with that stupid grin he always showed, when he thought he had something over on someone.

"Yah, I know," Willy said, "my dad used to say that he has a grin on his face like a wave in a swill barrel. You have to be a farmer to appreciate that one."

Philip continued, "Laura lost her twin brother about ten years ago from an overdose of drugs, and Lucy said that she can't be comfortable to be around or associated with anyone that has or had anything to do with drugs.

"That's rough," Willy said, "its bad enough losing a relative, or even someone you know, but a twin is about as close as you'll ever get to yourself. The poor girl must have been devastated."

"You know Phil," Willy continued, "for two cents, I'd fly up there and bust that creep Vince in the mouth. In fact, I'd do it for nothing. He has about as much charm as a fucking train wreck."

"You better not," Philip said, "you wouldn't get away with it like you used to when we were kids."

"You weren't involved with that drug thing." Willy said.

"I know," Philip replied, "but she needs her space right now. I saw her go through a hell of a lot of pain last summer. She almost lost her son Nick, so, at the time she didn't need any extra grief. That's why I'm leaving Valleyfield for a while."

He shrugged his shoulders and mildly said, "Maybe one day, when the time is right."

"Right now, I feel as if I've been dealt the queen of spades."

"Phil, you're running away from it. You love her and the kid, and by the sounds of it, she loves you. Why don't you stay and fight for her? Didn't you tell her you had nothing to do with drugs?"

Before Philip could answer, Willy said, "I'll bet you didn't. If I know you, and I do, you probably left it for her to make the decision. You know, she isn't Gray or me, she doesn't know you as we do."

"You could be right," Philip said, "but I feel that I have to get away. Maybe we'll get to know each other a little better, from a distance, and I also need the rest." He didn't say why.

Willy looked at him and said, "Phil, everything is going to work out, you'll see. By this spring, the three of you will be together again. Maybe the time away will be a good thing for both of you. By the sounds of it, you two started off in high gear, and time away will enrich your love for each other."

Philip surprisingly looked at him and said, "Willy, is that really you?"

"Sure," Willy answered, "I can be compassionate. Have I ever been wrong?"

"You really think so?"

"I'm sure." Willy replied.

"You and I have never talked about that drug bust, have we?" Philip said.

"No," Willy answered. "I always thought you would, when you were ready."

"Well, I wanted to, but I hardly ever see you."

"It was like this. Do you remember us talking about this friend of Michael's? His name is RJ Williamson."

"Yah I do. He boarded at that old farm house that Mike rented, didn't he?" Willy asked.

"Exactly," Philip replied. "Nice kid. He seemed to have a head on his shoulders, always ambitious. He kind of reminded me of myself, when I was his age."

"Anyway," Philip continued, "the cops in Valleyfield were notified by the State Troopers, who got their information from the U.S. Drug Enforcement (DEA) to keep tabs on him. Where he went, where he worked, whom he hung around with. They were pretty sure that he was involved in the dealing, and smuggling of drugs from Jamaica through Indianapolis, to Michigan, and across the border to Canada."

"He sounds really ambitious." Willy said. "How did they involve you in all this?"

"RJ came to me one day with a proposal about purchasing a warehouse, insulating it, and leasing it out to a large grocery company for cold storage." Philip continued. "In fact he already had a lessee, so he said. What he needed from me was a hundred and fifty thousand dollars, paid back with interest in two years, or an interest in the revenue that the building would create."

"I had Frank, our lawyer, look into it. He got back to me and said that the building was sound, no liens against it, and the overall price was a steal. The people that owned it needed the money. So I agreed. We turned the money into RJ's account, had all legal papers stating that if there was a default in the deal, then I had the option to purchase the building myself."

"So what happened next?" Willy asked.

"About a month went by," Philip continued, "and we hadn't heard anything. RJ wasn't living at the farmhouse, and Michael hadn't heard from him either."

"This is when everything broke loose. The shit hit the fan. It started with the R.C.M.P. in Canada."

THIS IS WHAT HAPPENED.............

chapter IV

**TILLERY, ONTARIO, CANADA
MARCH 13, 1984
11:00 pm**

Below air traffic control radar levels near Tillery Airport, just east of Sarnia, a pilot maneuvered a single engine Apache towards the one-runway airport. The small plane also included one passenger and six hundred pounds of Jamaican hash oil. Snow and freezing rain were swirling around the windscreen making it extremely difficult to see the highway that he had used in the past, as a visual guide.

Not knowing how low he was, a hill covered with pine trees suddenly came into view, and before he could pull the Apache up, the propeller severed into the branches. The trees trapped the wings, which reduced the speed as it plummeted through the pines.

The shattered $150,000 plane uttered a deep moan, as it hung in the trees, and slowly dropped to about three feet off the ground.

The pilot and passenger crawled out of the cockpit, luckily missing injury, and then retrieved the four containers of hash oil. Although they were only fifteen hundred feet west of the highway, they made three trips to haul their heavy cargo that they stashed in the bushes. After walking a couple of miles to find a phone, they called their associates, who within ten minutes picked them and the cargo up, and then they left.

It didn't take long for the hash to hit the streets. This was one of the largest amounts of that drug ever to be imported into Canada.

The drug was sold in ten-gram vials for an average of $80.00 a piece, that brought in approximately seven million dollars.

It wasn't until the day after the crash, since the area was so desolate, that the plane was found.

The site was on the glide path of Tillery Airport, four miles away. Later on, the authorities found out that the Apache had made the same flight many times before.

Usually the pickup vehicle would park at the end of the small runway, and flash the headlights. The night of the crash, the pilot used the radio microphone to turn on the runway lights, but never made it.

Within a week the Apache was traced to a private owner in Indianapolis, who had leased it to what they thought was a survey company from Louisville, Kentucky. Then the pieces started to fit together. The Indiana State Police were now keeping a closer watch on RJ. They even followed him to Florida, but he shook them off.

On March thirteenth an Indiana State Trooper, out on patrol on Highway 69, pulled over a vehicle for speeding. When he discovered that the license of the driver, Carlo DeMotto, had been suspended, he then arrested him and did a search of his car. Under the spare tire was a little box containing $18,000 in cash. The officer radioed for assistance and a tow truck to haul DeMotto's car to Fort Wayne, about four miles north.

At the police station they went through DeMotto's pockets, and in his wallet there were business cards with phone numbers written on the back. When the police called one of the numbers, a voice answered "Marriott Hotel," and when the other numbers were recited to the hotel clerk, he said that they were room numbers, and one of the occupants of the room was RJ Williamson.

The case was then turned over to the U.S. Drug Enforcement

Agency, led by Sergeant Bill Hanson, who obtained a search warrant, and raided the rooms.

Sitting around a large oak table, that looked like a board meeting, were RJ and five other men, two Americans, two Jamaicans, and a Canadian with approximately $250,000 stacked in little piles on the table.

They all gave up peacefully, without a struggle. They were arrested and charged with conspiracy to possess the proceeds of crime.

RJ's parents, for his release, put up twenty thousand dollars, and then he skipped the country to Jamaica, leaving his parents to forfeit the bail money. He held up in Jamaica for a few months, and then came back to Florida where he lived on a small cabin cruiser.

The D.E.A. wanted to nail them with conspiracy to import drugs, but they needed more information on the case.

Hanson had learned during his investigation that RJ had met up with a drug importer by the name of Richard Travis, who was wanted in several countries for drug related offences. His contacts to smuggle drugs out of Jamaica are many. He pays off the authorities to get you in and out of the U.S., Canada, and Mexico without any difficulty. He also uses a U.S. passport with a name that he copied from a gravestone in Georgia.

This is how it originated...

Travis and RJ constructed a plan to smuggle 1000 pounds of cannabis resin (hash oil) into the U.S. and Canada.

They would do it in two separate shipments. Travis would handle the shipment out of Jamaica and into the U.S., and RJ was to handle it into Canada.

The first shipment went well. It traveled by cabin cruiser from Port Antonio on the north coast of Jamaica, through the Windward Passage, and passed the Bahamas to Florida, then by car to Flint Michigan, and by light aircraft to Canada.

RJ had an efficient distribution network that would get the drugs on the streets of London, Ontario, and on into the large city of Toronto and the outlining towns. This proved that the operation could work, but the next shipment didn't go that successfully.

First of all, the three men that piloted the cruiser from Jamaica had strayed off course and found themselves in Cuban waters. Lucky for them they were rescued by the U.S. Coast Guard. The officers searched the cruiser, but even their well-trained dogs couldn't sniff out the drugs because they were so well hidden. They had no reason to hold them, so they got them back on course, and they were on their way.

When the three men reached Boca Raton, Florida, they put their cruiser into dry dock, and with the proper tools they cut open the hull and removed the oil. It was than transported to Indianapolis, where a pilot was waiting with a leased single engine Apache.

One of the men from the cruiser accompanied the pilot and the drugs to Flint, Michigan, and across the border to Tillery, Ontario, where it ended up in the trees.

Meanwhile, with the help of local police forces in Indiana, Michigan, and Ontario, Hanson poured through registration in various hotels, telephone records, and airline tickets, to see if anything matched up with any of the suspects that they had on file.

There's an abundance of information in between, all about computer printouts. On one printout alone the computer told them twenty-five transactions took place in one day, and it also suggested who did what.

By May of 1986 most of the charges had been laid, somewhere around eighteen. Some of them were allowed to avoid possible jail sentences by giving evidence.

"Otherwise squealing on their buddies," Willy said.

"Something like that," Philip answered.

Six of the eighteen charges were dropped.

RJ and DeMotto were caught holed up in a yacht, in West Palm Beach, and brought back to Indianapolis to stand trial.

One of the informers told the D.E.A. that Michael Mariano's father financed the whole operation from the beginning, and of course that was Headline News all over Valleyfield, and the state.

"That's when they came to my door, cuffed me, read me my rights, and charged me with 'financing a drug operation.' They also put Michael under arrest for harboring a suspected criminal, and conspiracy to traffic in narcotics. At that time, Michael was renting that old farm house on the outskirts of town. A contractor, who owned it, would in time subdivide it which he already has."

RJ lived with him when he was around. They both had dirt bikes, so it was convenient they had a hundred acres to tear around in.

When RJ was on trial, he swore along with the others that Michael was not involved in the drug operation, but the state had spent more than a million dollars in cracking the case, so they had to show the taxpayers that everyone involved got their share of jail time.

"Michael spent three months of a three year sentence in a minimum prison."

"As for me, they locked the doors of my office, and had auditors in to audit my books. My accounting staff are so meticulous, the auditors couldn't find one penny out of place."

"So you lost the $150,000.00?" Willy asked.

"No," Philip answered with surprise. "RJ or his lawyer bought the warehouse during the time that RJ skipped out on his bail. It was completely insulated and leased out to United Grocers. It was making a profit, and believe it or not they had it registered in my name. That was very ethical of him."

"When he was released from prison, where he spent two years of a six year sentence, I turned the warehouse back in his name. He still owns it along with a couple of others in Fort Wayne."

"You know, Willy, he has a good head for business. Too bad he got himself involved in crime. I guess it looked like a fast way of making a lot of money."

"It was for a while," Willy said.

"Don't be surprised," Philip said, "that he gets himself back into it again; he seems to love a challenge."

"Most of them do," Willy said.

"Soon after he was released," Philip said, "he came to the house. We were all there including Diana, who was Michael's girlfriend at the time, and he asked us if we would forgive him for getting us involved as suspects. Then Sarah lit into him about the rights and wrongs, and the effects that drugs have, especially on young people. But she was the first one to embrace him and forgive him."

"Did you ever ask him about the money from the drugs?" Willy asked.

"It came up in conversation," Philip answered, "he just said, 'the cost of lawyers are expensive.' Then he said, 'Mr. M (as he called me) it's better to put it behind us, and don't ask questions. Those fuckers in Jamaica shoot horses; they have no scruples.'"

"Wow, what a story," Willy said. "I guess we better get going."

"Yah, Susan is going to wonder where we are," Philip said.

"No, she knows when I'm with you or Gray, time stops," Willy said.

They laughed and continued on to Interstate 80 towards Sacramento.

chapter v

SACRAMENTO, CALIFORNIA

As they entered the driveway, you could see how Willy and Susan were enjoying their success. Their house was pinky-toned stucco, about twenty-five hundred square feet, with a tile roof. The semi-circled garden was filled with cactus plants including a cactus rose that was in bloom, and in the centre there was a fifteen foot palm tree.

While they were viewing the front yard, the door opened, and Susan ran out and flung her arms around Philip's neck saying, "Oh, its so good to see you again. We missed you so much. How have you been?"

"I'm fine." Philip answered, as he returned the big hug.

"It's been over two years since I saw you guys, and in that time, just last spring, I met a very lovely woman and her little boy, from whom, I am sad to say, have since parted. Only temporarily, I hope," Philip said.

"Gray told us a little bit about her, and she sounds like a great person," Susan said.

"Now you listen to me, honey," she continued, "the three of you will be back together again soon. I know it. Anyway, no woman would let a catch like you get away," she joked.

Willy shook his head and said, "It's getting a little mushy. I'll make up some drinks, while Susan gives you a grand tour."

"That's right," Susan said as she took his hand and led him in the house. "You've never seen this house!"

"No I haven't," Philip answered, "I only remember the other one. It was a couple of blocks from here, wasn't it?"

"Yes, we bought this lot, and had it built the way we wanted it," Susan said.

They walked through the foyer to the family room that had light hardwood cabinetry. There was flagstone and Berber carpet throughout the main floor, and nine foot vaulted ceilings. It had a luxurious master bedroom and bath with a Jacuzzi tub.

They walked down the six steps to the main floor again, and out to the back yard that was beautifully landscaped with a pool and spa. The work shed was attached to a double car garage, and behind that was a small embankment that led to their boathouse by the Sacramento River.

Susan is a very dainty type person, she's about five-foot four, dark hair and eyes, with a lovely tanned complexion. Always seems to be on the go, a real busybody, and you hardly see her without a smile.

She and Willy met in Sacramento about twenty-eight years ago. Willy was hired to do the electrical work at an estate that was being renovated, and Susan was in charge of the interior decorating.

After a few weeks of running into each other in the rooms and hallways, and brown-bagging it together, Willy asked her one day as they were looking over some blueprints, "Would you like to own a house like this?"

She answered by saying, "It would be nice, but it wouldn't matter where I lived, whether it was in a house like this, or a trailer, as long as I shared it with someone who loved me more than the house."

Willy didn't have to know or hear anymore about this woman; he knew right there and then that she was the one that he wanted to spend his life with. All he had to do now was to convince her that he was the man for her.

Before he realized what he said next, and he has never regretted it, was, "I could love you more than anything, and for eternity. Will you marry me?"

Her answer was, "In the four weeks that we've known each other, I was beginning to think you'd never ask. Yes, yes I will."

They were married within six months, and in two years their son Peter was born.

Willy brought out three gin and tonics, and after toasting to their good health and happiness, they had a barbecue and talked on into the night, when Susan said, "You must be tired, it's been a long day for you."

"It has been that, but I could talk to you two for hours. We have a lot to catch up on," Philip said.

"We still have a couple of more days, before you leave," Willy said.

With that, they retired for the night.

The next two days went by quickly. They went boating and sightseeing along the Sacramento River, took in a water skiing show, where a couple of Willy's students competed in ski jumping and parasailing. In the evening they dined out, but most of the time was spent on their deck, by the pool, chatting about what was going on in each of their lives.

Willy and Susan's son Peter, and his wife Heather came over the last night of Philip's stay, and Peter was pumping Philip's brain about stories of when he, his dad, and Gray were young.

The next day, Friday, they sat around talking, had a swim in the pool and Susan made up a late brunch. About two o'clock they drove Philip down to Oakland for his three forty-five flight to Los Angeles to connect with his eight o'clock flight to Sydney, Australia via Honolulu. As Willy was unloading Philip's luggage for the skycap to take to the counter, Philip was saying his good-byes to Susan.

She said, as they were embracing each other, "We wish you could stay a little longer. Who knows when you'll be back again?"

"I'll make you a promise," Philip replied, "when I'm through with the Australian visit, I'll be back to spend more time with you, but don't forget, Valleyfield is only two hours away, and I will be expecting you two to visit me at Millcreek."

Willy cut in and said, "When you come again, we will have accommodations for the three of you."

"I hope so, Willy," Philip replied, as he looked his friend in the eyes, and shook his hand, "and don't you guys go worrying about me, I'll be fine. I'll send you a card from Cameron's Station," he continued.

They watched and waved as Philip entered the terminal, and then they drove off. As they were driving out, Willy turned to his wife and said, "Honey, I've known him all my life, and now he puzzles me. There's something different about him. I just feel it. Something he's holding back. I guess I'll have to get it out of Gray."

Susan said, "He seems very distant, doesn't he?"

"Yah," replied Willy.

"He has a broken heart," Susan said. "Women's intuition," she added.

chapter VI

VALLEYFIELD, INDIANA
WEDNESDAY, NOVEMBER 15, 1995
8:45 pm.

Laura had just seen Nicholas off on the school bus that would take him to his school on the other side of town. When she arrived back home, the postman was there with her mail.

He greeted her with, "Good morning Mrs. Manning, it's a lovely mild day."

"Yes its nice and fresh," Laura replied.

"How is your little boy coming along?" asked the postman.

"He's fine, Fred. I can't keep him still anymore, not that I'm complaining," she said.

"Well, that means he's healthy, and I'm happy for you. Here's your mail," Fred said.

"Thank you, and have a nice day," Laura said.

As she entered the house, she kicked off her shoes, and was walking to the kitchen sorting the junk mail from the others, and shedding her coat at the same time. She placed the mail on the table as one letter fell on the floor. She picked it up and noticed that it was a personal letter with familiar looking handwriting. She opened it, and it began…

Dear Laura,

By the time this note reaches your hands, I will be in California. I'm spending a few days with my friend Willy, and his wife Susan. I've mentioned Willy to you before. I wish you had have met him, he's quite a character. From there, this Friday the seventeenth, I'm leaving for Sydney, Australia, and spending an unlimited time with some friends at their ranch. Hopefully, I will get to finish the novel that I had started a few years ago. My reason for writing is to apologize for not seeing Nick before I left. He must be wondering why I didn't. I was with him during his operation, and I thank you for allowing me to be there. Gray assured me that Nick is going to be fine, and grow up to be a healthy young man. He is a special little guy, and will always share a section in my heart, as will you.

So, I think this is for the best. I've spent my life in Valleyfield, and now, everywhere I go, everything I see, reminds me of you. You don't need that extra burden, so I am leaving and you can get on with your life. If you ever find a way to believe in me, you will know where to find me. I wish you happiness always, and I hope you find what you're looking for.

Keep well and safe, and close to Nick, he is very special.

I leave you with my heart,

Philip

P.S.

I have enclosed two open tickets. You will find that they are destined to Oakland and Sydney. I wish you happiness, whatever your decision.

Just as she finished reading the letter, she heard a car door close. With the letter still in her hand, she approached the front door to see her closest friend Lucy walking up the steps.

Laura opened the door and greeted her with a stern "Hi, come on in. I have coffee on."

Lucy accommodated and said, "Great, I could use one, what's up, what are you doing?"

"Nothing," was Laura's abrupt reply.

"Than what's the reason for the tears that are about to topple from your eyes; is it Nicholas?" she asked with concern.

"No," Laura answered, as she handed the letter to her.

After a minute or so, Lucy looked at her friend, and with her head shaking slightly back and forth, she said, "Look at you, you're all upset, you still love him, and you always will. You have to go to him. It's unfair, not only to him, but to yourself and Nicholas. Take these tickets, and get on the next plane. I'll look after Nicholas. Laura, this man loves you both very much. Don't take the word of that prick Vince."

"I'm not," Laura said, "I went through newspaper records at the library, and found out that there was an indication that Philip and Michael were involved. Michael even spent time in prison."

"I'm a little surprised that you went to all that trouble. Did you ask him, did he admit to you that he was involved?" Lucy asked.

"Yes, I asked him. He didn't say he was, but he didn't say he wasn't," Laura answered.

"Then I don't believe it for a minute, and anyway that was twelve years ago. Ryan and I consider him to be one of the nicest men we've ever met." Lucy said.

"Well, he left. He's out of our lives now," Laura replied.

Lucy looked at her with a frown, and half smile and said, "Is he, is he really?"

"He'll forget us after a while," Laura said.

"No, no he won't," Lucy remarked, "I know him, I know his kind. I see how he looks at you, and the warmth he has for Nicholas. He's the type that loves forever. Remember the first time you saw him at the hospital, the day he bumped into you."

"Yes," Laura answered, "he was quite upset, he had just lost his wife."

"Right," Lucy replied, "you said, 'The poor man, he must have really loved her.' His love for her lasted twenty-eight years."

"What about Nicholas? He adores him. He hasn't seen him for over a month, but he talks about him every day. He knows something is different between you, and that he's not just away on business," she continued.

"I'll cross that bridge when I come to it," Laura said.

"Maybe the bridge won't be there to cross," Lucy replied.

"I'm sorry!" Laura yelled. "Yes, I do love him, but I swore when my brother Lenny died that I would distance myself from anyone who was involved with drugs. How can I be with him with this on my mind all the time? Maybe Lenny died from drugs that Philip was involved with twelve years ago."

"I don't think so," Lucy said. "He made his money honestly. Ryan knows people in the business world who know Philip, and they all respect him."

"You haven't been with him since last August, but he stuck by, until Nicholas was better. When most of us were scared, and wondering if he'd pull through, Philip never let it enter his mind. I think they have a special bond with each other."

"Why didn't he visit the two weeks that Nicholas was in the hospital?" Laura asked.

"I think he made a promise to you that he'd leave after he saw him through his operation, and I guess that's why he left." Lucy suggested.

"I know you're upset, and I'm sorry for that, so lets not discuss it anymore," Lucy said, as she squeezed Laura's hand.

Laura smiled and said, "I'm so confused right now, but I'm glad to have you to lean on."

chapter VII

**LOS ANGELES INT. AIRPORT
FRIDAY, NOVEMBER 17, 1995
7:00 pm**

Philip checked his luggage, and received his boarding pass at the Quantas Airline counter. He still had over an hour before take off, so he decided to grab a bagel and coffee at the snack bar.

While he was sipping his coffee, he noticed a couple, three tables from his. They were perhaps in their late seventies or early eighties, but they were laughing, and he was holding her hands with both of his while looking her straight in her eyes. She was smiling back at him, and you could see the little wrinkles by her eyes, and a cute dimple on her cheek. They were probably discussing some passionate time in their life, and Philip thought to himself, how wonderful that two people their age still have romance.

He finished his snack, bought a magazine, and then went through security to the lounge. Ten minutes later he heard an announcement over the intercom. "May I have your attention please? Would Mr. Philip Mariano please come to the Quantas ticket counter."

The message was announced twice.

Philip's eyes lit up as he said under his breath, "Laura, you're here, you came to me."

He picked up his carry-on and headed at a fast pace for the counter.

On the way, there was a flower shop, so he bought a single red rose, (something he never missed for Laura) and handed the clerk a ten-dollar bill and said as he rushed out yelling, "Keep the change."

Within twenty feet of the counter, he was looking all around to see his beautiful Laura.

She wasn't anywhere in site, so he sauntered over to the attendant at the counter, and identified himself to the agent. The agent said, "Yes Mr. Mariano, you left your credit card folder on the counter." His head dropped in sadness as he said, "Thank you, miss."

She looked at him very inquisitively as she said, "Are you all right sir?" Philip hesitated for a few seconds and said, "Yes, I'm fine, I'm all right." He started to leave, and then turned around and said, "Thank you for the folder," and handed her the rose.

As he was walking towards the security gate, another announcement was coming over the P. A. system, "Flight 440 is now loading at gate 12 for Honolulu, Hawaii and Sydney, Australia."

After passing through security, he entered the loading ramp and on to the giant, Quantas 747, and was escorted by a flight attendant to his first class seat in the lounge. Philip didn't always fly first class, but on this occasion he needed the wider seat, and the privacy.

People were milling about, getting settled, storing their carry-on in the over head storage compartment, adjusting the air conditioning nozzles, and you could hear the clicking of seat belts being buckled.

Looking out his little port window, he could see the loading finger being hydraulically drawn back, and hear the door of the aircraft closing. Ground crews were removing the chucks from behind the wheels, while a tractor was hooking up to the front axle to tow the aircraft off the tarmac and onto the taxiing section.

All this was going on while the flight director was making announcements. He revealed the type of aircraft, and all the safety factors, while the flight attendants were demonstrating how the safety equipment was to be used, and where it was stored. Timing seemed to be an essence. When the announcements were completed the plane was on the runway.

All at once you could hear the roar of the Rolls Royce engines at full throttle. The brakes were released, and the aircraft eased its way down the runway, picking up speed rapidly, and within thirty seconds you could hear the groan of the plane as it left the ground. Then there was the sound of the wheels as they were lifted and locked in their compartments.

A few minutes later the aircraft was at its cruising height and speed. The "fasten seat belt" sign went off and flight attendants were handing out cushions and blankets to anyone who desired one. They were also taking orders for drinks.

One of the stewardesses, who identified herself as Lisa, was assigned to the section where Philip was. She asked him, "Would you prefer a drink sir?"

Philip answered by saying, "I would like a Pepsi, and maybe you could bring me a cushion."

Within seconds she was back with the Pepsi, poured it in a glass for him, and then reached up to the overhead compartment for a cushion that she also handed to him.

He said, "Thank you, Lisa, and if were going the same way for ten or twelve hours would you call me Philip or Phil?"

"Okay, Philip, how was that?" she asked.

"Excellent," he said with a smile. Then he placed the cushion behind his back.

The intercom beeped and the captain came on by identifying himself and informing the passengers the height they would be flying, the speed of the aircraft, and also the time-of-arrival to Honolulu and Sydney.

About forty-five minutes later, the flight director came over the intercom to advise the passengers that dinner would be served in half an hour, followed by a movie called *Sabrina* with Harrison Ford and Julia Ormond, a movie that Philip had already seen.

Philip spent the next half hour sipping his Pepsi and flipping through a magazine, but his concentration was miles away, back in Valleyfield. Dinner had been served and the attendants were gathering up the trays. The movie was about to begin that would last two and a half hours.

When Lisa took Philip's tray she asked, "Philip, would you like a brandy?"

"Thank you, but not right now Lisa. I think I will rest, and if I should fall asleep and snore, you have my permission to give me a kick."

She laughed and said, "Even if you do, there's no one beside you to complain. I'll wake you after the movie and pour you a nice cup of tea."

"Thanks, that would be nice," Philip said, as he thought how cute her Australian accent sounded.

Philip pulled down the window shade, and stretched his legs in front of the vacant seat beside him, placed the pillow behind his head, closed his eyes, and let his mind wander back to what took place after his Sarah died.

chapter VIII

VALLEYFIELD, INDIANA
JANUARY 1994

Three months had passed since Sarah's death. Philip spent most of that time alone. It was a very traumatic time for him, and he didn't feel comfortable being around anyone, and he wasn't good company anyway. He was quiet. When he did talk he seemed very moody. He missed her so much. Carol and Michael and his good friend Gray would try their best to console him, but he would just say, "I'll be okay."

Quite often he would drive up to Millcreek to spend time with Pedro and Juanita. This is where he was more relaxed. Juanita would cook up a nice meal, and would make sure that Philip kept up his appetite; she was also very comforting to talk with. He and Pedro would go for long rides. If you ever wanted to be with someone who didn't talk much, Pedro was that person. He had a special way with people like he did with animals. He would let the other person do the talking, and he would do the listening. When they would ask his opinion, he would answer them with a question, "What do you think?" Then they would feel better, because they felt that they solved their own problem, and he knew it.

At this time, Philip decided to sell the house in Valleyfield, and move to Millcreek, but first he had a great deal of work to do to get the old mill in shape.

He always meant to make it liveable, at least that's what his intentions have always been, but never found the time.

Millcreek is located in the rolling hills of Caledon. It's about a thirty-minute drive north west of Valleyfield. The entrance to the property is off County Road 13. At the entrance there's a sign on a post, beside a mailbox that reads, "Millcreek, Mariano & Lopez 6715." Norway maples line each side of the long wide laneway, and about fifty feet in you'll see a very attractive white frame and stucco house, with a picket fence, and a blue pickup truck in the driveway. This is where Pedro and Juanita live. Another fifty feet further down, there's a lane that leads to a small four stable barn, where Philip stables his horses.

As you continue on down the laneway, another two hundred feet, and over an incline, a small bridge comes in site, with a creek flowing in a thin gentle stream. Then across the bridge and over a small rise is where you see it, an old gristmill. These old mills always intrigued Philip; their subtle beauty, their ingenious technology, and their ultimate significance. He believed that they were remnants of our vanishing heritage; to ignore their purpose, and neglect their survival would be tragic, when so little remains of the beauty our ancestors created. Just think of all the romantic verses that were composed "by the old millstream," and the romantic walks taken by lovers of the past.

The mill was built in 1857, it's only two stories high, with the typical "old mill" windows (twelve-over-eight). It also has the original overshot wheel, made of wood.

This certain mill hadn't been operational since the late forties. Only a few are performing their original function. Many are still surviving, only to serve a new purpose, like museums, or homes as Philip's is.

So when the opportunity arose and the location was right, Philip took advantage and purchased the property of about fifty acres with the house and mill.

With Pedro's skill as an all round tradesman, they worked on it and had it restored by the end of April. Even the overshot wheel was repaired, and replaced to the millrace side of the mill.

The bed-stone, lower stationary stone, was still in place, and the revolving stone, called the runner, was placed on top of the bed-stone, which is now used as a pedestal to hold a large plant.

By May the house in town was sold, and Philip took up new residence in a place he had named Millcreek.

During the next few months he spent his time traveling for the company, working around his new residence, and taking long rides on his horse Phantom.

He was a very lonely man. He recalls the times when he'd return from his business trips; Sarah was always there to meet him. They would go for dinner, maybe take in a movie, and then spend the rest of the night in each other's arms. She used to tease him about having a girl at every port, and he would say, "And what do you think of that?" then she would say, "When they'd start looking good you'd rush home to me." And she was right about the latter. Sarah was the excitement in his life. Now he's alone...

By the end of November, Carol broke the happy news that she was pregnant, and would be expecting her baby by the following July. This is what Philip needed to build up his spirits. The next eight months couldn't go by fast enough, so he could spoil his first grandchild.

Christmas came and went, and January was cold, and slow. It was now nearing the end of February. Carol was in her fourth month. Philip told her and Jack that they better get out house hunting, so they could greet his grandchild with a new home. This was to be a wedding gift from he and Sarah. Michael and Diana preferred a cottage to a house, so his mother and father paid for one of their choice.

The next couple of weeks were spent looking at homes, but Jack and Carol couldn't find that "special one," so Carol decided to call the Indy State Realty to have an agent search the market for them.

She got in touch with a lady who seemed to be quite knowledgeable with the real estate market, and made an appointment to meet with her the following day. Her name was Laura Manning.

The next day Jack had an important meeting with the U.S. Customs Department in Indianapolis, so he would be gone for the day, and couldn't be with Carol to look at homes.

Around ten o'clock she drove down to the real estate office and parked her car in the visitors parking area, and went inside. There were three women sitting behind a counter; two were busy on computers, and the other was the receptionist, who also ran the switchboard.

When she saw Carol, she immediately stood up and said, "Good morning, may I help you?"

Carol answered, "Good morning, I'm Carol Dawson, and I'm here to see Mrs. Manning."

"Yes, I believe she's in," the receptionist said. "Would you like to take a seat Mrs. Dawson? I'll buzz her office. May I get you a coffee or tea?"

"No, I'm fine, thank you," Carol answered.

A few seconds later Carol saw a very attractive lady enter the foyer. She was about thirty-five years old, five feet six inches tall, auburn hair cut to her nape, and long at the crown. But what caught Carol's eye was her beautiful smile that seemed to reflect her smiling deep brown eyes. She was wearing a black leather skirt, just above the knees, a white blouse, buttoned to the throat and fastened with a mother-of-pearl broach, a red scarf, black panty hose, with black high heeled shoes.

Carol knew right away she was going to be very comfortable with her. She couldn't explain it, but it was apparent for their paths to cross.

The lady said, "Good morning, you must be Mrs. Dawson. I'm Laura Manning," as she reached her hand towards Carol.

Carol stood up and reached out her hand to meet Laura's and said, "Yes, I'm pleased to meet you. Please call me Carol."

"Only if you call me Laura," she replied.

After they got acquainted, Laura took her in her office, hung

Carol's coat on the coat rack, and asked, "Would you like a tea or coffee?"

"A coffee would be nice," Carol answered.

"Cream and sugar?" Laura asked, as she was leaving to go to the coffee station.

"Cream only, or milk." Carol replied.

Laura brought in a coffee for Carol, and a tea for herself, and then sat down in front of the computer and asked Carol to move her chair beside hers, so they could both see the listings that came across the monitor.

After a few minutes, Carol asked, inquisitively, "Have we met before?"

Laura sat back in her chair and looked at Carol and answered by saying, "I don't think so; have we?"

"You seem very familiar. I seem to know you from somewhere," Carol said.

Laura hesitated for a few seconds and said, "Maybe you've seen my picture in some of the real estate ads."

"That could be," Carol replied, but she knew it was something deeper than that.

As Laura was skimming the screen, they were filling each other in on what was happening in their lives, and when Carol was to have her baby, and if she knew what sex it was. Carol knew it was a girl.

Laura briefly told her about herself, that she had been divorced for two years, had a seven-year-old little boy whose name is Nicholas, and that he was born with only one functioning kidney.

Before long, an hour and two cups of tea and coffee had been consumed, they decided to take some printouts of resales, and check them out.

They spent another two hours looking at homes, mostly on the outskirts of the city, and also took in lunch. Then they realized the time, and Laura said, "My goodness, its almost two thirty. I have to pick up my son."

Carol replied, "Where did the day go?"

Laura drove Carol back to the real estate office to pick up her car, and they made arrangements to meet the next day. Laura said that she would call her around ten. For some unexplainable reason the two women, who had just met, got along like two best friends.

That evening at dinner, Carol talked to Jack about her day with Laura.

"Jack," she said, "something kind of strange happened today. When I met Laura, the real estate lady, we seemed to become instant friends. It's like I've known her for some time. We had so much to talk about, she is so nice."

"Of course she's nice and friendly," Jack said, "she's in a business where she has to be. If she finds us a house and we buy it, she will make a hefty commission."

"No, it's not that," Carol said, "I have a feeling about her. I think she's lonely, or she's hurting. Her son isn't too well; he has a kidney problem. Maybe that's on her mind."

"Or it's possible she's looking for a friend, and she found one in you."

"I don't know. We're meeting again tomorrow."

chapter IX

VALLEYFIELD, INDIANA
FEBRURARY, 1995

Carol knew that it wouldn't be long before she and Jack would be moving into their new home. This was the reason for her taking two weeks of her vacation from the Clearing Center where she's been employed for the past six years, so she could get a head start on some packing, and cleaning the apartment.

She had only got started washing down the kitchen cabinets when the phone rang. After stepping down from the step stool, she picked the phone up on the third ring and said, "Hello, oh hi Laura, how are you?"

"I'm fine," Laura answered. "What are you doing?"

"Just on my second day of cleaning and a little packing. I'm hoping you will find us a nice house," Carol jokingly replied.

"Well, we may have something," Laura said. "There's a couple of homes that were just listed, maybe we should take a look at them."

"Okay," Carol said, "will I meet you at your office?"

"No, I'll come over and pick you up. What's your address?" Laura asked.

Carol told her the address, and Laura asked, "How soon will you be ready?"

"I will meet you in the lobby in fifteen minutes, as soon as I take off these track pants that I wouldn't be seen dead in," Carol said.

"Okay, see you in fifteen minutes, and I'll buy lunch," Laura said.

Carol had just stepped out of the elevator, when she saw Laura drive up to the entrance. Laura reached over and opened the passenger door, and Carol quickly got in. They were both smiling, and seemed so excited, like two teenagers heading for a rock concert.

Carol said, "Hey, we timed that pretty good."

"I like to be on time," Laura replied. "It's not a good policy for the agent to be late for an appointment."

"I guess not, but you could be an exception with me." Carol joked as they both laughed.

"I have two nice houses that we should see." Laura said. "One is a three bedroom spilt level on a pie shaped lot, many upgrades, new furnace, new kitchen, new roof. The other house is a four bedroom, pool, finished recreation room. Maybe your husband, Jack should see them."

"No, we'll wait until we have the finished product, then we'll show him." Carol suggested.

Laura looked at her, and they both smiled, and then she said, "We'll surprise him."

"I received this information off the computer. It came in yesterday. I haven't seen them."

As they drove to the neighborhood where the split-level was, they noticed a lot of cars parked on the street. They looked at each other over their sunglasses and at the same time said, "Naw".

After a short drive, they approached the street that the second house was on. There were mature trees, sidewalks on both sides, and well-landscaped lots.

Laura parked the car in the driveway, and they both got out. An older lady came to the front porch that had a four-foot wrought iron fence around it, and said, "Good morning, you must be Mrs. Manning from the real estate."

"Yes," Laura replied, "and you are Mrs. McGilvery," as Laura showed her her credentials.

"This is my good friend and client, Mrs. Dawson," Laura continued.

Carol looked at Laura with a surprising, yet satisfying look, and smiled and said "How do you do? This is a lovely neighborhood."

"Yes it is, would you like to come inside?" said Mrs. McGilvery as she led the way.

It had only been listed a few days, so there hadn't been an open house for real estate agents. Every aspect of the house, inside and out, showed very well. Even the price was comfortable.

They thanked Mrs. McGilvery for her hospitality, and then left.

On the way to the restaurant Laura remarked, "It's a nice house, what do you think?"

Carol replied, "It's lovely."

Laura looked at her and said, "But it's not for you."

"How do you know that?" Carol asked.

"With any other client, I wouldn't. With you I just seem to know. It's hard to explain; when the right house comes along I'll see it in your eyes. Crazy, isn't it?" Laura said.

"I don't think so," Carol replied, as she thought, how odd that they sensed each other's feelings.

After their two-hour lunch, Laura drove Carol back to her apartment, and said that she would call her the next day.

Just about every day for the next week and a half they were either out looking at homes, or Laura would call her about a new listing that came over the computer. Most of the time, they enjoyed each other's company by having long lunches together.

One Friday night, around the middle of March, Carol and Jack were about to go out for a late dinner, when the phone rang. Jack picked it up and said, "Hello."

The voice at the other end said, "Hello, Jack, this is Laura."

"Hi, how are you?" Jack asked.

"I'm fine. I'm calling because I just found out that there's a lovely home down near the hospital, that will be on the market within a few days. It's a custom built home, and the owner has been transferred."

"That sounds great, Laura. When can we get to see it?" Jack asked.

"The house is empty, the people have already moved, and their company is selling the house. I can get the key first thing in the morning from their lawyer, and then come over and pick you up."

In the background, Laura could hear Carol getting all excited just by hearing part of the conversation, so Jack said, "Laura, I'll put Carol on, so you can tell her, before she has our baby right here."

Carol took the receiver and said, "Hi, did you find us a house?"

Laura answered by saying "I think I found your dream home. I haven't seen it, but by all the reports, it's supposed to be really nice." Then Laura told her, what she had told Jack.

"Can we see it now?" Carol asked.

"No, I can't get the key tonight. Don't worry, it won't burn down, and nobody is going to steal it," Laura answered. "I'll pick the two of you up at nine thirty tomorrow morning."

"You know damn well I won't get any sleep tonight," Carol said. They both laughed and said good-bye.

The next morning Laura picked up Jack and Carol, and on the way over Carol was pumping Laura about the house. "How big is it, how many bedrooms, what's the back yard like, does it have a pool?"

"I don't know much more than what I heard from Glen, the manager, and one of the other agents. It's in a beautiful area, I know that. I believe it's four bedrooms, and I think there is a pool. It will sell fast. The people that own it have moved to Texas."

"Do you know what they're asking for it?" Carol asked.

"I'm not sure, around three twenty-five, I think. The homes in the neighborhood are going for three seventy-five and up. The company would like to sell in a hurry, rather than have it sit around for a month or two, trying to squeeze a few more dollars. They don't mind breaking even."

Carol whistled, followed by a wow, "I wonder if Daddy will go for it."

"Laura said, "Hey, lets look at it first, you may not like it."

"Right," Carol answered.

The street was a large crescent that made it private from traffic.

When they were in sight of the house, Carol said, "Look, mature trees."

Jack responded with, "And many of them."

There was a large Chinese elm in the front yard near the road, a full size locust tree on the opposite side and closer to the house, and a well-pruned Mountain ash centering the two large trees. They turned in the driveway (that had to be sixty feet from the road) to the double garage doors, and on each side of the driveway were two weeping mulberries.

The two long steps at the entrance to the double front doors of the house, an English Tudor, were done in river stone with hedge on either side and a tall juniper to the left of the doors. You could see the shoots of many daffodils and tulips making their way through the surface of the ground.

Carol said, "If I don't go any further, I think I want it."

Laura answered by saying, "Let's not go by first impressions, there might be termites," as she unlocked the door.

"Not in Valleyfield," Jack replied.

As they entered, they noticed the foyer floor was a rich looking bluish, pinkish, white Italian marble that continued through the hallway and into the open concept kitchen. The kitchen cabinets were white and blue with brass handles. Everything seemed to be in its place.

Jack said to Carol, "Honey, take a look at this," as he held the French doors open that led to the back yard.

There was a huge deck with three steps at either end leading to the pool that had all the extras. Beside the pool there was a change room, with a sauna attached, and a bar that faced the pool, all done in stained pine.

On the other side of the yard there was a gazebo with a Jacuzzi in it. Beyond the pool, stretching back to the fence, another forty feet, stood a willow tree and a swing blowing in the breeze. The property backs onto greenbelt, with a wooded area of sugar maples beyond the fence.

Carol said, "Yes. I want it," as she grabbed Jack around the neck with both arms. "I can see us now, sitting by the pool, and our little girl swinging under the willow, and Nicholas will be pushing."

Laura looked at them, and said, "Thank you, I hope so. Now, let's take a look at the upstairs."

"Let's go," Carol answered as she and Jack made their way across the deck.

The rails of the winding staircase, which led to the upstairs, were stained in a light brown, with white pickets. The stairs were carpeted in a peach color. There were four bedrooms upstairs, with two ensuites and a washroom off the hall. There was also a small room, ten by twelve, that could be an office.

Carol, right away planned out the nursery, then she grabbed Laura's arm and said, "I am so happy that we met, and you found us this house. I hope you will be our friend forever."

Jack said, "Sweetheart, it's not ours yet."

Carol turned to Laura and said with emotion, "I don't want anyone else to look at this house."

"I feel the same way. We want it. Is that possible?" Jack asked Laura.

"Like I said to you a couple of weeks ago," Laura replied, "when we find the right house, I'll see it in your eyes, and I can see it in both your eyes. Yes, to your question, it's possible. We'll write up an offer and a check for about five thousand dollars."

"We can handle that right now," Jack said.

"Okay, let's go to the office. You won't lose your deposit, and you might want to get the house inspected, the wiring, the furnace—that's if we're accepted." Laura said.

"You know what, speaking of a furnace, we haven't seen the

basement," Jack commented.

When they reached the basement, Jack said, with excitement, "Wow, take a look at this."

The basement was completely finished with an oval bar with all the fancy lights, a large billiard table, and a stained glass light over a poker table.

"Now I have to bring the happy news to my father, who will look after the financial segment," Carol said.

"Your father's out of town. He won't be back until late Tuesday night, and then he's off to Kansas at noon on Wednesday," Jack said.

"We'll have to get him here on Wednesday morning," Carol said. "What if another agent wants to show the house to someone else?" she continued.

"Well, for one thing, the owner's lawyer won't be in his office until Monday. By then I'll have the offer to him, and besides, I have the only set of keys," Laura answered.

"I think we love you. I'm glad Carol found you," Jack said.

"Me too," Laura replied, "you both are so nice. I hope this isn't the beginning of the end for us."

"By no means," Carol said as she held her hand, "I haven't had so much fun and laughs in a long time, and that little boy of yours, Nicholas, he's a little sweetheart. You have to meet him Jack. He's going to break a few hearts."

"I'm looking forward to it, and if, no, I should say, when, we move to our new house, we will be expecting you both often."

They reached the office, and when all the signing of papers was finished Laura said, "First thing Monday morning, I will deliver the offer to the lawyer personally, so he can get it to his client. We should have a reply by the afternoon."

Jack and Carol both thanked her, and then left.

The remainder of the day and on into the night, they spent planning the baby's nursery, what furniture they would buy, and for what rooms. Around ten o'clock, by coincidence, the phone rang. Carol answered it. It was her father calling from Quebec

City. Before he could say, "hi, how are you honey," she started, "Daddy, we found the perfect house, our dream home. You have to get home here to see it, and you must meet Laura, our real estate agent. She is so nice, Daddy, she is the one."

Philip said, "Hold on a minute, pumpkin. First of all, how are you, and second, I am very happy that you found a nice house, and third, quit playing Cupid."

She said, "I'm fine, and so is the baby, and Jack is almost as excited as I am, and after you meet Laura, I won't try to set you up again."

"That's great, I'm delighted, now could I speak to Jack?"

"Okay, I love you, Daddy, and we'll see you on Wednesday morning."

"I love you too, and I'll be there between ten thirty and eleven. I'll call you for the address."

"Hi, Philip, how is everything in Quebec?" Jack asked.

"Cold, you sure have an excitable wife," Philip joked.

"Oh, she's really wound up about this house that's not ours yet, but it's a real beauty."

"Well, let's hope the offer goes through. Call Frank, our lawyer, first thing Monday morning and fill him in. I also want you to go to the office tomorrow and dig out the folder on the shipment of lumber that we're importing. I need some pricing," Philip said.

"Right, I'll do that first thing in the morning and fax it to you. I know exactly where it is," Jack replied.

"Thanks, Jack, and don't let my little girl have a heart attack," Philip said.

"I'll try to keep her calm. Don't freeze to death up there, and by the way, she is a classy lady."

"You too!!! See you next week."

chapter x

VALLEYFIELD, INDIANA
MONDAY, MARCH 1995
8:00 am

Laura was in the kitchen making breakfast for Nicholas, who was sitting at the table, finishing up some homework that he didn't complete last night, when the phone rang. Nicholas picked it up and said, "Hello."

The voice at the other end was Carol's, and she said, "Hi Nicholas, how are you this morning?"

Nicholas answered, "I'm fine, and how are you Carol?"

"I'm fine too. What are you doing?" Carol asked.

"I'm doing the rest of my addition that I didn't get finished last night and Mommy is making my breakfast and my lunch."

"Mommy said that you and Jack will be moving to a new house," he continued.

"I sure hope so, and if we do, I want you and your mommy to visit us as often as you can," Carol said.

"Really, oh that will be neat. We would like that. Here's Mommy now, good bye Carol."

He handed the receiver to his mother.

"Hi there, excitable woman. Did you get lots of rest over the weekend?" Laura asked.

"No, there was a house on my mind most of the time."

Laura laughed and said, "I knew that, and I'll bet that you and Jack went for a little ride or two."

"How do you know so much about me?" Carol asked. "We went over to the house four times."

"See, I knew that, I'm psychic, didn't you know?" Laura replied.

"I think you're getting scary," Carol joked. "How about us having lunch, or going shopping, or both?" she suggested.

"I like the 'both,' but first I have to get Nicholas off to school, and then run some errands, and you know what they are; 'offer to the lawyer', so I'll pick you up around ten forty-five."

"Great," Carol said, "I'll be here if their lawyer needs any more information."

Laura was earlier than she thought. She buzzed Carol's apartment at ten thirty. Carol answered the buzzer with, "Hello."

"Hi, it's me," Laura said.

"Come on up," Carol replied.

When Laura came in the apartment, she was smiling quite noticeably.

"Why the big grin?" Carol asked. "Either our offer was accepted, or you got laid last night, or I'm right on both accounts."

"Neither," Laura answered. "We will know about your offer around three o'clock. The lawyer said it looked respectable. And the latter, I haven't been with anyone since my ex-husband George, over two years ago, and he's the only man I've ever slept with."

"No kidding," Carol said with surprise.

"I have to have love and strong feelings for a man before I'll sleep with him," Laura said.

Carol looked at her for a moment, without saying anything. She was thinking about her father, as her thoughts were, "I wonder, my dad and Laura, how wonderful" as you could see a smile on her face.

"What's the matter?" Laura asked. "Do you find it strange that I feel that way?"

"Oh no, not at all," Carol answered, "I think that's wonderful. Is there anyone in your life now?"

"No, I've been out for dinner a couple of times, but I've never accepted a second date. Lucy has tried to set me up a few times, until I told her how I felt, and she understood. I will know when the right person is there. My first priority is my son; we will both know when the right man comes to share our lives. I think I'm talking too much, aren't I?"

"No," Carol said, "I believe you, and I respect you for what you just told me, (as she thought again about someone else, whose priorities are identical) and I have a confession. Jack's the only man that I've been with."

"What? A young fox like you," Laura joked.

They went out shopping, had lunch, and gabbed a couple of hours away, and on the way home they stopped to wait for the school bus, to pick up Nicholas. The bus stop was only two blocks down the street from Laura's house, but they timed it close, she had only parked the car at the curb when the bus arrived. Laura and Carol got out of the car to greet Nicholas when he stepped off the bus. His mother gave him a kiss on the cheek, and could tell that he wasn't in a good mood.

Carol greeted him with, "Hi, handsome."

When they got in the car, Laura asked him, "Are you all right? Do you have a problem?"

Nicholas answered by saying a sharp, "No!" and turned and looked out the window.

Carol turned around and asked, "Did you play road hockey again today?"

"Yah, but I wasn't very good," he said with a whine in his voice.

"Oh, that comes with a lot of practice," Carol said. "Isn't your favorite player Wayne Gretzsky?" she asked.

"Yes, he is," he said with pride.

"Well, Wayne's father built a small rink in their back yard when Wayne was only three years old, and he used to place pylons in a straight row along the ice. Every day, for hours, Wayne would start at one end with his hockey stick and go in and out of those pylons. He pretended those pylons were other players on the ice.

That's why he can stick handle around the other players so well, and that's why they call him The Great One.

"Really?" Nicholas said with excitement. "How do you know?" he asked.

"My dad told me, and he is one of his greatest fans," Carol said

"Your dad likes hockey?" Nicholas asked.

"Oh yes, he used to play when he was younger, but not professionally. He still likes to have a game with Jack, and my brother Michael, and some of their friends," Carol replied.

"I'll tell you what; hopefully, when we move into our new house, I'll round up all those guys, and Lucy's husband Ryan, and we will play road hockey on our driveway," Carol continued.

"That would be neat. Can we do that Mommy?" he asked.

"We sure can," his mother answered as they were getting out of the car.

Nicholas ran ahead and unlocked the door.

Laura said, "Thanks, you sure brightened up his day. Is this one of your special gifts?"

"Most likely," Carol answered. "It comes from my father. He always had a way to cheer people up when they were down. He'd say it's your 'excitement nerve'. When someone is sad, you talk about something that they like, or get excited about. It works every time."

"He sounds like a good guy to have around," Laura commented.

Carol thought to herself, "I only hope you find out," and crossed her fingers.

As they were closing the door, Laura's pager beeped. She called her office and found out that it was the secretary of the lawyer for the company that was selling the house. Right away she phoned them and was told to meet at their office at four o'clock.

"Great," Carol said, "I'll stay here with Nicholas, and beat him at a game of Crazy Eights."

"Okay, if that's all right with you," Laura said.

"Yah, that will be fun," Nicholas replied, "only I will beat her."

"Don't forget you have homework," Laura said, as she was slipping on her coat and boots and then left.

After six games of cards, where Nicholas won four of them, Carol decided to make herself a cup of tea, when the phone rang. Nicholas was busy sorting out the cards, so Carol picked up the receiver and said, "Hello."

It was Laura, and she excitedly said, "I'm picking up a bottle of champagne, you better call Jack, they accepted the offer."

"Oh, thank you Lord, thank you Laura, thank you whoever took the offer," Carol screamed as she hugged Nicholas.

"We can tie everything up definitely this week, and you will have the keys by the weekend." Laura said, "They informed your lawyer this afternoon."

"Okay," was Carol's answer. "I'll phone my father tonight. He's out of town, and won't be back until late tomorrow night, so I won't see him until Wednesday morning. Now you get the heck home. My baby and I want to give you a big hug."

"I'll be home in thirty minutes." Laura said.

chapter X1

WEDNESDAY, MARCH 15, 1995
7:00 am

Carol got up earlier than usual this morning so she could put on a pot of coffee and warm some bagels for Jack and for her brother Michael, who came over to pick him up. They were going to the office an hour earlier to prepare the paper work for Philip's business trip to Kansas.

He had a meeting with the Farmer's Association and the state government. It mostly involved customs duties, shipping, and customs regulations on a shipment of combines that were being imported from Brussels for a large farm equipment dealer in Kansas.

Carol served her brother a bagel and poured him a coffee while filling him in on their new home.

Jokingly, Michael said, "I know where Diana and I will be on the weekends— your pool, your sauna, and then I'll beat Jack at snooker."

Jack entered the kitchen, and was pouring a coffee and said, "Were going to be looking forward to you doing that. Not beating me at pool, because I'll be giving you a few lessons, but coming over when you're not at the cottage."

"Daddy's coming over before he leaves, to see our house," Carol said, "and I want him to meet Laura."

"I see you're still playing Cupid," Michael said. "When Dad's ready, he'll find the right woman, and I don't think he's looking right now," he added.

"Laura is different," Carol said. "I'm sure he will like her. She's his type of woman."

"How do you know what his type is?" Michael asked. "We've only known him with mother."

"Right," Carol answered with a satisfying smile.

Michael looked at her strangely, then asked, jokingly, "She's not an old retired school teacher, is she?"

"Quite the opposite, Mike," Jack replied. "Laura is a very charming woman, inside and out."

"Well, I hope he meets someone soon; loneliness isn't one of his traits," Michael said.

"I'm ready, if you are," Jack said as he gave Carol a kiss.

Michael grabbed another bagel, gave his sister a peck on the cheek, and said, "Good luck with your matchmaking, Sis."

"Tell Daddy to call me on my cell phone, around ten. I'll be at the new house with Laura."

Sometime around ten-thirty, they had all the paperwork in order for Philip to take on his trip to Wichita, Kansas. The months of preparation, along with the miles that Philip logged from Valleyfield to Kansas, and Valleyfield to Belgium, would surely profit about two-hundred thousand dollars on the eighty combines that were being purchased. So, before he left his office, he phoned Carol to say that he would be over to the house in fifteen minutes and asked her for directions.

Carol and Laura were busy planning room by room, measuring the windows for drapes and blinds, and what colors to choose, especially for the nursery, when they heard a car pull in the driveway. Carol looked out the upstairs window, and said, "It's my father," and then hurried downstairs to meet him. Laura followed her. Philip had already exited from his car when Carol opened the front door.

Laura, after staring at him for a couple of seconds, asked surprisingly, "Is *that* your father?" As her memory of this man went back almost two years.

"Yes," Carol answered, "do you know him?" she asked.

Before Laura could answer, Carol trotted out to meet her father, who was now walking faster toward the door.

She flung her arms around his neck and said, "I missed you. It's been over two weeks."

"I know," he said, "they keep sending me away on these trips. How have you been, and how is my little sweetheart?" as he patted her on her tummy.

"Oh, she's all excited about her new nursery," Carol answered.

When they reached the front door with their arms around one another, where Laura was standing, Carol said, "Daddy, I want you to meet my new friend. This is Laura. Laura, this is my father, Philip."

As she put out her hand to meet his, he was staring into her eyes, and unconsciously his other hand came forward to entrap hers. He was encircled by the scent of her eau de cologne, Obsession, that captured her body as if it was made for her. For what seemed to be moments, Philip didn't say a word. His thoughts were, "She is, without question, the most beautiful woman that I have ever seen." It was something beyond her beauty that caught at him. There was an almost palpable force that pulled him to her. Some unexplainable reaction that made him feel as though he had known her forever.

Laura said with a smile, "How do you do? It's nice to meet you."

Philip was still holding her hand, with both of his, and looking very strangely into her eyes.

Carol was looking at both of them with a satisfying look on her face, and then said, "Daddy," as though she were trying to pull him out of a trance.

At that moment, Philip came out of his composed thoughts, and said, "I'm sorry, you seemed to have taken me away. I'm glad to meet you. Carol speaks well of you."

"Why, thank you," Laura replied. "We have met before."

"Oh no. No." Philip said. "My eyes would have had to be clouded to not notice the beauty that stands before me now."

"They were." Laura answered softly. "It was almost two years ago, at the Valley Hospital. I was the woman you bumped into when you were coming out from the chapel. You likely don't remember."

"Yes, I do. It was the day my wife Sarah died. I was a little clouded up that day," Philip said.

Carol whispered to herself, "My God, I can't believe she started so soon. Now it all makes sense, or does it?"

Laura heard her, and asked, "What started so soon?"

"Oh nothing, I was just thinking out loud," as her thoughts went back to what her mother told her. "You will meet someone who will make you happy, and become friends, and in time, your father will too." She didn't think much of it at the time, because she couldn't picture her father having an interest in any other woman but her mother.

As Carol and Laura were giving Philip the grand tour of the house, and characterizing each room, he was listening, but not hearing. His mind and eyes were on this beautiful person, and Laura knew it.

Carol was greatly pleased, not only because of her new home, but also for her father. She could see that the change from loneliness to happiness had transformed.

"What time is your flight, Daddy?" Carol asked.

"Are you trying to get rid of me?" he asked jokingly, then said, "It's one o'clock. I guess I'd better be on my way."

What do I say to her now, he thought to himself. It's been so long since I've courted. Should I ask to see her again?

Carol saved the moment as she asked, "When you get in on Friday, do you think the three of us could have lunch?"

"I think that's a great plan," Philip said, thankfully, "I'll look forward to it."

"I thought you would," Carol said, as she looked at him with a sneaky smile.

"That would be nice, and I'll treat," Laura replied, as she was also grateful that Carol mentioned the lunch.

"No," Philip said, "it would be my pleasure."

"Now, now children," Carol said with authority, "you two just met, and it's so cute that you're having your first quarrel. I'll splurge for lunch, period." They laughed and agreed.

"You'd better be on your way, Daddy," Carol continued, "you don't want to keep those farmers in Wichita waiting. They may get angry."

"You're right honey, and how old are you going to be when you stop calling me 'Daddy'?" he asked, jokingly.

"Well, I could call you Phil," Carol replied, "but you always said that I'm your little girl, so you're my daddy. Anyway, I'm comfortable with it."

He shook his head with a smile, and asked, "Laura, do you call your father 'Daddy'?"

She lowered her head, and took a breath, and said, "I did, but he was killed in Vietnam. He was a helicopter pilot. My brother and I were only eight."

"I am so sorry. It must have been very traumatic for you all," Philip said with deep concern.

"Yes, it was," she answered, "and then I lost my brother in eighty-five."

Carol came over and put her arms around her and said, "I am sorry too."

Philip said, "Me and my big mouth. I apologize for rekindling such a sorrowful time in your life."

"Oh no, don't be sorry," Laura said, "I can handle it now . I believe that they are together in heaven and are watching over us."

Philip looked at her with compassion, and replied, "I'm sure they are, and I do mean that."

"My mother is now remarried to a wonderful man, and is living in Seattle."

"I must leave. It's been a real pleasure to have met you,"

Philip said.

"You too," Laura replied. "We'll see you on Friday."

"I'm looking forward to it," he said smiling.

Carol walked her father to his car. As he was getting in she said, "You old hound dog you. Isn't she nice?" she asked.

"She is beautiful; do you think she might like me?" he asked.

"I believe it started over a year ago, but none of us knew it. Women know women; I'm sure she does, and daddy," (as she looked at him with sincerity) "she is a wonderful person."

"I'm sure you're right, and I'm glad you didn't give up trying." He gave her a kiss, and said, "See you Friday" as he waved to Laura, who was standing on the porch.

When Carol entered the house, Laura said, "I had no idea who your father was until I saw him. I know you mentioned your mother, who passed away over a year ago, but I never connected one with the other, and you never mentioned his last name."

"You're right. I don't think I ever did," Carol answered. "So, what do you think?" she asked.

Laura thought she'd toy with her and asked, "About what?"

"About my dad," Carol said with expression.

"Now let's see. I think he's a little handsome, he's most likely very shy, he has a nice personality, but it's really hard to tell," Laura said.

"Tell about what?" Carol asked with wonderment.

"I think he was in cloud nine," Laura answered.

"Yes, he was, wasn't he? I've never seen this side of my father. He and my mother used to show their affection very openly. Hell, he was always at her. Michael and I grew up with it, but seeing him with you, I don't know, kind of brought him back to me again.

"He's been extremely lonely since my mother died. Doesn't go anywhere, except on business. Most of his time is working, or at his farm. He likes you, a lot. I saw the change in him the moment he set eyes on you."

Laura cut in by saying, "Remember when I said, 'when the right man comes into my life, I will know it'? Well, I have that feeling now."

"Really," Carol commented, "as she gave Laura a squeeze on the hand. "He's a good man, and he loves kids. You will see when he meets Nicholas. If he knew I was building him up like I'm doing, he would turn me over his knee."

Both Laura and Carol had appointments. Carol had a two o'clock with her doctor, and Laura had a meeting at her office. But what she really wanted to do was tell her friend Lucy all about meeting Philip Mariano. That would have to wait because Ryan and Lucy were in Chicago and wouldn't be back until Friday night.

chapter XII

WICHITA, KANSAS

The next two days in Wichita seemed to drag by, in Philip's mind. It's a miracle how he got through the meetings with the Farmer's Association, but everything worked out well.

Physically, he was there, mentally his mind was back in Valleyfield with Laura. He couldn't wait for those big wings to fly him back to her.

The meetings were over by ten o'clock Friday morning. Philip's luggage consisted of a carry-on, which he had with him, so he grabbed a cab from the Association headquarters and was at the airport to catch a ten thirty-five plane that got him into Fort Wayne by twelve o'clock noon.

He was at the exit door before the engines were shut down, was like a school boy waiting for recess. Philip was off the plane, hurried to catch the shuttle bus to drive him to the parking lot, paid the attendant and then on to Interstate 69, for the thirty minute drive that took him twenty.

Was she just being nice to him, because he was Carol's father. That would be proper. She's seventeen years younger than him, only seven years older than his son Michael.

"Hell," he thought, "I'm only having lunch with her. I'm not asking her hand in marriage. What a lovely thought."

At twelve twenty-five he walked in his office to the cheering of "hip, hip, hurrah" from his office staff.

A large smile came over his face, as he asked, "Are there no secrets in this town. I see my lovely daughter has been filling you all in," he added.

Theresa, his secretary and office manager, said jokingly, "Carol tells me everything. She always has, you know that, so be careful," as she followed him in his office.

Theresa Hayes is an African American lady in her sixties, who has been with the company for thirty-five years, back when Stefaniac was the owner. She is always completely candid, a marvelous human being, and a fabulous employee. There isn't an import or export that goes through the company that she isn't involved with. Philip learned from the beginning to lean on her and love her as a person. She is one of the main contributors to the success of the company. Philip grabbed her by the arms and did a little twirl around his office.

Theresa said, "Okay, okay, who is she? I want to check her out. No, never mind. You have my approval. It's gratifying to see you back to your old self again. Are you all right?" she added.

"Yes, I think so," Philip answered. "You know, Theresa, I can't keep her off my mind. It's like I've been given special permission from Sarah to perceive this through. She's telling me to go ahead, it's all right." He started to break up a little. "Does that sound demented?"

"No, not at all," Theresa answered. "I've known Sarah almost as long as you have. She and I have spent many special moments together, and she was a big believer about when something or someone dies, others shouldn't carry on their lives as if life has also been taken from them. She taught me after my Howie died, that I must live on and prevail. This is what Sarah would want you to do."

"Thanks Theresa," Philip said as he gave her a hug. "When I need comfort, or motherly advice, or both, why do I always come to you?"

"I don't know," Theresa answered. "I can't remember 'motherly advice' on my resume."

"I've never seen your resume," Philip replied.

"That's possibly because you were too young to read," she said with a smile.

"Okay," he said, "how would you like to get me my talkative daughter on the phone. She's presumably at her apartment. If not, call her cell phone."

"Right away, boss," Theresa joked.

Philip looked at her and shook his head, and said, "By the way, the lady's name is Laura Kaitlan Manning. She is a real estate agent with the Indy State Realty."

"How nice," Theresa commented from her desk. "Do you think we can get a discount on a new home?"

Philip looked out his office door towards her desk and said, "Your home is this office."

A few seconds later Theresa said, "Carol's on line two."

"Thank you," Philip said as he picked up the receiver. "Hi sweetheart, how are you?"

"Fine, Daddy. Did your meeting go well in Wichita?" Carol asked.

"Very well. The farmers up in Salina and most of them in the state of Kansas are going to be very happy when they receive their combines this summer in time for the harvest," Philip answered. "What's new on the house?" he asked.

"Everything is in motion," Carol answered. "Jack and I signed the papers yesterday; the house is now ours."

"Great," Philip replied. "I'm really happy for you both, I should say you three."

"Daddy, I don't have to see you to know who's on your mind." Carol said.

"Is that right? I didn't know that I had such a brilliant daughter," Philip answered. Well, do you think a gentleman could take two lovely ladies out to lunch?" he added.

"Unlikely," Carol replied, "but I'm sure we'd love to have lunch with you."

"I'm going to shower and shave here at the office," Philip

said, "so I'll meet you at the club about one thirty."

"We'll be there," Carol answered.

Philip reached the Valleyfield Golf and Country Club, where he had been a member for many years, at one twenty-five. After saying hello and having small talk with a couple of friends and other members, he entered the dining room where he saw Carol sitting alone at a table by the window.

When he reached the table, he bent over and kissed his daughter on the cheek, and said, "Hi, nice to see you again."

"You too," Carol replied. "That western air suits you well. You look very, how will I say, bright, and don't worry, Laura will be here. She had to drop off a letter of permission to the school so her son Nicholas could go on a bus trip to the museum in Fort Wayne next week."

"Now, did I look worried?" her father asked.

They didn't have long to wait. You could almost feel her entrance. The room seemed to glow as she entered the dining room.

The host was escorting her to her table. Philip was watching her, as he stood up. You could see her full smile from across the room, and she walked as though she was walking in late for a church service, not wanting to cause attention, but that wasn't to be. Heads were turning, but not only men; women were also looking at this very graceful lady as she made her way to Philip's table. He was, without a doubt, the most envied man in the club as he held Laura's chair for her.

"Thank you," she said. "It's nice to see you again. Was your trip successful?" she asked.

"Yes, it was, but it was too long," Philip replied. "You look lovely today," he continued.

"Why thank you again," Laura said.

"Hey, what am I, chopped liver?" Carol asked.

Laura reached over and touched her hand and smiled. Philip took her other hand and said, "Tell you what—since you're eating for two, we'll let you order lunch."

"Okay, we'll have Italian," Carol replied.

"That sounds pretty good to me," Laura said.

"Italian it is," Philip replied.

Lunch went well. Philip got to know a little more about Laura, her work, what she liked to do away from her job. But what pleased him the most was the love she had for her son Nicholas. He was her life.

It was getting close to three o'clock when Laura mentioned that she had to pick up Nicholas from the bus stop.

Philip motioned to the waitress, and when she came over, she asked, "Will there be anything else, Mr. Mariano?"

"No, we're okay, Fran," Philip answered as he handed her a twenty dollar bill, "charge the bill to my account, and thank you."

She said, "Thank you, and I'll look after it."

As they were leaving, Philip was racking his brain on how he was going to ask her to go out. Then it hit him, the tickets that he had bought a month ago to a play in Fort Wayne this Saturday night.

So he found himself saying, "Laura, would you like to accompany me to a," then he hesitated for a couple of seconds, "I guess you would call it a play? It's called *Love Letters* with Robert Wagner and Stephanie Powers. It's playing at the Convention Center in Fort Wayne tomorrow night."

Laura's thought "Thank you for asking," as she answered, "I would love to. I'll have my friend Lucy look after Nicholas."

"Oh, if that's a problem," Philip said, "the three of us could go to a movie."

Then Carol spoke up and said, "If Lucy is unavailable, I'd be glad to. You know how great he and I hit it off, and were not doing anything."

"Thanks, Carol," Laura said, "I'm sure Lucy and Ryan will take him. They're always at me to let him stay."

"Then it's settled," Philip said, "I'll pick you up, say about six-thirty tomorrow night. That will give us time to have dinner, before the show."

"That will be fine," Laura replied, "six-thirty, I'll be ready."

On her way to the bus stop to meet Nicholas, she called her friend Lucy. Lucy wasn't at the office or at home, so Laura left a message on her pager for her to respond. Within two minutes, Laura's cell phone rang. It was Lucy saying, "Hi, what's the panic?"

Laura said, "I have something very exciting to tell you. Where can we meet?"

"I'm a few blocks from your house," Lucy answered. "I was on my way over to see you."

"Okay, I'm at the bus stop," Laura replied, "I'll be home as soon as I pick up Nicholas. Let yourself in. You have your key, don't you?"

"Yes, I also have to pee, so I'll let you go," Lucy said, "and yes, although you didn't ask, we had a good time in Chicago."

"Sorry," Laura said, "I'm a little excited."

As Laura reached home, Lucy met them at the door, and said to Nicholas, "Do I get a big hug from my favorite guy?"

Nicholas answered, while giving and receiving a hug, "I'm not your favorite guy, Ryan is."

"Can't a girl have two favorites?" Lucy asked.

Nicholas smiled, and then asked his mother if he could call on his friend Bobby, three doors down, to play some road hockey.

She agreed and told him to be home in an hour for dinner.

He took off down to Bobby's house. Laura and Lucy watched until they saw him go in the house, then they went in, and Laura plugged the kettle in to heat some water for tea.

"So, why the big smile, and what's the exciting news," Lucy asked, "Did you get laid?"

"No, you goof," Laura answered. "You know the Dawsons, Carol and Jack," she continued, "the couple that bought the Brown's house."

"Yes," Lucy answered, "we met at the office, a lovely couple."

"Well, I met Carol's father Wednesday morning, at the new house," Laura said, "and the three of us had lunch today at the Valleyfield Country Club."

"That's nice," Lucy mused.

"His name is Philip Mariano, he's buying the house for them, it's a wedding gift that he promised them. Do you know who he is?" Laura asked.

"Should I?" Lucy replied.

"Remember the time, about a year and a half ago, when you and I picked up Nicholas at the Valley Hospital?" Laura asked.

"Yes," Lucy answered, "the two days that he was there for tests on his kidney."

"Right," Laura said. "Do you also remember a man bumping into me as we walked by the chapel on our way out?" she asked.

"Yes I do," Lucy replied. "There was a group of people coming out of the chapel, and the man that bumped you apologized a half dozen times."

"That's him, Philip Mariano, Carol's father," Laura said with a big smile. "He asked me to go to a play with him in Fort Wayne tomorrow night."

"Hey, slow down a bit, you just met him." Lucy said.

"I know," was Laura's reply, "but I just feel so good, I can't help smiling. The moment I saw him, something seemed to tell me to go ahead, it's safe."

"Well, I can see that he's put the smile back on your face," Lucy said, "something I haven't seen for years."

"Lucy, he's such a nice man, you have to meet him," Laura said. "When he first saw me," she continued, "he stared into my eyes with a half frown and half smile and didn't say a word for about ten seconds, like he was looking beyond my eyes, and instead of shaking my hand, he held it with both of his, and after Carol pulled him out of his trance, he told me that I was the most beautiful woman that he's ever seen, and he raised my hand and kissed it. I knew, right then, that he was a kind, loving, and passionate man."

"Look at you," Lucy said smiling, "you're like a giddy school girl going on her first date. By the sounds of it, you accepted to go."

"Yes I did," Laura answered, as she was preparing dinner.

"How about Nicholas?" Lucy asked, "you haven't dated anyone since your divorce. He may take offence."

"I'm not running away and marrying the man," Laura sternly said. "If we see more of each other, you know that Nicholas will sure be a part of it."

"I'm sorry for being so negative," Lucy said (as she hugged her friend), "I'm acting like your big sister. I'm happy for you, I really am. You've been carrying a lot of sadness for too long. It's time you had a little, I should say, a lot of happiness."

"Thanks," Laura said, "I can feel it already. By the way, how would you and Ryan like to look after Nicholas tomorrow night."

"We'd love to," Lucy replied. "I'll pick him up tomorrow at noon, and take him shopping with me, and he can stay the night. I'm sure you'll have some preparing to do for your 'Big Night'."

"Philip said I was beautiful enough, so what preparing could I do?" Laura said as they laughed.

"I don't know if I could have survived the last two years without you and Ryan by my side. I love you both, I mean, we, Nicholas and I love you both. You spoil us crazy, especially him," Laura said.

"Sure you would survive," Lucy replied, "and he's an easy little guy to love and spoil. Ryan and I couldn't love him more, if he were our own, and he is our godchild."

"I still want to see a resume on this guy," Lucy added with a smile.

chapter XIII

VALLEYFIELD, INDIANA

Saturday night at six-thirty, the temperature was about thirty-eight degrees and snow was falling lightly, when Philip entered Laura's driveway. She lived on a quiet crescent in a split-level, four-bedroom house, a settlement from her divorce.

He had no sooner left his car, and was walking to the entrance when the front door opened, and Laura made her appearance.

Philip's first impression was, "My God, she's more beautiful than when I first saw her." She was wearing a soft, yellow, knitted tank top dress, with a matching cardigan. The highlights in her hair seemed to glimmer in the light. Her gold earrings and matching bangles on her wrist set off the beautiful dress, and her smile was full showing off beautiful white teeth.

"Hi, come in," Laura said. "I just have to put on my coat," as she reached in the closet. "You look very handsome."

"Thank you, best compliment I've had this year. No one ever gets used to seeing me in a suit. Most of the time, where there's a dress code, the host usually finds me a tie or jacket or both, and they never match." They laughed, and Philip handed her a single red rose.

"If I were to tell you how lovely you look tonight, we would be here for hours, and I would bore you." Philip said.

"No you wouldn't, go ahead," Laura replied.

"Well, you do look very lovely," Philip remarked. "I'm going to be the envy of every man we see tonight."

"Thank you," Laura said.

As he helped her with her coat, he noticed a boy's picture on the end table and said, "This good looking guy better be your son Nicholas, or I'm going to be very jealous."

"Yes," Laura replied, "that's my right hand man."

"He has your eyes and smile," Philip remarked.

Do you think so?" Laura asked.

"Absolutely," Philip answered. "I would love to meet him."

"He was funny this morning," Laura said. "I told him that I was going out with a nice man, and he started to give me the third degree. He said, 'You haven't been on a date for a long time, some men you can't trust.' Then I told him that I was going out with Carol's father, and he asked, 'Is he as nice as Carol?'" They laughed, and as they were going out the door Laura said, "Oh yes, Carol volunteered all your family, Ryan and Lucy, and myself to a road hockey game on Jack and Carol's driveway, as soon as they move in."

"Great," Philip replied. "I'll look forward to it. Boys against girls."

"That's not fair," Laura said, "there's more of you than us."

On the way to Fort Wayne, Laura said, "I've been doing most of the talking, so how about you telling me a little about yourself."

"Oh, I'm boring," Philip replied. "You'll certainly fall asleep."

"I promise not to," Laura said. "I might yawn—just kidding."

"Well, let's see. I have an import/export company that my son Michael and Jack run. I don't live in Valleyfield anymore. I have a little place in the Hills of Caledon that I've named Millcreek. I play some golf, but not as much as I used to. I have horses, so I ride quite often, it's relaxing, and I am now with the most beautiful girl in the world. Now, except for that last sentence, did you find it boring?" Philip asked.

"No, not at all, I think it's exciting," Laura replied. "Carol said that you do a lot of traveling."

"I do a fair bit, mostly for the company," Philip said.

"Do you like hockey?" Laura asked

"Yes, I do, I try to keep up with the teams as much as I can. Any opportunity I get, I'll see a game. Why do you ask?"

"Just curious," Laura replied. "Nicholas likes hockey. His favorite player is Wayne Gretzsky. He has a hockey sweater with Gretzsky's name and number 99 on it."

"Isn't that nice. I guess Wayne Gretzsky is most any kids' and adults' favorite player," Philip replied.

Laura continued, "He loves playing road hockey with the kids, but he gets frustrated because he gets out of breath real fast. He was born with only one functioning kidney, and it's been giving him problems for the past two years."

"That's too bad," Philip said. "Is he being treated?"

"He's on medication," Laura replied, "and also a diet. He has good days, but he also has bad ones, real bad."

"One of my two best friends is one of the best surgeons in the country. He's the chief of staff at the Valley Hospital. Maybe you've heard of him. His name is Dr. Graham West."

"Yes, I have. Our family physician, Dr. McAllister, mentioned him to us," Laura said.

"Any time you're ready, I will set up an appointment for you," Philip said.

"Thanks, we may have to do that. Our doctor said that he was going to see him," Laura said.

The evening was magnificent. They had dinner at a little Italian restaurant called Franangelos, in the small Italian section of the city.

Following dinner, they went to the theatre.

It was different. The play was called *Love Letters*. Two actors sat at a table, across from each other, and read aloud 'letters' that they presumably had sent to each other over the years. Some of the letters were passionate, some were funny, and others were argumentative.

It's one of those plays that you don't dash out every Saturday night to see, but Robert Wagner and Stephanie Powers were very elegant.

During the intermission, while Laura visited the ladies room, Philip took the opportunity to go to the stage manager's office, a man whom he had known for years, when he and Sarah spent many evenings at the playhouse. His name was Alfonce. Alfonce wasn't there at the time, so Philip told his secretary that he and his date would like to visit the stars after the show. She told Philip to be at his office after the performance, and Alfonce would likely personally escort them to their dressing room.

The show was over, and the aisles were crowded, so Philip and Laura remained in their seats until the crowd subsided.

He turned to her and said, "What would you like to do now? Anything you want."

Laura thought for a few seconds, and answered by asking. "Do you think it's too cold to have some ice cream?"

"Absolutely not," Philip replied, "I can eat ice cream at any temperature. As soon as we leave, we'll visit the ice cream parlor. They still call it that, don't they?"

"I think so," she answered.

"First, if you don't mind," Philip said, "there's a couple of people I'd like you to meet."

"Oh, that would be nice, friends of yours?" She asked.

"No, not really. I've never, personally seen them before." Philip answered.

Laura looked at him, with a slight frown, and then Philip said, "Okay, I won't keep you in suspense," he smiled," it's the stars of the show."

"Are you serious, you wouldn't be kidding me? You mean we're going to meet Robert Wagner and Stephanie Powers?" she asked with excitement.

"No, no kidding," Philip replied, "I'm trying to make a good impression, and I also know the stage manager."

Laura smiled, and said; "You sure know how to 'awe' a girl. I'm a little nervous," she added

"Me too, but maybe they are as well," Philip said.

The stage manager's door was open. Alfonce was sitting at his desk when Philip and Laura arrived. When he saw them, he got up and walked toward the door and said, as he shook Philip's hand, "Philip, it's nice to see you again. It's been a long time, we missed you."

As he shook his hand, Philip said, "You too, Alfonce. I haven't been going out much, but I hope to start again," as he looked and smiled at Laura.

"I understand," Alfonce replied, as he looked a little sad.

"I'd like you to meet a friend of mine," as he introduced Laura to him.

After the introductions, Alfonce escorted them to a dressing room and knocked lightly on the door and said, "Mr. Wagner, it's Alfonce, I'm with two special fans of yours and Ms. Powers'."

The door opened, and there stood Robert Wagner. Laura stood with her arm clutching Philip's, and for a couple of seconds, just stared.

Robert said, very casually, "Hi, come on in." He thanked Alfonce, and closed the door.

Over by a small table and sitting in a very comfortable looking chair was Stephanie Powers. She was pouring a diet Coke into a glass.

Philip introduced Laura and himself, and they all shook hands. He addressed them as Mr. Wagner and Ms. Powers, so Robert said, "Just call me Bob, and my partner here likes Stephanie."

He then offered them a drink.

They talked about the show, and Robert said that they were taking it global, noting that it's been very successful.

After about twenty minutes, Philip thanked them for seeing he and Laura, and said it was an honor to see them. Laura said that it was an unexpected pleasure that she wouldn't forget, and also told them that she enjoyed their show *Hart to Hart*.

Robert said, "It's always a pleasure to perform for such devoted fans."

Stephanie agreed by saying, "Yes, we always feel so comfortable, it makes our work so easy." Then she added, "We'll be back in Fort Wayne next year, and we'd be delighted to have dinner with you both."

Philip and Laura left, but not before Robert and Stephanie signed their programs.

Next stop was the ice cream parlor, where Laura had a butterscotch sundae, and Philip's choice was chocolate.

On the drive back to Valleyfield, they talked mostly about the play, a little about Jack and Carol's house, and by then, they were in Laura's driveway.

Laura looked at Philip and asked, "Would you like to come in for a cup of tea?"

"I would love to," Philip said. "How did you know I preferred tea to coffee?" he asked as they were getting out of the car.

"Because you look like a teetotaler," Laura replied, and your daughter told me." She added.

"Really," Philip said, "and what else has she been telling you?"

"That, I will keep to myself, right now," she replied, smiling.

Philip helped Laura off with her coat, and hung it in the closet along with his own.

She said, "Make yourself comfortable, and I'll make the tea," as she walked to the kitchen.

Philip replied, "Would you mind if I come in with you?"

"Not at all, I'm only going to heat water," she said.

"Well I've never seen that done before," Philip joked.

Laura laughed and said, "Okay, we'll sit by the table."

"I'm a kitchen person," Philip said. "I would rather sit and carry a conversation here than anywhere else in the house. Did my daughter tell you that too?" he asked, with a smile.

"As a matter of fact," Laura started, and than said, "No just kidding."

After two cups of tea and an hour of conversation, there was no doubt that they had a strong, mutual attraction and matching personalities.

It was now almost two in the morning when Philip said, "I don't want to overdo my welcome, but I should get on my way and let you get some rest. I think I've been talking too much, making up for lost time, I guess. I haven't enjoyed an evening, or being with someone like you in a long time. See what I mean, I can't shut up."

"I don't want you to, when you say things like that," Laura said. "I feel the same. I didn't think I ever would."

From across the table, Philip took both her hands in his, and before he could say anything, Laura looked him in the eyes, with her head slightly tilted, and a half smile she asked, "Are we going to see a lot of each other?"

She could see by the look on his face that she had her answer.

Philip squeezed her hands gently, and replied, "I certainly hope so. I feel as though I'm on a first date. I really don't know what to do."

"You're doing fine," Laura said, "I would like to take it slow. Is that all right?"

Philip shook his head slowly from side to side, and said, "Absolutely, that would be nice, I would like that too."

"There's just one thing," Philip said, "I have to confess something to you about tonight."

Laura looked at him with a frown, and said, "Already, you're being unfaithful."

They both laughed, and Philip continued, "I wasn't trying to impress you, or put on an act. I think I knew when we met, that we would have been comfortable, if I had taken you to a dog fight, and had dinner at McDonald's, and you would have been blithely unconcerned. I don't think it matters what we do or where we go, as long as we enjoy each other's company."

"Well," Laura replied smiling, "first of all, I've never been to a dog fight." They laughed. "And second, I'm sure that were going to see a lot of McDonald's."

"Of course, with Nicholas," Philip sighed, "what a relief. What a load off my mind."

As Philip was putting on his coat, he said, "Maybe we could meet somewhere tomorrow."

"I'd like that," Laura said, "I have a house showing, and I'm bringing Nicholas with me."

"That would be great," Philip replied, "it will give us a chance to meet."

"Okay," Laura agreed, "I'll write down the address." She reached in her purse for a pen and a business card. "The showing is between two and four."

"All settled. I have some work at the office that I have to catch up on, so I'll see you shortly after two."

He took the business card from her and put it in his pocket, and said, "Of all the blabbering I did tonight, right now I'm stumped for words. I only know that you made me feel like I've never felt in a long time, and never thought I ever would. So thanks for spending this evening with me."

Laura came closer to him, and put her hands on his arms, and said, "For someone who is stumped for words, you sure say some nice ones." They both came forward and kissed on the lips.

Then she said, "Nice—I'll look forward to seeing you tomorrow."

"Me too," Philip replied.

His thoughts turned to picking her up, carrying her to her bedroom and making passionate love to her. They were also hers.

On his way to Millcreek, the song on the radio was Rod Stewart's "Have I Told You Lately That I Love You."

chapter XIV

MILLCREEK
MARCH 19, 1995

Sunday morning brought with it a lovely sunny day. Any snow that had previously been on the ground was now a light mist, hovering about a foot off the ground. You could hear the faint drips of water as it found its way along the eaves and down the side pipes of his house.

He was never one to sleep in, but this was an exception. It was nine o'clock when he rose from a very peaceful sleep.

So after a shower and shave, and pulling on his Levis with a white sport shirt, Philip downed a glass of orange juice, put on his cowboy boots and a lined denim jacket, and headed for Pedro and Juanita's house. He had to tell them about Laura.

As he drove in their driveway, he noticed Pedro coming from the stables.

"Hey Philip!" he yelled, "Long time, where have you been?"

"I did a couple of back-to-back trips, so I stayed in town." Philip replied. "How are the horses, any problems?" he added.

"No, nothing I couldn't handle." Pedro answered. "Buck had a heavy wheeze. I think he got into some bad water down by the flats."

"Are you thinking of riding today?" Pedro asked.

"Yes, but first, there's a special lady I want to see. I have something to tell you both," Philip said.

"She's inside making cookies," Pedro said, "and I'll be there in a few minutes."

As Philip walked in the back entrance, he called out, "Juanita Maria Catherina Lopez, where are you?"

Juanita came out from the kitchen as Philip was taking off his boots. He then embraced her. "I missed you and your cooking, mostly your cooking," he joked.

"We meesed you, Mr. Philip. You've been gone two weeks."

"I know Juanita, but I have some wonderful news to tell you."

Before he could say anything else, Juanita said, "I know, I can see it in your eyes and feel it in my heart."

"I could never fool you, could I?" Philip said. Then he looked at Pedro, and asked, "Is she that way with you?" he asked.

Pedro shook his head, looked at his wife, and smiled, and said, "I don't even try."

"She is a wonderful lady. Her name is Laura. Carol introduced me to her. I think she had her in mind for me some time ago. Laura is a real estate agent. Jack and Carol bought their house through her."

Juanita came over to him with a tear in her eye and said, "I, I mean we, are so happy for you, my prayers have been answered."

Pedro came over and shook his hand and said, "I think we should go riding."

"I think so too," Philip replied. "I will tell you more later," Philip added as they were going out the door.

"Be back in an hour," Juanita said, "I'll have breakfast ready."

Philip and Pedro exercised their horses well. They left the stable with a trot, down past the corral along the fence, through the gate and into the open field, where they put their horses to a gallop until they reached the bush.

As they were sauntering along the trail in single file, Philip was telling Pedro about Laura's son Nicholas, and how he was looking forward to meeting him.

He said, "I sure hope we can be friends. There hasn't been any other man in his life except his father, who he doesn't see that often."

Pedro, who is the world's best listener and can usually answer a question before its asked, said, "It's been a long time since I taught a little boy the fundamentals of riding and taking care of horses. It would be an exciting challenge for me again."

Philip turned ninety degrees in his saddle, and said to Pedro, who was riding behind him, "Thank you, my friend. Again, you put my mind at ease."

They followed the river for another couple of hundred yards, and then headed back up the other side of the property to the stable. The horses were stripped of their saddles and bridles, were groomed down, watered, and turned loose in the field.

Juanita had a large brunch made up when they came in, and as they were eating, Philip told her all about Laura and their first date.

Juanita said, "We must have her and her son here for dinner soon."

"I will invite them to come next Sunday," Philip suggested. "We will have dinner at my place, and I will cook."

Pedro looked at him with raised eyebrows, and then turned to his wife, who caught the hint, and she said, "I would be glad to do the cooking, if you don't mind."

"Not at all," Philip replied. "Thanks for volunteering."

They all laughed, then Philip said, "I must be on my way. I have some work at the office to do before I meet with Laura."

Before he left, Juanita came over and gave him another hug and said, "Again, we are very happy for you. You have come back to us again."

Philip kissed her on the cheek and said, "Thanks for waiting."

Sunday, 12:00 noon, the phone rang, once, twice, and on the third Gray picked up the receiver, and said "Hello."

"How are you doing, buddy?" Philip asked.

"Why, it's lover boy. On your first date in two years, did you have to stay out all night?" Gray asked, jokingly.

"Isn't anything sacred anymore?" Philip asked.

"Not in this town, and not when your darling daughter and

Betty get together. We are really happy for you. Carol said that she is a combination between a best friend and a mother to her."

"Yes, her name is Laura," Philip said, "and she is all of that and more. Gray, when I first saw her, it wasn't like I want this woman, or I need this woman, it was like, she is part of our lives. It was like our paths had crossed for a purpose. If you had told me six months ago, or a month ago, or last week that I would one day feel this way about another woman, I would have sent you to see one of your neurologists."

"When do we get to meet this lovely lady?" Gray asked.

"Hell, I only met her myself," Philip replied. "I'm not in too big a hurry to set her loose amongst the wolves. I believe you will certainly see a lot of us, socially and professionally."

"What do you mean, professionally?" Gray asked.

"She has a son. I'm going to meet him this afternoon," Philip said. "His name is Nicholas, and he has a kidney problem. He was born with only one that works. Their family doctor is Doctor McAllister."

"Dan McAllister," Gray said, "I know him. He came to see me a couple of weeks ago about a little boy with a kidney problem."

"That little boy was Nicholas," Philip said. "Laura said that he had gone to see you."

"Say, why don't you drop by and have lunch with us, and we'll talk more on it. I know we can do something," Gray suggested.

"I just had lunch with Juanita and Pedro, and I'm on my way to the office to do some work on that combine deal," Philip said. "I'll see you tomorrow, and we'll make plans to get together next Saturday."

"You mean we have to wait all week," Gray said.

"Have patience, my friend. You have a few of those, don't you?" Philip replied.

"A few," Gray answered. "And bring the little guy in anytime," he added.

chapter XV

VALLEYFIELD, INDIANA
9:30 am

She was lying, peacefully awake, hugging her pillow, and listening to Vanessa Williams on the radio singing "Save The Best For Last," and tossing the idea around in her mind, whether to rise from her bed and commence with the day, or let her thoughts of the night before carry on for a little longer.

After a few moments of visualizing her future with Philip, Laura quickly jumped from her bed, thinking, this is silly, I've only met the man, and yet I'm counting the hours and minutes when I will see him again.

She looked out her bedroom window and saw her neighbor washing his car, and kids playing road hockey on the street; so she knew it was a nice day. After putting on her house coat and turning on the taps for a hot bath, she then went downstairs, filled the kettle with water for a cup of tea, and buttered a bagel with cream cheese.

Within a few minutes her breakfast was ready, so she took the Sunday paper, her tea and bagel and enjoyed them while soaking in the tub.

At eleven o'clock Laura left for the office to pick the essential items she needed for her open house. As she was getting out of her car, her cell phone rang. She took the phone out of her purse, and said, "Hello. Hi, Lucy. How is my boy?"

"Oh, he's been a real sweetheart, as always." Lucy replied. "He and Ryan are assembling a racecar set that he bought yesterday. I don't know who the bigger kid is. Ryan seems more anxious than Nicholas."

"You guys are spoiling him," Laura said.

"Where are you now?" Lucy asked.

"I'm about to go into the office to pick up my 'open house' signs for my showing today, then I'm going over to your place." Laura answered.

"Well hurry," Lucy said, impatiently, "I'm aching to hear about your big night. I want to know everything."

"Your version of 'everything' didn't happen," Laura replied. "I'll be over in twenty minutes."

Just before noon, Laura arrived at Lucy and Ryan's house. As she entered, Nicholas ran over and gave her a hug and a kiss, and asked, "Did you have a good time last night?"

"Yes, I did sweetheart," Laura answered. "We went out for dinner, and then we went to the opera house to see a play, and after the play, we went to the ice cream parlor and had an ice cream sundae. Most of the night, we talked about you."

"You did?" he asked with a big grin.

"Philip is a really nice man, and he wants to meet you," Laura said. "Would you like to meet him?" she asked.

"Yes, I'd like to meet him. When?" he asked.

"I'm having an open house this afternoon," his mother said, "and Philip said that he'd drop by around three o'clock, so you can come with me. Is that okay?" she asked.

"That's okay, Mommy, but come and see our race car set," Nicholas said, as he took her hand and led her in the dining room where Ryan was putting the last of the tracks together.

"Hi Laura," Ryan said, "how was your evening at the opera?" he asked.

"We had a great time, but it wasn't an opera. It was more of a play called *Love Letters*," she answered.

"Yes, I've heard of it. A lady in our staff and her husband

went last Wednesday night."

Lucy entered the room, and said, "I have tea and some hot biscuits, on the table, why don't we leave these two Andretti boys to winning the Grand Prix," as she hurried Laura into the kitchen to pump her on her date with Philip.

"Okay, spill it, all of it, did he pass the 'Laura' rules?" Lucy asked.

"The 'Laura' rules never entered the picture last night," Laura replied. "Lucy, I can't remember when I've had a nicer evening, he is so nice, there wasn't a dull moment all evening. He is such an exciting man to be with. We started with dinner at a little Italian restaurant called Franangelos, and after a five course meal, we left for the theater. Great seats, we were so close, you could see the expression on the actor's faces. Robert Wagner and Stephanie Powers are truly professionals. They were great in the reading of *Love Letters*."

"I'm really happy for you. Do you think he is the one?" Lucy asked.

"I hope so, Lucy," Laura replied.

"That's not everything," Laura continued, "listen to this. After the show, Philip surprised me by taking me to meet the stars, in their dressing room."

"Get out of here," Lucy said with surprise.

"No kidding," Laura said, "we spent about twenty minutes with them. They are really wonderful. They said that they'd be back next year, and invited us to have dinner with them."

"Wow, how much pull does this guy have?" Lucy commented.

"Apparently he knows the stage manager quite well," Laura said, "I think he and his wife used to frequent the theater often."

"So, continue, what happened next?" Lucy asked.

"That's when we went to the ice cream parlor," Laura answered.

"What—you wanted ice cream?" Lucy surprisingly asked.

"Yes," Laura replied. "It just came out of me. He asked me what I'd like to do, and before I could think, I said that I wanted ice cream. Crazy thing, he wanted some too."

"You must be in love or reverting back to your teenage days," Lucy joked.

"I wonder," Laura thought.

"On the way out of the parlor, guess what he bought me?" Laura asked.

"If the ice cream parlor sold them, I wouldn't be surprised if it was a diamond." Lucy replied.

"No, something better," Laura said, "a Kit Kat chocolate bar. In fact, he bought three of them."

"No shit," Lucy remarked. "That's your favorite."

"I know," Laura said, "it's his too, weird, eh? Then we drove to my place."

"Ah, now the good stuff." Lucy said.

"We had tea and talked for about two hours," Laura replied.

"No 'hanky panky'?" Lucy remarked.

"No 'hanky panky,'" Laura answered. "He was a true gentleman. In fact, when he was leaving, I kissed *him* good night. He was fumbling around with the belt on his coat that he never did do up, and was running out of good-byes, so that's when I reached out and kissed him. He's going to meet me at my open house around three, so he can meet Nicholas."

"Lucy, I don't know what it is," Laura expressed. "I can't keep him off my mind. It's like I was destined to be with him. I want to be with him, and yet I'm a little afraid."

"I think it's called love," Lucy said. "Take your time, play it slow."

"That's what we came up with last night," Laura said. "I know he has strong feelings for me, so we agreed that if we were going to see a lot of each other, there wasn't a need to rush into anything. We both feel comfortable with that."

At that moment Nicholas came into the kitchen, so Laura said, "I guess we should be on our way."

"Why don't you go ahead," Lucy suggested, "and I'll drive Nicholas over about three o'clock. That will give me a chance to meet Mr. Wonderful."

"Is that okay with you Nicholas?" Lucy asked.

"Yeah, then I can play some more with the racecar," Nicholas said.

Laura gave him a kiss, and said, "I'll see you both later."

There wasn't much action at Laura's open house. Two couples stopped by, and Laura gave them a tour of the house and a brochure, then they left.

At two forty-five, Lucy and Nicholas came with a box of donuts that they had stopped to pick up on the way. As Lucy was taking off her coat, she asked, "Has there been many over?"

"Two couples showed up," Laura answered, "looked around, took the information and left. They didn't show much interest, but you never know."

"That's right," Lucy said, "last summer I gave a woman some information about a condo over the phone, and she had me write up an Agreement of Purchase before she saw it."

"Oh sure, but that's you, Mrs. # 1 Seller of the Year Award."

At that moment, they heard a car door close. Nicholas looked out the window and asked, "Mommy, is that Philip?"

Laura looked out, and as she was opening the door, she replied, "Yes, Nicholas, that's Philip."

When Philip saw Laura, he said, "Excuse me Miss, I understand you have a house for sale."

"Yes sir, I do. Are you interested?" she asked.

"No, I bought one last week," Philip replied," I'm only here to see the sales agent."

She took him by the hand, and gave it a little pull, and said, "Get in here. There's a couple of people I want you to meet."

Philip took off his rubber overshoes, hung his coat on the wooden coat rack that was standing by the front door, took Laura's hand and followed her to the kitchen where Lucy and Nicholas were sitting at the table.

Laura said, as she placed her hand on Nicholas's shoulder, "Philip, I'd like you to meet my son Nicholas. Nicholas, this is

Philip."

Nicholas stood up and took a step forward, and said, "It's nice to meet you Mr. Mariano."

A satisfied smile came to Philip's face, as though this little guy was someone he had been searching for, and he thought, "What a well disciplined young man he is," as he reached out his hand and said, "How do you Nicholas? I've been looking forward to meeting you, and please call me Philip."

"Is that okay, Mommy?" he asked.

"Yes, that's okay," she said.

"Thanks for the Kit Kat chocolate bar," Nicholas said.

"You're very welcome," Philip replied.

Laura then turned to Lucy, who was sitting by the table with a cup of tea, and said, "This is my very best friend, Lucy. She and her husband Ryan are our guardian angels."

Lucy stood up to meet Philip's outstretched hand and said, "It's nice to meet you Philip."

Philip took her soft hand in his, and remembered what Laura had said about her beauty, and then he thought about his friend Willy, and how he had such a passion for tall women and said, "It's a pleasure to meet you Lucy. Laura speaks highly of you, and Ryan."

"Why, thank you, and I hope we can get together some time soon," Lucy said.

"I'm looking forward to it," Philip replied. "Does Ryan play golf?" he asked.

"Yes, but not as often as he'd like to," Lucy answered.

"Well, my friend Gray and myself are usually looking for a fourth player," Philip said.

"So now you've found one," Laura said.

They talked for another half hour. Philip and Nicholas were hitting it off really well, and Lucy could see why her friend was so attracted to this man, and she was happy for her.

Lucy stood up and said, "I must be on my way. It was nice to meet you Philip. Perhaps we can get together at our place, this coming Friday night."

"I'd like that," as he looked at Laura, who agreed.

Lucy had her coat on, and was giving Nicholas a hug, when Laura said, "I'll walk you to your car."

Lucy was opening the door when Philip said, "Oh, by the way Lucy, I'm working on the resume."

Lucy looked at Laura with surprise, and Laura burst out laughing, which got the three of them laughing.

As they reached Lucy's car Laura asked, "Well, what do you think of him?"

"He's gorgeous," Lucy answered. "Are you sure he's Carol's father?"

"She calls him Daddy," Laura replied.

"You have my approval," Lucy said as she got in her car and left.

When Laura came back in the house Philip said, "Your friend Lucy is a lovely lady. You must be honored to have her in your life."

"Yes, you're right," Laura replied, "I can't imagine not having her and Ryan in our lives. They would do anything for us."

"She's also a very attractive woman," Philip added.

"That, she is," Laura said. "She seems to capture the attention of most men."

"Well, I can see why," Philip answered. "That's the penalty that beautiful women like you and her have to pay."

"I'm going to tell her what you said," Laura joked. "She and Ryan are nuts over each other. They've been married over eighteen years," she continued.

"That's wonderful," Philip commented.

There hadn't been anyone else in to see the house, so Laura gathered her paper work, and put it in her briefcase.

Philip and Nicholas were talking about the National Hockey League, when Laura asked, "How would you two hockey players like to retrieve my signs from the curbs."

Nicholas looked at Philip, smiled and said, "Okay mommy,

we can do that, can't we Philip?" Nicholas added.

"I don't know," Philip joked, "do hockey players pick up signs?"

"They do for their mother," Laura answered.

After the signs were retrieved and stored in the trunk of Laura's car, Philip suggested, "If you two don't have any plans, I'd like to take you to dinner."

"Oh boy, can we mommy. We don't have plans, do we?" Nicholas asked.

"No," his mother replied, "we don't have any plans. That would be nice."

"Okay it's your choice, where would you like to eat?" Philip asked.

Before Nicholas could answer, Laura said, "We've been to McDonalds twice in the past four days, so I think we should have a dinner with vegetables."

"Yes mommy," Nicholas said, "then lets go to Rosey's Place." He added.

"If that's all right with Philip." Laura said.

"That's fine with me". Philip replied. "Rosey's Place it is."

We have to drop by the house first, to pick up your pills." Laura suggested.

"All right," Philip said, "I'll meet you both at your house."

The evening was fun. They talked school and sports, and Nicholas wanted to know about Philip's work, and the different places where he traveled.

Philip learned that Nicholas was very knowledgeable, and for an eight year old, he was very easy to talk with.

Laura remembered, Carol saying to her that her father was great with children.

chapter XVI

**VALLEYFIELD, INDIANA
2nd WEEK IN APRIL**

As the days flew by, the signs of spring were truly visible. The air was warm; the blossoms were sprouting on the trees. The birds that arrive back in spring were upon us, and the grass had turned from brown to a glistening green.

Philip and Laura were seeing each other most every day. If he was out of town, he would call her, and they would talk for hours.

One day, he was in New Mexico on business. When he returned, he brought with him a hand-stitched wallet for Nicholas, and a cactus-rose, a favorite of Philip's, for Laura. On the ceramic pot, there was an inscription in Native American that read, "Be kind, be gentle, and give me love, and I will be with you forever."

Nicholas and Philip were hitting it off marvelously. They took to each other like good friends, and that made Laura very happy. About a week and a half ago on a Sunday afternoon, it was a little uncertain if this friendship would take place.

Philip, Laura, and Nicholas were in the park. Philip was leaning with his back against a tree, and Laura was leaning with her back to him. He had his arms around her waist, and his chin leaning on her right shoulder "cheek-to-cheek."

They were watching Nicholas throwing sticks in the river. The current was running quite rapidly. His mother called to him, "Nicholas, don't go too close to the water."

He ignored her, so she hollered again, "Nicholas, did you hear me, come back a few feet from the shore."

Again, he continued to ignore her.

Philip said, "I'll go over to him."

When he reached where Nicholas stood, he said, "I think your mother's right buddy, that river is running pretty fast, and the banks are slippery, you might slip in."

Well, Nicholas went into a little rage and ran past them, yelling, "I don't have to do what you tell me, you're not my daddy."

Laura was shocked. She started to walk over to where he was, and said, "Nicholas that was very rude. You get over here and apologize to Philip. I don't know what's got into you."

Philip turned to her, put his hand on her arm to console her, and said, "Would you mind if I talked to him? Apparently he's upset and tense and doesn't know how to tell us."

"All right, but I'm upset as well," Laura said.

"I know, but I'm 'the new kid on the block,' so maybe I should explain why I'm here," Philip replied.

Philip walked over to the picnic table, where Nicholas was sitting, with his head bowed, and asked, "Are you upset with me?"

"Well, you're not my daddy, so you can't tell me what to do," Nicholas answered.

"I know I'm not your daddy," Philip said, "but I'd like to be your friend, if you will let me."

Nicholas didn't say anything. He just sat with his head still bowed, picking at a small sliver of wood from the picnic table, hoping Philip would carry on with the conversation.

Philip sat on the opposite side of the table, and said, "You love your daddy, don't you?"

"Yes," Nicholas replied.

"I have never met him," Philip continued, "but I know that he is a nice man because he loves you very much, and he would be extremely sad if anything happened to you."

"I know he would," Nicholas said, as he continued picking at the loose sliver.

"So would your mommy," Philip said.

"Yeah, I know she would," Nicholas said as he looked up at his mother who was sitting on a large rock, by the shore of the river, watching two gray squirrels chasing each other along the branches of a willow tree.

"Do you have a good friend?" Philip asked.

"Only Bobby, who lives two doors from me," Nicholas answered. "He's older than me, but he lets me play on his side, when we play road hockey. The other kids don't want me on their team. They say I'm too slow, because I get out of breath."

"Bobby sounds to me like a real cool guy. I would like to meet him some time. I don't have a lot of good friends either," Philip said. "Dr. West, his name is Gray, and Willy, he lives in California, are my best friends. We grew up together, right here in Valleyfield, but my very best friend was my wife. Her name was Sarah."

"Are you divorced, too?" Nicholas asked. "No, Philip answered, "my Sarah died; she had cancer."

"Oh," Nicholas said, "were you sad?"

"Very much, for a long time," Philip replied, "until I met your mother and you. I believe that Sarah became an angel, and God gave her a job to see that I was happy again, so somehow she made our paths cross, and I think that's why I'm here."

Nicholas's eyes lit up, as he looked at Philip and said, "That's cool."

"My friends, Gray, Willy, and myself used to have a special code," Philip said. "We used to join two fingers and a thumb together, as he showed Nicholas with his fingers and thumb touching his, and we'd say, 'buddies forever.' We could tell each other secrets, and know that we could keep them."

"If you and I were good friends," Nicholas asked, "could we have a special code?"

"Absolutely," Philip replied, "it would be just like my friends and I have. And Bobby could join us too."

Getting all excited Nicholas said, "I would really like that, and so would Bobby."

"You see Nick, you don't mind me calling you Nick, do you?"

"No, I like it," Nicholas said

"I think it's a cool name," Philip said.

"Anyway," Philip continued, "I love your mommy very much, but if you don't want to be my friend, than I will leave, and not see you or your mommy, ever again."

"I want to be your friend, but how will we know that we're friends?" Nicholas asked.

"We will put it on trial for two weeks, and in that two weeks we have to gain each other's trust; like if I tell you a secret, I wouldn't want you to tell anyone else, and the same goes for me. But it doesn't always have to be a secret, just being nice to people is trusting enough."

"Okay, lets do it," Nicholas said with excitement.

"Then we better shake on it," Philip said.

They both reached their arms over the table, and shook hands.

"I guess Mommy is still upset," Nicholas said. "I better tell her I'm sorry."

They stood, and with Philip's hand on Nicholas's shoulder, they both walked over to where Laura was sitting.

The first thing that Nicholas said was, "I'm sorry, Mommy, for upsetting you." Then he turned to Philip and said, "I'm sorry, Philip, for saying what I said to you. It won't happen again."

Laura hugged him, as she gave a strange look to Philip.

Philip shrugged his shoulders, but at the same time felt very proud of Nicholas as he said, "It's a man thing."

From that day on, Nicholas and Philip were friends, not just an adult and child relationship, but good friends. They made the code, many times.

Philip taught him to have responsibility to whatever he should be doing, whether it is sports, or schooling, or taking care of animals, like Philip's horses.

He looked up to Philip, like you would to your favorite celebrity, or a big brother.

chapter XVII

MILLCREEK
FRIDAY, APRIL 21ST

Philip and Pedro spent most of the week clearing up the property that had its share of destruction from the hazards of winter.

They took down the snow fencing, that ran parallel to the laneway, and straightened up the regular fence, that had been bent by the drifting snow. Tree trimming had to be done, especially down the driveway, where there were broken limbs caused by the winter winds. As these repairs were being executed, the horses in the field were looking on curiously, while pounding the ground with their forefoot, searching for new shoots of spring grass.

By one o'clock the work was finished, the tractor and tools were put away in the shed, then they sat down to a hearty lunch that Juanita had prepared. After lunch Philip left for his house to have a shower and shave, called his office for any messages, and then phoned Laura. She had been out with a client since ten o'clock that morning, and was glad to tell him that she was pretty sure she made a sale.

Philip was happy for her, and after talking for twenty minutes he said that he would be over at six. They had plans to drive to Fort Wayne for dinner and a movie, neither knowing that they wouldn't be seeing a movie tonight.

Philip and Laura had known each other for about four weeks,

and in that time, other than walks in the parks, dinners, and visiting friends at their homes, riding the horses at Millcreek, they had really only been on four dates by themselves. Tonight would be the "unforgettable fifth."

Nicholas was staying with Carol and Jack. Michael and Diana left early to open their cottage, and of course have a romantic evening by the lake.

A few minutes to six, Philip rang the doorbell on Laura's house.

The door opened and Laura said, "Hi, come on in."

Philip stepped in, and thought what an extremely beautiful woman she is. If there was one thing, other than her beauty, charm, and personality that he noticed, it was the elegant way she dressed to make a man feel delighted to be in her company, and immediately kissed her on the lips. Laura kissed him back, and then they kissed again, not a complete passionate kiss, but one that gave promise for them both to think about.

They drove to Fort Wayne, and decided to dine at Franangelos, the little Italian restaurant where they had dinner on their first date. As always, the dinner was superb. The piano player was playing soft music, as they were enjoying a glass of red wine. The lights were dim, and the flickering of the candles made their eyes sparkle, as he could see himself in hers, and she in his.

It was the elation that had been sparked some weeks ago. Two hearts were beating fast, as their pulses were racing.

At this time, the waiter came to their table with a dessert tray. Without losing focus with Laura's eyes, Philip said, "No thanks, just bring the check."

They left, and by the time they reached the car, without a word spoken, they were in each other's arms, kissing passionately, as he walked her to the passenger side of the car. With one arm around her neck, and without releasing his lips from hers, he reached in his coat pocket, took out his keys and unlocked the door. They broke off the kiss as he opened the door, and she entered.

By the time Philip got behind the wheel, Laura was leaning

over the console, with her arms out, and her lips parted, waiting for him to take her in his arms again.

The wish was granted, as he took her in his arms and kissed her feverishly on her waiting lips, and lifted his left hand, that was around her waist, to the back of her head and drew her closer. Their mouths parted, as she whispered, "Philip, I want you tonight, right now."

"Yes," he breathed, "I want you too. Let's get to the nearest hotel."

They released each other, as he started the engine, put it in gear, and in three minutes they were at the door of the Monte Carlo Inn. Philip registered, and the clerk handed him the room card to a third story room.

On the way up the elevator, they couldn't keep from tearing off each other's clothes. When they reached the room, Philip inserted the card in the slot, turned the handle, and opened the door, took the card out and placed it on the nearest table, came back to the hallway and picked up Laura to carry her over the threshold.

As he picked her up, the door to their room closed, because it was spring loaded to close automatically, leaving the key-card inside, and Philip standing outside with Laura in his arms.

"Shit," he said as they both broke down laughing.

He set Laura down, and left to retrieve another key.

This time, everything went well. They were inside, the door was bolted, and they were again in each other's arms. Their mouths met, and their hands were undressing each other quickly and eagerly, leaving a trail of clothes from the door to the queen size bed.

Within seconds, Laura had Philip's shirt off and was unzipping his trousers, and unbuckled his belt. His trousers fell to the floor. She then reached both hands down the front of his shorts, and could feel the growth, as she tenderly stroked him.

Laura's skirt was also at her feet, her blouse was completely unbuttoned, and Philip had her black laced bra unclipped, and was kissing and moving his tongue ever so gently over her now tight, hardened nipples, as her breathing was getting heavier and faster. He than removed his mouth from her breasts, and covered her lips with his, as he kicked off his trousers, picked her up, and lowered her onto the bed, like a priceless piece of China.

Her head was resting on a pillow, and her eyes were coaxing him to come to her. Seconds later, her desire was answered. His hands were on her face, gently holding her head as his mouth again found hers. Her arms were around his neck as she lightly caressed his back and pushed herself hard against him.

They were totally absorbed in each other. It was the alternating current, building up, and they could both feel it. There was a sensual tension between them that was overwhelming.

Laura's thoughts were, "How different it's going to be, to make love to someone who I'm truly in love with, and I am in love with this man."

With his arms wrapped around her, all her worries and fears of not being a good lover for him had left her.

Philip continued to explore this beautiful woman, as he moved his mouth from her burning lips over her throat, and then again, with the point of his tongue, he teased first one, then the other nipple into two hard points.

At this time, nothing excited him more, than the inauguration of this woman that he knew had never experienced the passionate pleasures that he could grant her.

He released his hand from her tightened breast, while his mouth remained, and moved it slowly down her side, until it rested on her left knee. He then let his hand lead the way up the inside of her leg as she gently gave him room until it reached her black lace panties that were damp with love passion, and he then slipped them down partially over both her hips.

He moved down her body, kissing his way to her waist, and with both his hands now under her hips lifted them towards him. She spread her legs a little further apart to give him space.

Laura's loud whispers of, "Oh yes, yes, yes" echoed the room, as her hands and nails were caressing his shoulders.

With her help, he lifted her legs and removed her dampened panties. Her legs were now resting on his shoulders, and his two hands were back under her hips. Love had joined with lust as he had an inordinate desire to kiss her left knee all the way up until his lips and tongue reached the most tender and exciting organ which she yearned he would find.

Her head was thrown back over the pillow, as she was fondling Philip's head, and her moans were now loud with an exquisite joy that she had never dreamed possible, an explosion that became a delicious ecstasy.

Now, the need became wild, as he released his mouth from her beautiful passionflower, and slowly kissed his way up to her dry open mouth. With her legs now tightly around his waist, he reached down and pulled her hips up to meet him, as he gently entered her.

Laura was aware, only of the most intense delight. She felt herself pausing on the edge of another orgasm, and while she was throbbing and jerking her hips forward, Philip rolled her over on top of him, and cupping her round bottom with both hands, he pulled her closer to him, until they both came quickly into the masterful orgasm that they had been holding back for so long.

He brought out feelings in her that she had suppressed, passion that she had been afraid to let loose, a pleasure that she never dreamed possible. Moments went by, they lay motionless. Laura was cuddled up to Philip's left shoulder, his arm was around her neck and his hand was resting on her left breast that was covered with a blanket.

There wasn't an after-sex cigarette to smoke because neither of them smoked. There was only the stillness of the night, and the sweet fragrance of sex in the air.

Laura broke the silence by saying, "Philip."

Philip answered with a weary, "Aha," as he kissed the top of her head.

Then she said, as she turned her head slightly to look at him,

"I never knew love making could be so beautiful and exciting."

Philip was about to say something, when she reached up and placed a finger over his lips, and than continued, "I'm thirty-five, and this is the first time I've experienced an orgasm. It was so great, my body just seemed to rush, so many rushes, and then when we both came, it was total explosion. Is that the way it's supposed to be?" She asked.

"I certainly hope so." Philip answered with a satisfying smile.

"You mean, not even the seven years that you were married to Gord?" he asked.

She replied by saying, "Gord is the only man I've ever been with. He's not a passionate man. His lovemaking was, 'on' and very quickly 'off' and that was about once every two weeks. No hugging, no kissing, and no foreplay."

Philip wondered how could a man be with such a beautiful woman as Laura and want to end the lovemaking.

Laura continued, as she asked, "If a man isn't circumcised, does that have an effect on him not being passionate? Gord isn't circumcised."

The question caught Philip by surprise, he never dreamed that Laura, or anyone else would throw a question like that at him, as he answered, "Wow, I don't really know. I've never thought about it, I suppose it could be uncomfortable at times, maybe a little embarrassing." As he thought to himself, how can a woman be entirely passionate with a man that isn't circumcised? You never know what's up there, or for how long

"I'm not one to ask questions, or pry into anyone's affairs," Philip continued, "but was that the reason for your divorce?"

"Not really," Laura replied. "I suppose I was expecting more in that field, but I likely could have lived with it. The main cause was that we didn't have anything in common. His friends were his friends, not mine. He had his work that he was dedicated to, and after that, on weekends and holidays, it was golf and his friends again. Gord should never have gotten married. He's more comfortable being single."

"You both seem to get along well," Philip suggested.

"Oh yes, this divorce is good for both of us. We are still good friends, and he loves Nicholas, although he doesn't see him that often." After chatting for a while longer, and sipping on Laura's favorite drink, (kahlua and milk) they got dressed and left for Valleyfield.

Philip spent the night at Laura's, where they made love again, and then fell into a deep sleep in each other's arms until the phone woke them at nine o'clock. It was Nicholas, calling to tell his mother not to pick him up until noon. Jack and Carol were taking him to Fort Wayne to do some shopping for the baby nursery.

Laura got up and went to the kitchen, to heat some water for tea, as she heard Philip singing in the shower.

After their tea, Laura showered and got dressed, and they went out for breakfast at a local Waffle House. They both had work to do at their offices, but had made plans to meet at Jack and Carol's house to pick up Nicholas, and the three of them would then drive to Millcreek.

On her way to her office, Laura's cell phone rang, she clicked it on and said, "Hello. Hi Lucy."

Lucy answered with, "Well, you sound pretty cheerful. How was your evening?"

"There was never one like it." Laura replied.

Lucy said with excitement, "Listen girl, you get your ass right over hear and tell aunt Lucy all about it."

Laura said, "I'm on my way to the office to finish up some paper work on that house that I showed yesterday."

Before she could say anything else, Lucy said, "I'll meet you there in twenty minutes."

At eleven o'clock Lucy arrived at the Indy State Realty, and went directly to her office, that she shared with Laura.

Laura was working on the computer when Lucy walked in. Her first question was, "Last night was 'The Night' wasn't it?"

She could tell by the unending smile on Laura's face, as she said, "Tell me all."

"I don't kiss and tell," Laura answered.

Lucy's remark was, "Bullshit, we tell each other everything."

Laura said, "Lucy, I never knew love making could be so beautiful. He moved me to a place I never knew existed. He was so gentle and compassionate with me, and neither one of us wanted it to end."

"Welcome to the real world," Lucy said. "It won't end, if you don't want it to."

"Is it that way with you and Ryan?" Laura asked.

"Yes, for the past twenty or so years, and it's better every time."

"So that's why you always look so content," Laura remarked.

"Now you know, girl," Lucy replied.

"You know, Laura," Lucy continued, "they say there's a match for everyone. Some people wonder if they missed out on the one that was right for them. I know that Ryan and I didn't. All the harps in heaven can't equal what goes on between a man and a woman in love."

"That's so beautiful," Laura whispered, "I never knew. It feels that way with Philip and me. I hope it always will."

"What movie did you see?" Lucy asked.

"We didn't." Laura replied. "We were eating dinner at this little Italian restaurant called Franangelos where we ate on our first date. About three quarters through the main course, our eyes met, and it was like we were mesmerized. We both knew right then and there that we had to have each other. I've never had a feeling like that. It just seemed to be right."

"So, what did you do?" Lucy asked. "Did you drive all the way back to Valleyfield?"

"No, we were lucky to make it to the car," Laura replied. "We went to the nearest motel; I think it was the Monte Carlo. Then we came back to my place and he spent the night with me."

"Wow, you sure make up for lost time," Lucy joked.

"Now, don't go telling Ryan all this," Laura said.

"This is girl talk," Lucy replied. "Ryan doesn't like to hear about other people's love affairs anyway."

"What are your plans for today?" Lucy asked.

"After I'm finished here," Laura answered, "I'm going to meet Philip at Carol and Jack's to pick up Nicholas, and then we're going to Philip's place to go riding, and later on have dinner with Pedro and Juanita. How about you?" she asked.

"Ryan and I are going to a Buck and Doe dance, for some guy at his office. He's getting married in a couple of weeks," Lucy said.

They talked for a while longer, and then they left.

chapter XVIII

MILLCREEK
LAST WEEK IN MAY

Spring was now moving into summer. The trees were losing their blossoms, to give way to the buds that would soon bear fruit. The birds were busy gathering twigs to build their nests, and the grass in the fields were a deep green, and almost long enough to be cut and bailed.

Philip and Laura were seeing each other just about every day, and with each day their love grew stronger. Weekends were spent at Millcreek, where Nicholas enjoyed working with Pedro. He would let him drive the tractor, and teach him how to take care of the horses, and of course, he would love to fill up on Juanita's home made cookies.

One Sunday morning Philip and Laura were having their usual walk (hand in hand) along the millstream, when Philip asked, "How would you like to have an Italian dinner cooked by two good friends of mine?"

"I would love to," Laura replied, "you know it's my favorite, but aren't we having dinner with Pedro and Juanita tonight?" she asked.

"I don't mean tonight," Philip answered. "Next weekend, a week from today."

"Well, let me check my little black book," Laura joked, as she reached in her pocket. "Nope, no one's asked me out for dinner next Sunday."

Philip stopped, looked at her and smiled, put his two hands on her shoulders, kissed her gently on her lips, and said, "I have to leave this Thursday for Italy, and I want you to come with me."

Laura looked at him with her wide smile, and said, "I'd love to," as she wrapped her arms around his neck.

"Great," Philip said, "we'll talk to Nick at dinner tonight."

"It's a business trip," he continued, "that will only take two hours a day for two days, but we'll be gone for a week. Do you think you can put up with me for a week?" he asked.

"I'm sure I can, and I promise I'll be on my best behavior," Laura said.

Philip drawled out a large, "No. I want you to be bad," he joked.

"Oh, I'm all excited. I can't wait," Laura said.

"We'll be leaving this Thursday and returning the following Thursday to prepare for Nick's birthday on Saturday."

That evening they had dinner with Pedro and Juanita and talked about the trip to Italy. Nicholas was happy that his mother and Philip were spending some "private time," as he called it, together. Philip told Nicholas that he and Pedro had a very special birthday surprise for him. He got all excited and started to guess what it was. One of his guesses was that Philip and his mother would get married, and they would all live together.

Philip's remarked, "That's not the surprise, Nick, but it sounds like a great plan." He smiled at Laura, and she returned it with an enthusiastic look.

The next few days went by fast. Laura made arrangements for Lucy and Ryan to look after Nicholas. Although she knew that he couldn't be in better hands, she was also apprehensive about being away from him for seven days. They'd never been apart for any longer than two days, and she was concerned about his new medication that he was having a slight problem getting adjusted to.

Lucy put her mind at ease by telling her that she and Ryan

would be with him every moment except for his time in school. She would take him there and pick him up after class instead of him taking the bus.

At six thirty Thursday morning, Carol dropped her father and Laura off at the departures level at Smiths Airport in Fort Wayne for a seven thirty flight to Chicago, which would connect with an Alitalia flight at nine o'clock, destined to Rome, an eight-hour flight that would arrive in Rome at eleven o'clock, in the evening (Rome time). The flight to Chicago was about thirty minutes, and their luggage was transferred on to Alitalia Airlines while they checked in at the Alitalia counter.

When that was all confirmed, they decided to have a tea, while Laura, excitedly wanted to go over the itinerary for the fourth time.

Philip said, "I have a couple of calls to make; one to the office, to make sure our fax got through to my friends in Verona, and another to Pedro to confirm about Nick's birthday present. I meant to talk to him yesterday, but for some reason it slipped my mind."

"Oh," Laura said, as she raised her eyebrows, "and what would that be?"

"Do you really want me to tell you, or do you want it to be a surprise?" Philip asked.

"I think you better tell me," Laura said with a smile, "or I'll have it on my mind for the whole trip."

"Well, we can't have that in our way," Philip said jokingly. "What fun would I have knowing that I don't have your full attention, so I'll tell you. It's a colt; it's five months old and has already been weaned from it's mother. Pedro is picking him up this weekend."

"Nicholas will be so happy," Laura said, "you're spoiling him, even more than Lucy and Ryan do."

"No," Philip replied, "he's going to help Pedro train him, and Pedro will put him through the apprentice stage of cleaning the stables, grooming the horses, and feeding and watering them."

"Pedro is great with horses, isn't he?" Laura asked.

"He's a professional horseman. He seems to have a psychological gift with animals," Philip said, "not only training them, but also caring for their health. He knows their moods, their likes and dislikes. I'm really fortunate that he's with us."

"Have you known him long?" Laura asked.

"About seventeen years. We bumped into each other in a small town in New Mexico, called Santa Rosa," Philip answered. "I was looking for someone to care for my horses, and do odd jobs, and he was looking for work. I believe he and Juanita were a Godsend to Sarah and me."

"I love you, you know," Laura said.

"I know," Philip replied, "and you know that I love you too."

They leaned across the table, and their lips met, then Philip asked, "Do you want to call Lucy?"

"Yes," Laura answered, "I better call her car phone. She'll be on her way to the school with Nicholas."

After the calls were made, they went through customs and sat in the lounge, where they talked about their vacation *again.* At that moment, Philip could feel warmth on his face, and brightness appeared to be in his eyes. He opened them and realized where he was, and how long he'd been asleep.

The aircraft had made a turn slightly south, and the bright setting sun, reflecting off the wing of the aircraft, seemed to be forcing its way through the window blind.

He straightened himself up in his seat, and caught the flight attendant's attention and asked her to bring him a warm cloth, so he could wipe his face, and since his last thoughts were with Laura, he decided to have a Kahlua over ice.

When she arrived with his drink, he asked what time they'd be landing in Honolulu. She told him it would be in two and a half hours and asked if he'd like a snack. He declined, but asked how long the layover would be.

Lisa told him, "Only the time it takes to discharge some passengers and take on fuel, approximately an hour. Passengers would be allowed to rest in the airport lounge, if they wished," she added.

He thanked her, used the lavatory, and then returned to his seat to relax with his thoughts of he and Laura on their romantic trip to Italy.

An eight-hour flight would normally seem long and boring, but with Laura by his side, time seemed to stand still, and in no time they were about to land in Rome. By the time they retrieved their luggage, took a taxi to their hotel, and got settled in their room, it was after eleven o'clock, Rome time.

Philip said, "It's only about five o'clock Valleyfield time, if you'd like to give Nick a call. He'd be happy to hear from you, and while you're doing that, I'll take a shower."

"You mean, were not having one together!" Laura commented.

"If we did, we'd be in the tub all night." Philip replied.

"That would be different," Laura said as she dialed the phone.

Philip was out of the shower and was brushing his teeth as Laura finished her call, and after talking to Nicholas and Lucy, she was content everything was all right.

Laura took a shower, put on a beautiful, sexy, powder blue nightgown with a matching negligee, and after a nightcap, they retired to the sheets.

As they were lying arm-in-arm, Philip said, "I wonder if it's any different making love in Italy than in Valleyfield."

"Gosh, I really don't know," Laura replied, "I wonder how we could find out?" as she rolled on top of him, undid his pajama top, lowered the straps of her nightgown, and gently covered his breast with hers.

They then embraced in a long kiss, shook off the rest of their night-wear, and made passionate love.

After a few minutes of relaxing, Philip said, "Tante grazie, Signora."

Laura answered by saying, "Grazie, Signore."

They then fell into a deep sleep.

Philip was up early, showered, shaved, dressed, and went downstairs to rent a car and ordered breakfast to be brought up to their room.

When he arrived back, Laura was just waking up. Looking around the room she said, "Oh my, I thought I was dreaming. Am I?" she asked.

Philip answered by saying, "Naw, what you see is true." He bent over and kissed her, and then said, "Buon giorno, Signora, amoré."

At that moment the bellman was at the door with their breakfast. Philip opened the door, tipped the bellman, who said, "Grazie, Signore," and left.

Philip then pushed the cart to the bedside, pulled up a chair for himself, poured two cups of tea, and he and Laura enjoyed bacon and waffles with syrup.

"Breakfast in bed," Laura commented, "I must be dreaming. I never get that."

"You've never lived with me," Philip replied.

"Where have you been all my life?" Laura asked.

Philip said, "We'll leave Rome this morning, take our time to see the sights, while we head north to Venice."

"You make everything sound so romantic," Laura said.

"I sound like a tour guide," Philip replied. "Italy is romantic, and it's more romantic when I'm with you," he added.

"Maybe we'll spend a night between here and Venice," Philip said, "and spend the weekend in Venice, then off to Verona where we'll meet my friends, Tony and Eva."

Laura leaned over and kissed him and said, "I better get up and shower, so we can get going."

After her shower, and while she was getting dressed, Philip continued to tell her about his friends. He said with a smile, "They are a great couple, always happy. Both in their late sixties, but you'd never know it. They're always romanticizing with each other, and they both speak fluent English."

"I know they're going to expect us to party with them," he continued, "I mean eating, drinking, dancing. He always brags about how he makes the best wine in Italy."

"They sound like a terrific couple," Laura said.

"They are, and they'll take to you right away," Philip replied.

"I hope so," Laura said, "then we go to Italian Lakes."

"Right," Philip said. "After a couple of days with them, we'll need to rest up, and enjoy the beauty and tranquility of the lakes."

That morning, they left Rome. The temperature was 23°C, with not a cloud in the sky as they headed north. On their route to Venice, they crossed olive groves and the Chianti vineyards, and then crossed the Apennine Mountains, had lunch in Bologna, then decided, because they made such great time without even hurrying, to cross the Veneto plains and drive directly to the magical city of Venice.

They checked in at the Hotel Torino, formerly a 15th Century Venetian villa, early in the afternoon. The hotel is only a short walk from St. Mark's Square. So after resting for an hour, they took a gondola ride, which took them under the Bridge of Sighs, and later they combined a lagoon cruise with a delicious seafood dinner.

Saturday was filled with sightseeing, a lovely lunch, and a romantic candlelit serenaded dinner.

Venice is like a poem.

Sunday morning started off with breakfast in the hotel, and a short drive to Verona. It's been named as Shakespeare's Verona.

They arrived at Tony and Eva's around eleven o'clock, and just as Philip said, they took to Laura with heartfelt feelings. Philip and Laura joined them at mass, and the rest of the afternoon was spent at Tony and Eva's little twenty-acre mini farm, where Tony had almost ten of those acres as a small vineyard.

Eva made a delicious dinner that she started preparing early that morning. A garden pasta toss to start with, and a scrumptious penne marinara with sausage, and of course a bottle of Tony's red wine. They talked on into the night and the wee hours of the morning before retiring.

The next morning Philip and Tony had a few hours of business to discuss at Tony's shoe factory. Philip was importing a couple of hundred thousand dollars, two hundred million lire worth, of Italian shoes to the U.S.

After their meeting at the factory, they visited an orphanage school where they both donated a considerable amount of money to buying computers.

Eva showed Laura some of the sights of the town, like Juliet's balcony, and the 1st century Roman arena, and then had lunch at one of the outdoor cafes.

When lunch was over Eva said, "Now were going shopping, on me."

"Oh no," Laura said, "I couldn't let you."

"Oh yes," Eva replied, "my husband's orders. We've been married forty-eight beautiful years, and there are two things that he's never left me short of. One is his dedicated love for me. We have shared the same bed every night. And two, thirty years ago when our business took off, he's never left me short of money."

That evening they had dinner at one of Tony and Eva's favorite restaurants. It was a night to remember. A seven-course meal, and dancing to live music. Tony even had Laura up dancing a polka. One of the musicians, at Philip's request, came to their table and sang a song in Italian called "Dance Me To The End Of Love."

After the place had quieted down, Philip and Laura were in each other's arms dancing to a slow waltz

He looked at her and said, "Isn't this a beautiful place? I don't just mean this restaurant, I mean the whole country."

"Yes," Laura replied, "it's so romantic, and Tony and Eva are the perfect couple. I've only known them for a few hours, and they make me feel as though we've known each other for years. I love you for bringing me here to meet them. I can't explain it, but I feel it in my soul."

Philip looked in her eyes and said with a smile, "I love you very much, Miss Manning," as he kissed her on the lips.

Eva turned to her husband and said, "I'm so happy that he has found her."

Tony answered by saying, "Yes, my sweet, you're right," as

he rubbed his hand on hers.

Then he got up, told the maître d' to have a cab for the couple on the dance floor when they were ready to leave.

Tony and Eva left shortly after midnight. About forty-five minutes later, a cab dropped Philip and Laura off.

As they entered the house, Tony said, "We thought you two would be dancing all night. You both seemed to be in another world."

Philip laughed and replied, "We certainly were, and some other time we will, but Laura wanted to call home to check on her little boy Nick."

"Would you mind?" Laura asked Tony. "It's about six o'clock back home."

"Of course you can, any time, don't even ask," as he escorted her into his office where she'd have more privacy.

She talked to Nicholas for a few minutes, and with Lucy for ten minutes longer, and when she came out of the office she looked distraught. Right away Philip could see it in her eyes, he asked her, "What is it, is something wrong with Nick? If so, we'll leave on the next plane."

Laura answered, "No, it's all right. Last night was a little uncomfortable for him. Lucy said that she and Ryan were up with him for a while, but he got up bright and early this morning, and felt good all day."

Philip asked, "Would you mind if Gray examined him? This is his field, he's the best in the state. I wouldn't be surprised that he's the best in the country."

"That's what Dr. McAllister said to me a couple of weeks ago," Laura replied.

"I'll call Gray tomorrow," Philip said, "and when we return home, we'll take Nick to see him."

Laura hugged him and said, "I feel better already. You're worried about him too, aren't you?" she asked.

"I sure am," Philip replied, "and he's going to be fine," as he held her tight.

Tony and Eva were looking on at the conversation, and Tony said, "If there's anything we can do, we would be hurt if you didn't ask us."

Laura hugged the both of them and said, "Thank you, you're very kind."

Eva smiled and said, "He will be in our prayers, and one day we would like to meet him."

"You will, and I hope soon," Philip replied.

Eva excused herself, as she gave her husband a kiss, said good-night to Philip and Laura, and retired to her bedroom.

Philip showed Laura to theirs, and a few minutes later he joined Tony who was on the patio enjoying a cigar with a carafe of red wine and two glasses. Tony poured wine into both glasses, as the two men toasted their friendship.

He looked at Philip and said, "You look a little concerned my friend. Is it the boy?" he asked.

"Yes," Philip answered as he explained to Tony about Nick's condition.

They talked for about an hour on the subject, while finishing off the carafe and then retired to their bedrooms.

The next morning, after a hearty breakfast that Eva cooked up, they left for the Italian Lakes, where they had a well deserved day and a half of relaxation.

At eleven o'clock Wednesday morning they left the Lakes, drove across the Plains of Lombardy, over the Apennine Mountains en route to Genoa, the birthplace of Christopher Columbus. After spending an hour having lunch in Genoa, they traveled down the coast to Pisa to see the Leaning Tower, and then across to Florence where they spent a couple of hours sightseeing and shopping. Philip bought Laura a lovely gold ring, placed it on her finger, and asked her, smilingly, if she would go steady with him.

She said, "Yes, I will." Then jokingly remarked, "What are all those other guys going to do?"

Philip kissed her and said, "They will just have to suffer."

They then left Florence and drove south through Siena and

the Chianti wine-producing region of Tuscany, and then on to Rome where they reached their hotel about five in the afternoon.

Philip showered and then ran the tub. He knew Laura would like to relax with a hot bath.

Afterwards, Philip said, "There's one more place I'd like you to see before we leave for home."

Laura, wearing just a house coat, looked at him, smiled, and thought, "He is so emotional, he never ceases to arouse the excitement in me." Then she asked, "And where could that be?"

"Well," Philip answered, "you put on something casual, I'd suggest slacks, and maybe bring along a sweater, and I'll show you."

Philip called the front desk to have his car brought out, and in a few minutes they were heading southeast through Monte Casino, and then south again to the Bay of Naples. He parked the car by the large marina, and they entered the ferry to the idyllic Isle of Capri, where they explored this enchanting island with its orange and lemon trees, and fashionable shops. Before leaving they visited the Blue Grotto, and then returned to Sorrento and back to Rome.

The next day they left Rome, but before they left, they threw a lira into the Trevi Fountain, following a tradition that says the spirit of the fountain will see that you return to Rome one day. But that wasn't the only reason. They promised each other when they returned again it would be for a much longer visit, with the idea to buy a small villa for them to stay.

chapter XIX

CHICAGO ILLINOIS
FIRST WEEK IN JUNE

Eleven-thirty a.m., the big seven forty-seven was thirty minutes early as it touched down at O'Hare International Airport in Chicago.

After Laura and Philip retrieved their luggage, Philip called Carol notifying her that they would be in Fort Wayne in about an hour, if she was available to meet them, and she was.

They were waiting at the arrivals section when they saw Carol. She could tell instantly by their big smiles, and the way they held each other's hands, that the trip sealed their love for each other.

All the way to Valleyfield, Laura didn't let up about what they did and what they saw. When they reached the outskirts, Philip told his daughter to drop him off at his office, so he could get the paper work started for the shipment of leather goods from Verona.

Philip gave the two girls a kiss, and told Laura that he would drop by her house later. As they drove off, Carol and Laura carried on their conversation about Italy, Carol's baby, and the new house.

When they reached Laura's house, Carol walked her to the front door carrying a small piece of luggage and said, "When you get a chance call Lucy, and the two of you meet me at my place tomorrow morning around ten for coffee and maybe some girl talk."

"That sounds like a plan to me," Laura remarked, "I'll drop

Nicholas off, and check my mail, and come right over. I have a gift for you both."

"Oh, I love presents," Carol said. "Can I have it now?" she asked.

"No," Laura said, "you'll have to wait, and don't pout. I'll see you in the morning."

Philip came by around two-thirty, just in time for the both of them to drive to the school to pick up Nicholas.

Laura had called Lucy to let her know that they were home, and that they would pick up Nicholas, and also to tell her to meet at Carol's house in the morning.

They heard the school bell ring, and Nicholas was one of the first to exit the door. He ran over and kissed and hugged his mother and gave Philip a hug as well. Laura could tell that there was a change in him. He looked a little tired and out of breath, so she decided there and then to have him examined by Gray.

Nicholas was all excited about his birthday party at Millcreek.

The next day Laura saw Nicholas off to school, and then called Gray's office to make an appointment. Gray's secretary told her that Dr. West was expected in at any time from a three day seminar in Chicago, and that arrangements had already been made for an appointment for Nicholas today at three thirty. She also told her that Nicholas' medical records had reached their office from Dr. McAllister. She said that Philip was talking to Dr. West a few days ago.

That set Laura's mind at ease, and she thought how wonderful and caring Philip was to make these arrangements. He must have called from Tony and Eva's house.

She then went to her office to check her mail, and then over to Carol's where she saw Lucy's car in her driveway. Carol had a pot of coffee brewing when Laura entered, and Lucy was helping her put away some glasses on a top shelf. There were still a few boxes from the move that weren't unpacked.

So after the hi's, and how-do-you- do's Lucy came right out and said to Laura, "Okay, give it to us, and don't take any shortcuts."

"You seem to be more excited than I am," Laura said, knowing that she wouldn't go into any intimate details about her and Philip.

"You did have a great time," Carol said (as she poured the coffee for the three of them), "I could tell just seeing you both at the airport."

"Yes, excellent," Laura replied. Then she went through the trip from beginning to end.

Afterwards she handed them a gift that she bought in Italy. The girls opened them, and thanked her. The gifts were silk blouses.

Laura then put her hand on the back of Carol's and said, "Carol, I fell in love with your father, even more than I knew."

"Oh," Carol groaned with her eyes sparkling with tears, "he has a way of rubbing off on you, doesn't he?"

Lucy said, "I'm really happy for you. I'm sure you're both meant for each other."

"Thanks Lucy, I knew you'd feel that way, and I'm glad I'm sharing this moment with my two best friends," Laura said.

"He is such a wonderful man," she continued. "Everyone we met, all the people he did business with, seem to treat him and trust him like he was their brother. His two friends in Verona, Tony and Eva, treat him like he was their son."

"Does this mean that I will soon be calling you Mom?" Carol asked, as she glanced at Lucy, who laughed and said, "That, I would like to hear."

"Well, what about it, did he pop the question?" Lucy continued.

"Hey, hold on you guys," Laura said. "No, he didn't pop the question, as you put it. I'm sure when the time is right, and then she hesitated, as she thought, the time couldn't have been any more "right" then the evening they spent at a little "ristorante" in Verona.

"Does he know that you love him? Have you told him?" Lucy asked.

"Yes, I have, but I really didn't have to, I'm sure he knows."

Laura replied. "All the emotions are there," Laura continued, "I was sure, well let me rephrase that, the time was appropriate one evening when we were having dinner with Tony and Eva at a little restaurant just outside of Verona. After what seemed like a six course meal, with a violin, and an accordion player playing at the tables, and so many glasses of wine, we danced the night away.

"Tony and Eva left around twelve-thirty, but we just couldn't leave. Everything was so beautiful—the setting was perfect: a dim-lighted candle, a red rose that Philip bought me, two glasses of wine, and a man and a woman crazy in love."

"Oh my God," Lucy said, "He didn't ask you…"

"Hold on, there's more," Laura said. "We had just finished a nice slow dance, and we're sitting at our table when the violin and accordion player came over, by Philip's request. The accordionist sang a song to me in Italian; it was called "Dance Me To The End Of Love." It was so beautiful I cried, not only because of the song, but while the man sang, your father interpreted it to me in English."

She looked at Carol and said, "Carol, if I ever had any doubts about my love for your father, which I don't, they would have disappeared at that moment."

"What a romantic," Lucy said, "and he even dances!"

"That's what I asked him," and he said, "Someone had to teach Fred Astaire."

They laughed, and Lucy asked Carol, "Has he always been so romantic?"

"Always," Carol replied. "I can remember parties that we all attended. Women liked to talk with him. He was always very charming to them, no matter who they were or what they did, or what they looked like, but there was only one woman in his life, my mother. They couldn't keep their hands off each other."

Laura then told them about the Isle of Capri with the fashionable shops where she bought their gifts.

"The whole trip was so exciting," Laura said. "You know, the beauty of it all is that you don't have to speak or even understand the language to love it."

"So, enough about me. What's been happening back here in Valleyfield?" Laura asked. "Anything new at the good old I.S.R?"

"Yes, matter of fact," Lucy replied. "That bitch Madge left her husband."

"Well, by the rumors that were floating around, and I hate rumors," Laura said, "you could see it coming."

"Is this an agent, someone you don't like?" Carol asked Lucy.

"I can't stand the little tart," Lucy answered. "She's not only screwing Glen, the manager, she also sleeps around with half her clients and a couple of agents, one that I had some respect for."

"Lucy, you don't know that for sure," Laura commented.

"I heard it from a good source," Lucy replied. "When she came here two years ago, it took her eight months to make two transactions, and she slept with both of those clients."

"Really," Carol said. "I hope she got a good commission."

"She shares it with the agency, it's an agreement that pays her office space." Laura said.

"It's been rumored, and I wouldn't be surprised, that Glen has tossed her a few listings," Lucy remarked. "She's always running in and out of his office."

"Maybe its business," Laura said. "She could be getting advice from him."

Carol looked at Lucy, Lucy looked at Carol, and then they both looked at Laura and shook their heads up and down, and at the same time said, "Yah, right."

"Ah, you guys aren't being fair," Laura said.

"If Glen's wife, Connie, ever finds out, he'll be in the cleaning business because that's where she'll take him," Lucy commented.

"Wow!" Carol said, "This Madge sounds like a popular girl."

"With the men," Lucy replied. "She even bleached her hair. Now it matches her personality."

"Hey," Carol jeered, "I'm a blond."

They laughed, "You know what I mean," Lucy replied.

"That's too bad," Laura commented. "Didn't we meet her

husband at the Christmas party?"

"Yes, we did," Lucy answered.

"He seemed very nice. His name is Gary, isn't it?"

"That's right," Lucy replied, "and he is a great guy. It's cruel what she did," Lucy continued. "She not only left him, but she also deserted her little girl, Christina. The little sweetie is only seven, same age as Nicholas, and she has asthma. I can picture her crying in the night, calling for her mother because she can't catch her breath, and where is her mother, laying beside some fat bellied bastard because he has a few dollars to spend on her, and probably drives a mortgaged Mercedes."

"Oh Lucy, don't you think you're magnifying a little?" Laura suggested. "I don't like to see you upset like this."

"No damn it! She couldn't wait to get her hands on her share of the money from the sale of their house, and it pisses me off." Lucy continued with tears in her eyes. "I can't have children," she went on, "and here this little strumpet abandons hers. I know, Ryan and I adore Nicholas like he was ours, and that's why we spoil him, but it bothers me so much to hear of anyone leaving their children," she scowled.

"Well," Carol said," I think I speak for Laura as well as myself when I say that no man, or all the money on earth, would separate me from my child, so we do understand how you feel."

"That's right," Laura said, "I'm sure there will be a time when Madge will realize what she's doing, and I hope she will get her life together again."

"I imagine she's having some sleepless nights," Carol added.

"I'm sorry for shooting off my mouth and spoiling your homecoming. Maybe I shouldn't have run her down like I did." Lucy said.

Laura put her hand on her friend's and said, "That's okay, we understand, and I'm glad we discussed it."

Carol said, "It's called relieving pressure. I've never seen this side of you before. It's kind of exciting."

Lucy touched Carol's arm and sadly said, "I'm sorry."

"No, you don't have to be," Carol replied. "It's really all right."

"Well, I'm still going to spoil your little girl," Lucy commented.

Then she looked at her watch and said, "I hate to break up our little gathering, and I'm overjoyed at Laura's pre-honeymoon, but I have an appointment at one o'clock."

"Yes," Laura said, "I'm meeting Philip for lunch, and then we're picking up Nicholas at two, and I still have a half dozen things to do for his party tomorrow. Of course, I could do them with Philip."

"Sure, why not," Carol added. "He loves to shop."

"Do you want to come with us?" Laura asked.

"No, I'll leave you two love birds alone. I don't think my dad wants his kids hanging around." Carol joked. "I also have a doctor's appointment at one forty-five." She added.

They left and went their separate ways.

At that moment Philip was awakened by an announcement from the captain.

"May I have your attention ladies and gentlemen. We will be landing in Honolulu in thirty minutes. The temperature there is a balmy eighty-two degrees, and the time is ten o'clock p.m. Our stay will only be for approximately one hour while we take on fuel. There is a lounge at the terminal where you may rest if you wish to leave the aircraft. Thank you, and my apologies if I awakened you."

Philip thought that this would be a good time to write Nick a letter, and send it via Lucy and Ryan. His letter starts:

Dear Nick,

I guess by now you're wondering where I am and why I wasn't with you when you woke up from your operation. I am now in Honolulu, just a stopover on my way to Australia, to visit some friends, and do some business.

One day, I hope I can explain to you why I wasn't with you at the hospital. If I could have been, I would have, believe me, but there was an emergency so I had to leave. Gray told me that you're coming along great, and I'm so happy to hear that. Remember what we talked about after Davey died, how God would put him in charge to make you better. Well I guess it worked; Nick, I honestly believe that. Davey has now earned his wings. He is now an angel. Maybe you could tell his mommy and daddy. It will make them feel better, and that is good.

I don't know how long I'll be away, but I hope you will invite Lucy, Ryan, and of course your mommy, out to Millcreek to ride the horses, and maybe if it's okay with your mommy you might stay over at Pedro and Juanita's house. They would love to have you, and Pedro could always use an extra hand on the farm, and Silver Dollar needs to get to know you again.

Most of all Nick, and I know I don't have to ask you, look after your mommy, if she feels sad, you cheer her up, if she makes a decision, you honor it. You're the man of the house; I'm counting on you buddy. Keep in touch with Dr. West. You can also share secrets with him. He's one of the good guys....

I miss you Nick, and I love you. Keep strong, and hug your mommy every day. Don't worry about me; I'll be okay, I promise....

Love Philip

He then placed it in an envelope, addressed it to Ryan and Lucy's address, and when they landed in Honolulu he would exit the plane, and place it in a mailbox at the airport lounge.

After an hour and fifteen minutes, they were off again. Next stop would Sydney, Australia.

Philip was now again deep in his thoughts, cataloguing his memories with Laura.

chapter xx

VALLEYFIELD HOSPITAL
JUNE 7, 1995

Since Dr. Graham West is the chief surgeon, and also chief of staff at the Valley Hospital, it would be appropriate that his office would be there as well.

When Philip, Laura, and Nicholas entered the office, Gray's secretary, Valerie, who was at the filing cabinet filing some records, greeted them. A lady in her late thirties, about five foot four, with lovely brown hair, done back in a French roll. Although her figure could be classed as a number nine, her beauty is in her sparkling deep brown eyes.

Laura noticed right away how attractive she was, and a sort of jealous thought entered her mind, and then it left as fast as it entered.

Valerie has been Gray's secretary for over fifteen years. She is divorced, and has a sixteen-year-old daughter. Her personality is first class, and Gray regards her as his right armed person.

As they approached her desk she said, "Philip, how nice to see you again."

"You too, Valerie, it's been quite a while."

"Last Christmas," she replied.

"I'd like you to meet Laura," Philip said, "Laura this is Valerie."

"How do you do?" Laura asked as she reached out and shook her hand.

"I'm good," Valerie replied, "I've heard nice things about you."

"What?" Philip asked. "Is Gray telling stories again?"

They laughed and Valerie said, "This has to be Nicholas," as she came around her desk to shake his hand. "I am really glad to meet you. Dr. West is always bragging about his new friend. He refers you to "Agent #4."

Nicholas smiled his comforting smile and said, "Really, does he really?"

"He sure does," Valerie replied.

"You are very pretty," Nicholas remarked.

"Oh, how nice of you to say so, thank you." Valerie said. "If only I were ten years younger, and you were ten years older."

"Make it thirty," Philip joked.

"Don't get smart," Valerie quipped.

At that time Gray opened the door of his office, as one of his patients was leaving. He said to him that Valerie would make an appointment for next week.

He then came over to where Nicholas was sitting and pointed his thumb, index finger and little finger towards Nicholas, and Nicholas did the same until they touched each other's fingers and they said together, "'*Secret Agents*' forever."

They all laughed, and then he led them into his personal office and closed the door. His office was like most doctors', with degree plaques hanging on the wall, a couple of other pictures, and a computer on a separate table behind his desk. On his desk there is a picture of Gray, his wife Betty, and their son Jason, who is now attending the University of Chicago, studying (what else) medicine. He wants to go into research.

Nicholas was staring at a picture that was hanging above a cabinet in the corner next to the window. He asked, "Who are those kids?"

Philip came over and took the twelve by ten wood framed picture of three young boys in their bathing suits down and replied, "This is Gray on the left, this is me in the middle, and this is Willy on the right."

"Holy cow," Nicholas said, "look Mommy it doesn't look

like them."

Laura smiled as she looked at the picture and said, "That was a long time ago."

"Forty years," Gray said.

"Yah," Philip laughed, "we were twelve years old."

"Well," Gray said to Nicholas, "we are going to give you a 'big' checkup, to see what we have to do to make you feel better again, and you know what?" he asked.

"What?" Nicholas asked.

"It's not even going to hurt, one bit," Gray continued.

He focused his eyes towards Laura and said, "I have all his records from Bob, Dr. McAllister, and we had a talk the other day. So, if Monday afternoon is okay with you, we can get most everything done in a couple of hours. I'm free from appointments all afternoon, so whatever time is convenient for you, it's okay by me."

"How about two o'clock?" Laura asked.

"Two o'clock will be fine." Gray agreed. "Is that all right with you Nick?"

"Yep, that will be okay," Nicholas answered. "You're coming to my party, aren't you Gray?"

"Try and keep me away," Gray replied. "Betty and I will be at Millcreek at noon tomorrow, so don't start without us."

"We won't," Nicholas said as he snuggled up to his mother and Philip.

They then got up, and Gray ushered them out and said to Laura, "Try not to worry. I know it's a parent's instinct, but we're going to give him a thorough examination."

"Thanks, Gray, you put my mind at ease." Laura said.

"We'll get to the bottom of it and then we'll know what to do, and we'll do it," Gray sternly said. "Now you guys get out of here, and Betty and I will see you tomorrow."

On the way out, Nicholas said, "Good-bye Valerie. If you wish, I'd like you to come to my party tomorrow."

"Oh, thanks Nicholas. We usually go for a drive in the country on Saturdays, and we'll definitely drop by," Valerie said.

"By all means," Laura said, "we'd be glad if you could."

"Thanks, Laura, you have a darling son," Valerie commented.

Laura smiled and said, "Thank you."

On the way to the car, Laura said to Philip, "Valerie is a very attractive woman."

"Yes, she is," Philip replied as he looked at Laura and squeezed her hand.

"Does she have a man in her life?" Laura asked.

"Not as far as I know." Philip replied. "She and her daughter go to a lot of functions together. Gardening is her favorite pastime, and she likes to golf."

Laura, smiling, looked up at him, and at the same time squeezed his arm with both hands and said, "You know a lot about her."

"I've known her for about eighteen years. She had a bad relationship with her husband."

"That's too bad," Laura said. "She seems like a wonderful person."

"Both she and her daughter are great," Philip said.

As they reached the car, Laura just had to ask, "Have you ever dated her?"

At that moment Nicholas jumped in the back seat and was doing up his seat belt. As Philip was about to open the door for Laura, he turned her around, smiled, kissed her on the lips and answered her by saying, "No, not a date. I've had lunch with her a few times, and we've had a few rounds of golf. It isn't that I wouldn't have, but I think I was a little messed up the last couple of years."

"I'm sorry for asking," Laura said as she kissed him back.

"That's okay, I don't mind," Philip replied.

"I guess it's a '*woman thing,*'" Laura continued, "When we entered Gray's office, I could see her eyes light up when she looked at you."

"Really?" Philip said excitedly.

"Well, of course! You're a very handsome man," Laura said.

"That's likely why," Philip joked. "Beauty is only in the eye of the beholder."

"Your eyes are only for me, right?" Laura commented.

"Right, only for you, and yours for me," Philip replied.

chapter XXI

MILLCREEK
SATURDAY, JUNE 8, 1995

Pedro and Juanita spent a week preparing for Nicholas's birthday party. They affixed a huge banner across the entrance of the laneway, that read "Happy Birthday Nick," and all the way in there were ribbons and balloons hanging from the trees. Tables and chairs were set out, and the barbecue was ready to be lit. The party was to take place on the grassy area near the corral. The wooden fence around the corral was also decorated with ribbons and bows.

Juanita baked a batch of cookies and a large birthday cake, along with numerous salads. Everything was ready. All that had to happen now, was the guests and the birthday boy to show up.

Last night wasn't one of Nicholas's best nights for sleeping. It wasn't his kidney that was keeping him restless, it was the persistent craving of the next day, of his best birthday ever. At seven-thirty he rushed into his mother's bedroom, waking her from a sound sleep and said, "Mommy we better get up, we have to get ready, Philip might be waiting for us."

"No," his mother replied, as she stretched and gave out a large yawn, "it's early, it's only seven thirty. We're not to be there until noon; the party starts at one o'clock. That's when everyone will show up. But I'll tell you what," she continued, as she sat up in her bed, gave him a hug wishing him a happy birthday, "we'll get up, have breakfast, shower, get dressed, and after we take the books back to the library we'll drive up to Millcreek, okay?"

"Okay," he replied. As he walked to the kitchen to prepare his cereal, he asked, "What time will Ryan and Lucy be leaving?"

"They both have to go to their offices this morning," Laura cried out from the washroom, "but they'll be there before one."

"I phoned Daddy last night," Nicholas said. "He told me that he was playing golf this morning, but he'd be at Millcreek by one o'clock. I gave him directions on how to get there."

"I know," Laura replied as she plugged in the kettle, "he phoned me after you went to bed."

"I told him about our visit with Dr. West, and your appointment next week."

"What did he say?" Nicholas asked.

"He said that he'd meet us there," Laura answered.

"Oh goody!" Nicholas yelled as he started eating his breakfast.

Philip was out of bed by seven, had a quick shower, threw on a pair of jeans, a sweat shirt, and his riding boots, opened the fridge, grabbed an apple for himself and a carrot for his big black seven year old Arabian stallion Phantom that he and Pedro raised and trained from a colt, and headed for the stable.

The other horses in the stable included Pedro's ten-year old Roan, Big Buck, a very gentle nine-year-old mare called Delila that Sarah and the kids used to ride, and the newest addition, a one-year old colt that would definitely have a name today.

While Phantom was enjoying his carrot, Philip was saddling him. He then led him outside, mounted him, and rode off at a gallop down through the valley, over the creek, and in through the woods.

Riding was one of Philip's passions. For hours he would be borne along by Phantom through his farm. Quite often, he would take a book with him, dismount in a quiet domain in the valley, and read for an hour, and then walk his steed along the fences, back to the stable.

After about an hour he headed for the stable, unsaddled Phantom and pulled off his bridle. While the horse was gulping down water, Philip groomed him, and then set him loose in the field with the other horses.

Philip walked back to his mill-house, took a shower, changed into something casual, and then over to Juanita's where he knew he would have a meal of her delicious Mexican hot-cakes covered with butter and maple syrup.

Twelve o'clock rolled around, and the first to enter Millcreek were Laura and Nicholas. She parked her car in Pedro's driveway, and then walked over to the lawn where Pedro and Juanita were setting up a table and some folding chairs. Philip was getting the barbecue ready.

Laura stealthily came up behind him, put her two hands over his eyes and said, "Guess who!!"

Philip stopped what he was doing, put his two hands up on each side to his shoulders, raised his head a little and asked, "Julia, are you back again?"

"Julia," Laura said, "Who's Julia?" she asked.

"Julia Roberts," Philip replied, "she's always sneaking up on me and kissing me on the back of my neck."

"Oh really," Laura said. "Like this?" as she tipped up and rubbed her tongue below his ear.

"Ah," Philip sighed, "you must be Pamela Anderson. That's what she does."

Laura released her hands, smacked him on the butt and said, "You're not nice."

Philip turned around, put his arms around her neck, kissed her on the lips, and said, "I love you, and I knew it was you. I could smell the scent of 'Obsession', and you know what that does to me."

At that moment, Nicholas, who had shaken hands with Pedro and received his usual hug from Juanita as they wished him a happy birthday, came over to where Philip and Laura were affectionately teasing each other and said, "Hi, Philip."

"Hi to you and happy birthday," Philip replied, as he shook his hand. "We're going to have a ball today, right?"

"Yep!" Nicholas answered excitedly, looking at Philip and his mother.

"He had ants in his pants all morning," Laura said. "He couldn't keep still. If he had his way, we would have been here at seven o'clock."

"Then you could have gone riding with me," Philip replied.

All of a sudden Nicholas cried out, "Here comes Bobby and his mom and dad."

They looked over as a car was being parked along the side of the lane. Bobby was out of the car first and ran over to Nicholas, who met him half way.

He said, "Happy birthday, Nick," as he handed him a gift. "This is a neat place."

"Yeah, it sure is neat," Nicholas replied.

Bobby's mother and dad caught up to them and Nicholas said, "Hello Mr. and Mrs. O'Neil, how are you?" he asked.

"We're fine thanks," Mr. O'Neil replied. "Happy birthday to you," they both said together.

"Thank you," Nicholas said. "I'd like you to meet Philip," as Philip and Laura were walking towards them. "Philip you've met Bobby, this is his mom and dad."

"How do you do?" Philip asked.

"Very well, thanks. My name is Ken, and this is my wife, Donna."

They shook hands, and Donna said, "This place is beautiful. You must really enjoy it."

"Yes we do," Philip replied. "We did a lot of preparation to make it like it is, but I love it. I've owned the land for over twenty years, but only fixed up my living quarters three years ago. Later on I'd like to show it to you. It's a one hundred and fifty year old gristmill that we made livable."

"We'll look forward to it," Ken replied.

Philip offered them a drink, as Laura and Donna were carrying on a conversation.

It was now getting on to one o'clock and most of all the guests had arrived.

Nicholas's father hadn't arrived as yet and Nicholas was getting a little concerned. Philip assured him that he would be here shortly, telling him that it rained at the golf course this morning and it most likely set them back an hour. Nicholas had no sooner thanked him for his concern, when his father drove in the driveway.

The burgers, steaks, and chicken wings were ready, and the salads and baked potatoes were on the tables. There was a large tub filled with soft drinks and beer if anyone wished one.

The party went well, but not quick enough for Nicholas. He wanted to get at his presents, but first he made a surprising announcement. He got up from his chair that was between his mother's and Philip's and said, "I would like to thank everyone for coming today and sharing my birthday, but most of all I want to say a special thanks to Pedro and Juanita for making all the food and decorations."

He walked over to where they were sitting and said, "I love you," and kissed Juanita on the cheek, and shook Pedro's hand. There were tears in Juanita's eyes, and Pedro's were glistening as well, as they hugged him and she said, "We love you too."

Laura couldn't get over the emotion that her son had just displayed as she took Philip's arm and squeezed it and said, "He sure is growing up fast."

"In a very nice way," Philip added.

The tables were cleared, the paper plates and napkins went in the garbage bin, and Juanita was placing a large birthday cake she made on the picnic table. The inscription on the cake read "Happy Birthday Nicholas #8."

Everyone gathered around and sang "Happy Birthday."

Nicholas very shyly said, "Thank you," and added, "Can I open my gifts now, Mommy?"

His mother agreed, so the gifts were put on and around the table. First there was the gift from Bobby, who was now sitting next to Nicholas. It was a Louisville baseball glove. They both touched each other with clenched fists to emphasize their emotion.

He opened Gray and Betty's gift next. It was camping equipment along with a large tent.

Gray said, as Nicholas was hugging Betty, "We got the large tent because when you go camping, us guys want to go with you."

His father's gift was a complete set of junior golf clubs and one year's golf lessons. Nicholas went over and hugged him with, "Thanks, Daddy, now I'll be able to go out with you."

"That's what I'm counting on," his father said.

Lucy handed him a large box, beautifully wrapped with a big blue bow. Nicholas gave her a smile and looked over at Ryan who just shrugged his shoulders, and then he gently took off the ribbon and bow, and then tore the paper and opened the box.

To his surprise there was a pair of blue jeans, a shirt, a belt, and a special buckle, and under all that there was a pair of brown cowboy boots. Right away he kicked off his sneakers to try on the boots, and they fit.

Ryan came over with another box and said, "This goes along with it."

Nicholas then looked at his mother with amazement and she said to Ryan and Lucy, "You guys."

As Nicholas was opening the present Ryan said to Laura, "It's okay Laura, I cut back on three of my salesman's commissions."

They all laughed as Nicholas was admiring a white cowboy hat and a colored bandana. Lucy received a kiss, and Ryan a handshake and a big thank you.

Then Juanita very shyly handed him her gift, and kissed him on the cheek. He hugged her back and then opened the present. It was a knitted wool sweater with the face and neck of a white colt on the back.

He loved it, and wanted to wear it, but Juanita said, "Oh no, Neek. I think maybe when you go to school in the fall or on a cold night."

Nicholas took it off and handed it to his mother who put it back in the box and thanked Juanita, and told her it was lovely, and that he would sure get a lot of use from it.

The next gift was from his mother, but it wasn't wrapped, as Pedro brought it out from behind his house. It only had a big bow attached to the handlebars. He thanked her with a hug and kiss and then jumped on the bike and rode around the yard, and gave it to Bobby to try out.

Just then, a car came down the driveway. As it got closer, Gray said, "That's Valerie's car. She has her daughter with her."

Valerie parked; they got out and she said, "We were out driving around at yard sales, and I just had to come in and wish a special guy a happy birthday."

"Thanks," Nicholas said, "I'm glad you came."

"Well," she said, "we have something for you," as she caught Nicholas looking at her daughter. "No, it's not my daughter, Vanessa, she's too old for you."

Everyone laughed.

Gray introduced her and her daughter to everyone, while Philip got a cold drink and a piece of cake for them.

Valerie handed Nicholas an unwrapped gift. She had just purchased it at a yard sale. She said, "I know that you like hockey, so you might like this."

He opened the box to find a large collection of hockey cards. As he searched through them, he found some of the greats, like Gretzsky, Hull, and he even found an old one of Rocket Richard.

Valerie received a large hug, and Nicholas didn't forget to give Vanessa one as well.

Gray's remark was, "Everything else is working well. All we have to do is to get his kidney in good shape."

"You got that right," Philip added.

"Nick," Philip said, "there's something here that Pedro and I have for you."

Nicholas stood beside Philip with the widest smile, and his eyes open wide as Pedro came over and said. "Nick, you've been a great help to me, and I know that you're going to be a good horseman, so I made you something and I'm sure you will get a lot of use from it."

He handed Nick a box that was neatly wrapped, most likely by Juanita. Nick opened it and discovered a beautiful handmade bridle with his name engraved on one of the straps. He looked it over, and handed it to Philip who passed it around, and everyone marveled on the beautiful workmanship.

While Nicholas was thanking Pedro with a big handshake, the bridle found it's way back to Philip's hand. Philip handed it to Pedro and said, "Pedro, the bridle isn't any good unless we can put something in it."

"You're right, amigo," Pedro replied as he walked across the corral and into the stable.

Less then a minute went by when Pedro was seen coming out of the stable door, and along beside him was a beautiful silver gray colt. Pedro's right hand was holding the bridle while his left hand had a grip on the reins as he was now running with the colt that was at a fast trot.

When they reached the fence where Nicholas was standing on the second rail and leaning over the top one, Pedro pulled the colt up to a stop. Nicholas's eyes lit up like the lights on a Christmas tree, as he could only stare at this graceful little animal.

Philip came over and patted the horse on the forehead as Nicholas did the same, then Philip said, "Didn't I say that the black bridle would look good on your horse?"

Nicholas looked at his mother with amazement and then turned to Philip and said.

"He's mine!" Nicholas cried. "Is he really mine?"

"Yes," Pedro said, "he's really yours."

"How old is he?" Nicholas asked.

"He's five months old," Philip answered. "He was born on January 12th, and he's from New Mexico."

"Yes," Pedro said, "he belonged to an old friend of mine who sold his farm and wanted a good home for this colt, so Philip and I thought that he should come here to Millcreek."

"Do you like him?" Philip asked.

"I love him," Nicholas replied.

At that moment, the colt stretched out his neck toward Nicholas and seemingly kissed him on the head. Nicholas spurted out, "Mommy, did you see that? He kissed me, right here," as he pointed to his head.

"Yes, I saw him," his mother replied, "he must like you too."

"Well now," Philip said, "We have to stop calling him 'he' and find a name for him."

"You're right," Gray said, "It's your horse Nick, so you should give him a name."

"Okay," Nicholas said, still patting the colt between the eyes, and Laura clutched Philip's arm. "I like the name 'Silver' because he is silver, but that's the Lone Ranger's horse's name, so I can't call him that."

"Maybe you could think of something with the name silver in it," his mother said.

"Yeah like 'Silver Star,'" Nicholas suggested.

"Sure, that's a nice name," Laura said.

"He doesn't have a silver star," Philip said. "He's all silver."

"How about 'Silverdollar'?" Nicholas suggested.

"That's a lovely name," Lucy said, "don't you think so, Ryan?" she asked.

"It suits him. I think it's a great name," Ryan replied.

"So, can we have Pedro engrave 'Silverdollar' on the other side of the bridle?" Philip asked.

"Yes, I'm calling him Silverdollar," Nicholas said.

Everyone seemed to be getting ready to leave, so Nicholas thanked them for coming, as did Laura and Philip.

"You know Nick, Jack and Carol and Michael and Diana are going to want to see you tomorrow. I believe they have something for you," Philip said.

"Oh boy!" Nicholas replied.

chapter XXII

VALLEYFIELD, INDIANA

Philip and Laura were without doubt in love. Their trip to Italy enhanced the love they had for each other even more. Every day was like a honeymoon.

While Nicholas was in school, they'd go for long walks in the surrounding parks. On most occasions their walks would take them to a trail that would lead through the bush until they'd reach an isolated little spot where they'd be in each others arms making love in the most appropriate and pleasurable pose.

A little incident they often laughed about was the time they decided to go for a drive in the country. After driving for the best part of an hour, they decided to park off the country road on a makeshift driveway leading beneath large hydro lines beside a large field of fresh cut bailed hay.

As they strolled across the field hand-in-hand, they found themselves cuddled behind one of the large rolls of hay, and it wasn't long before passion took over, and Philip's jeans were lowered to his feet, Laura's shorts were off and her panties were dangling on her left ankle as they were positioning themselves.

The plovers were crying out their penetrating killdeer sound as they were searching for places to build their nests, and you could hear the moaning sound of a distant freight train as it was climbing up the long grade to reach the top of the escarpment. Even the hydro towers were sending out their approval with the musical humming of their wires.

Without notice, a pickup truck entered the driveway with two hydro employees in the cab. When they were within one hundred and fifty feet from the loving couple, one of the men hollered out that they were on private property, and that they would have to leave.

Philip pulled up his jeans and zipped up in such a hurry that he caught a little piece of himself in the zipper, letting out a silent ouch. He wasn't accustomed to zipping up while in such a rigid position.

Poor Laura was having a battle of her own. While trying, in a panic, to pull up her panties, they kept getting caught between her toes. She was begging Philip to help her, not knowing that the men had left for the line shack. Philip's previous pain had left him for an amusing smile as he gently slid her panties up around her hips, as she retrieved her shorts.

Then there was the billiard table event. One Sunday afternoon, Laura had an open-house showing just outside of Valleyfield. For the first hour only two couples showed up, and they only picked up a brochure and left. Laura decided to call Philip and ask him to drop by for tea. Of course he never had to be coaxed. Within a half hour he was sitting in the kitchen having a tea with Laura.

After talking about the sale of the house, Laura suggested that he should see how professionally they fixed up the rec room. So they departed the kitchen for the basement. She pointed out the beautiful wet bar with colorful stained glass lighting. A section of the floor directly in front of the bar was done in parquet, and the rest of the floor was tiled. In one corner, under a large colored light was a poker table, and at the other side of the room, Philip was attracted to a large billiard table.

While he was marveling at the beautiful design and workmanship of this table, Laura was standing behind him, rubbing the small of his back and caressing his right arm that was resting on the rail. Of course, he became aroused as he usually did when she would draw close to him, so he turned and wrapped his arm around her waist and drew her to him and passionately kissed her on her parted lips.

His lips were still on hers as he lifted her up and gently laid her across the pool table. They could have used any one of the four bedrooms, but they were at a point of no return. The buttons on her blouse were now undone and his lips had left hers and were now between her breasts, while his right hand was under her skirt lowering her panties. He was about to join her by getting himself in a more comfortable position when they heard a rustling upstairs.

The front door closed and a female voice said, "Hello, is anyone here?"

They both scrambled off the table as Philip pulled up Laura's panties that had been only lowered to her knees. The triangle rack that held the billiard balls was kicked and the balls went scattering all over the table and most of them found themselves in the pockets.

Laura was in another little panic as she straightened up her hair and called back to the voice that she would be right up. Unknown to her or Philip was that when she left the rec room, the back hem of her skirt was caught in the waist of her panties.

Fortunately the couple only wanted a brochure, and then they left.

As Laura was showing them out, the lady said (in private from her husband), "I've heard of 'strip-poker' but was that 'strip-pool' you were playing? Your skirt is caught in your panties." Then she smiled and said, "Good luck."

Laura, embarrassed, replied with, "Thanks."

When she told Philip, they laughed and Laura said, "If that couple ever makes an appointment to see the house, I think I will send Lucy to deal with them."

There were so many fond memories. The most favored location where two people lost themselves in each other, where, in one magic moment her heart was his, and his was hers, was a little unpopulated parcel of land just outside of Valleyfield, called 'Pumpkin Hill.' It was nestled between railroad tracks at the top and a small stream that trickled through the meadow and flowed into the Credit River at the bottom.

There, many times, they would climb to the top, spread out a blanket where the grass was long and soft, and lay in each other's arms and make passionate love. The only sounds were the buzz of summer insects in the meadow, and the whisper of the breeze wafting through the pines.

One time, while they were in a very intimate position, a large freight train was chugging its way out of Valleyfield. As it was passing Pumpkin Hill, the engineers had themselves quite an eyeful. They thanked the lovebirds with a couple of toots from the air horn.

Wherever they were, wherever they went, if there was a carnal desire, nothing stopped them from making love.

chapter XXIII

VALLEYFIELD, INDIANA

In the days that followed, summer continued to sweep across Valleyfield. Temperatures were in the mid eighties. Nicholas was in the hospital a few hours, three days a week for tests and treatment, and the rest of the time he was at Millcreek with Philip, working with Pedro who had started to train Silverdollar. Laura had a few listings that she had to attend to, but they managed to spend the weekends either at Michael and Diana's cottage or at Millcreek.

On July 11th, Carol gave birth to a beautiful baby girl. The following Saturday, Jack and Carol had everyone over to their house for a barbecue, swim, and of course to show off their little girl. Diana and Michael took a break from the cottage to celebrate with them, along with Philip, Laura, and Nicholas. She also invited Pedro and Juanita, Betty and Gray, and Lucy and Ryan.

After they finished eating, they were sitting around the patio, except for Nicholas who was still trying to throw the darts in the ring, when Diana spoke up and asked. "Have you decided what you're going to call this little darling?" as she cradled her in her arms.

Jack answered by saying, "That's one reason why we're all here. Carol and I wanted you all to assist us on a name. We tossed around just about every name we could think of. We even went through the *Baby's Name Book*, so we're hoping that before anyone leaves we would have a real name for our princess."

"Hey, what's wrong with that? Princess Dawson," Michael said.

Carol looked at him with a strange look and said, "Move on."

Then everyone was firing out names, some were agreeable to some but not to others.

Philip said, "Juanita must know some romantic Mexican name."

Juanita answered by saying, "We Mexican girls have too many names, and they're usually all too long. For instance mine, 'Juanita Catherina Maria Lopez'."

"You have beautiful names," Lucy said to Juanita. "I think any one of them would be nice."

"Yes," Betty said, "that would be nice."

As she looked at her and smiled, Carol said, "We've heard from everyone but Laura."

Jack agreed by saying, "Yes, Laura, you must know some lovely names."

"Oh," Laura replied, "she's so beautiful I think her mother should."

Before Laura finished what she was going to say, Carol spoke out and said, "I know, Laura, and we will name her, but I wanted you to have a say. It means a lot to me."

"Well," Laura said, "when I was expecting Nicholas, of course we didn't know he was going to be a Nicholas, I thought of some lovely names in case I had a little girl, but," then she hesitated and Jack said, "Go on, we really want to know."

She then looked very serious, as she put her hand on Philip's wrist, looked him in the eyes and said, "This may sound silly, but I feel that I've been drawn to your family, and I love you all very much. It's as though Nicholas and I are part of you."

She then shook her head, and was about to apologize when Carol said, "No, please, Laura, go on," as if she knew what Laura was trying to say, and she wanted everyone to hear it.

"I know how much you all loved and adored your mother," Laura continued as she looked at Carol and Jack, and Michael and Diana, and the great friends she had in Gray and Betty and Pedro and Juanita.

"And I can see now how much you all meant to her, and I know she was your life," as she looked up at Philip, her eyes watering as she squeezed his hand, and he looking at her so serious, everyone else was in awe at what she was saying, "so I can only think of one name for this little angel—Sarah."

Then she stood up, fighting back tears as she said to Philip, "I'm sorry, I had no right."

They all comforted her and Philip said as he held her close, "I thought I had gone to my limit of loving you, and then you say something like this to make me love you more."

Carol reached out to her, kissed her on the cheek and said, "I had a feeling that you held the secret that I wanted to hear, and I'm sure that my mother would be honored for you to be my baby's grandmother."

"I think so too," Philip said.

"Do we hear wedding bells?" Gray asked.

"Not yet," Philip replied, "we have to get Nick healthy first."

Jack looked at Carol, and Carol asked, "Is it okay, Daddy, that we call her Sarah?"

"By all means," Philip replied. "I would like that very much."

Michael said, "All in favor raise your hands."

Everyone agreed.

So Jack made an announcement: "Ladies and gentlemen, I'd like you to meet our daughter, Sarah," and then he hesitated, and Lucy said, "Maria."

Jack continued, "Sarah Maria Dawson."

Everyone said, "Glad to meet you, Sarah."

Juanita turned to Lucy and said, "Thank you, Lucy."

Lucy said as she put her hand on Juanita's, "You were her closest friend."

At that moment Nicholas came over, and his mother who was now holding the baby said, "Say hello to Sarah."

Nicholas leaned down and kissed Sarah on the forehead and

said, "I like your name, Sarah."

After the dishes were all cleaned up, and the games were put away, Michael and Diana left for their cottage to spend the night and following day. Pedro and Juanita, and Ryan and Lucy also left.

Nicholas was having a game of pool with Jack, and Carol was putting little Sarah to bed.

Laura asked Gray, "Do you have any results from Nicholas' tests?"

"Yes," he answered. "I was about to talk to you about it. Looks like he has an infection."

Laura's face dropped as she asked, "Is that dangerous?"

"Well," Gray answered, "I want him on a strict diet for a week."

"What does the diet consist of?" Laura asked again.

"Drinking large quantities of fluids so as to flush out the pelvis and ureter," Gray answered. "He has what is called *uremia,*" he continued.

"What's that?" Philip asked inquisitively.

"It's something that denotes abnormal chemical changes in the blood, and the kidney is unable to eliminate waste products," Gray answered.

"So what are we going to do?" Laura asked.

"We're going to try and treat it," Gray replied, "and if it is caused by an obstruction of the ureter, or the kidney outlet, and it's promptly relieved by what we're going to do, meaning the diet, the uremia will subside and Nicholas will get well. I have the diet written down," as he reached in his pocket. "Keep it as close as possible."

"Don't worry," Laura said, "if I have to be at his side every minute, I will."

Gray read the instructions that he wanted followed. "Drink large quantities of fluid; restrict having fruits that carry a lot of acids like oranges, grapefruits; bed rest and a bland diet. I'll put him on antibiotics to take care of the infected kidney, and also on medication for the relief of any pain he might endure."

"How would he have gotten an infection?" Philip asked.

"Since he has only one functioning kidney, there's considerable pressure put on it," Gray answered. "It's important to discover whether there is an underlying obstruction of the ureter," he continued, "like I mentioned before, which might have caused the urine to dam up and become infected. It is also important to eradicate any infection elsewhere in the body that might have precipitated the kidney infection. So let's try this diet for five days, and then we'll do more tests."

chapter XXIV

VALLEYFIELD, INDIANA

The week seemed to drag by very slowly. Laura stayed home to be sure that Nicholas had his proper rest, and was kept on his diet. She made a few sales calls and scanned the computer for any new listings.

Philip was busy working out a deal with the Citrus Growers of Florida to export fruit to parts of Canada. He flew to Florida for two days to present his proposal with the Citrus Developers.

By the end of the week Nicholas didn't seem to be getting any better. He was very weak, tired, and looked pale. There were now visible traces of blood in his urine, and it was difficult and painful when he urinated.

Philip arrived back from Florida on Friday afternoon, and after an hour at his office he spent the remainder of the day with Laura and Nicholas, and then left for Millcreek, stating that he would be back early the next morning.

As he entered Laura's house around nine o'clock, Nicholas was lying on the sofa. Philip noticed how frail he looked, so without hesitation he phoned his friend Gray at his house to enlighten him on Nicholas's condition. Gray told him that he would be right over.

In thirty minutes the doorbell rang. Philip answered it to find Gray with his little black satchel.

He said, "Hi, Bud, come on in."

Gray returned the greeting, and then said, "Hello, Laura," as he touched her arm in a gesture of comfort.

Laura answered by saying, "I'm sorry for having you give up your Saturday morning to make a house call."

"Hey," Gray replied. "Anytime. We have to get our buddy back on his feet again," as he focused on Nicholas, and at the same time lifting back his eyelids.

"I haven't been feeling good this week," Nicholas said. "I feel weak and really tired, and sometimes it hurts me to go to the bathroom."

"Well," Gray commented, "that's one thing I like in a patient, to have them come right out and tell me what ails them. That gives me a better idea of what to do."

Then he turned to Laura and asked, "Did he use all the medication for the pain?"

"No, not all of it," Laura replied, "he never complained until Thursday, so I gave it to him twice a day. It seemed to relieve the hurt," she continued as she looked sadly at Nicholas.

"Keep him on it today and tomorrow," Gray suggested, "and we will check him in to the hospital on Monday morning. We'll do tests for two days and then we'll know for certain what the problem is."

"What time on Monday?" Laura asked.

"Between nine and ten," Gray replied.

"So, how about it buddy?" Gray asked Nicholas. "How would you like to spend two days with me at the hospital, and I'll show you what I do?"

"I would sooner spend two days with you out of the hospital, if I was healthy," Nicholas answered.

"Okay, I'll make a promise to you," Gray said. "When we get you well again, you and I will spend two days doing whatever you want to do. Go camping, go riding, anything you want."

"That's a deal," Nicholas said, as he held out his hand for Gray to shake.

"Then I'll see you all on Monday morning." Gray said. "Come

right to my office."

"We will," Laura replied, "and thanks for coming over."

"Anytime at all, and I mean that Laura," Gray replied.

Philip showed him to the door and out to his car, and as he shook his hand in appreciation he commented, "You said earlier that 'we will know for certain what the problem is'. Is there something you know?" he asked.

"I think so Phil," Gray replied, "and it isn't good, but I don't want Laura in a panic. We will know after the tests, and we'll go from there . Keep them both comfortable."

"I will do that," Philip replied.

Philip left Millcreek early to get his people at the office started on the Citrus Growers account. A transaction had to be completed by the end of the week so they could start moving produce to various food terminals in Ontario, Canada.

Before Laura left to take Nicholas to the hospital, she called his father, Gord, to fill him in on the situation, but he was out of town on a three day golf tournament, and wouldn't be back until Thursday. They entered the hospital at nine-thirty where they met Philip who had been waiting for them in the lobby, and then they continued to Gray's office on the second floor.

As they entered, Valerie was busy on the phone, setting up an appointment for a patient. When she saw them, she waved and threw Nicholas a kiss. He smiled his innocent smile, but was thrilled because, even at his young age, he noticed how attractive Valerie was. She continued talking on the phone but motioned to the coffee pot in the corner of the waiting area. Philip and Laura both waved it off, as to say "not now thanks". In a few seconds she was off the phone and got up to greet them.

She said, "I understand were going to have this handsome gentleman with us for a few days," as she motioned to Nicholas.

"Yes, you are," Philip answered, "aren't you lucky?"

"I sure am," she replied. "Dr. West will be about five or ten minutes," she continued, as she whispered, "he's with a very despondent couple, whose eight year old boy has leukemia."

"Oh, how sad," Laura said, "they must be devastated."

"They knew for more than two years, and now it's at the critical stage," Valerie said. "He's such a brave little guy and a real sweetheart," she continued.

"What's leukemia, Mommy?" Nicholas asked.

"It's a blood disease that's very dangerous," Laura replied.

"Will he die?" Nicholas asked again.

"I don't know, I hope not," his mother answered.

"I'm sure Dr. West is doing everything he can for him," Philip said.

At that time Gray opened the door to his private office and stepped out, escorting a man and lady in their early forties, and a little boy who looked very frail. He was wearing a cap, and you could tell that he had lost his hair from the results of the medication.

As they passed the waiting area, the little guy smiled and waved his hand at everyone, and then looked at Nicholas and said, "Hi, my name is Davey, what's yours?"

Nicholas looked at him with surprise and said, "Hi, I'm Nicholas."

Davey in return said, "It's nice to meet you Nick."

Nicholas smiled and said. "That's what Philip calls me," as he pointed to Philip, "and that's all right."

"Hope to see you again," as he followed his mother and dad out the door.

Laura and Valerie's eyes were sparkling with tears, and even Philip was biting his bottom lip, as he said, "Wow, how about that."

Gray walked them to the elevator, and when he returned his right hand was on his forehead, and at the same time let out a sigh as he shook his head in sorrow.

Then he directed his attention to Nicholas and asked, "Are you flirting with my secretary again?"

"No," Nicholas answered, "I'm too young."

Valerie cut in and said, "I'm the guilty one. I'm flirting with him, but I'll get back to work right away boss."

They all laughed as Gray guided them to his office. He explained to them all about the tests that they'd be doing, and how long it would take. He also told Laura that if she wished, she could stay with Nicholas during these tests.

Nicholas spoke up and said. "It's okay, Mommy, you don't have to stay. I will be okay with Dr. West. He's going to show me all the neat machinery."

"Sounds like your little boy is growing up, Laura," Gray said. "We will get along fine. Maybe Nick can do my rounds with me?" he continued.

Shortly after, Valerie came in and said that she had him registered, and with her was a nurse to escort him to his room. Laura went with them to assist Nicholas with his pajamas.

Philip and Gray were carrying on a conversation when Laura and Nicholas returned.

Gray said, "Well, here's my best patient, so we'll have to say good-bye to you two."

Nicholas turned and gave his mother a kiss and said again, "I'll be okay. I want to get better as soon as possible."

"That's the attitude I like to hear," Gray uttered.

"Me too," Philip said as he gave Nicholas a hug. "We'll be over later."

In the x-ray room, Gray told Nicholas exactly what they were going to do, and also said that the needle might hurt for only a second.

Nicholas said, "I've had plenty of those, I don't mind."

"I wish all my patients were as brave as you, and I really mean that," Gray replied.

So the tests began. He took an angiogram, which is a method of obtaining an x-ray of blood vessels by injecting into them a substance such as iodine that shows up as opaque on an x-ray picture.

Those tests lasted until four o'clock, and when he arrived back in his room, his mother and Philip were waiting for him to go for dinner. Laura hugged her son, and asked if he was all right.

Gray spoke up and said, "He's fine, the best patient I've ever had."

"Yeah, Mommy," Nicholas cried out excitedly, "you should see all the neat machinery that they tested me with."

"Is it too soon for any results?" Philip asked.

"Yes, I'll be examining the x-rays this evening," Gray answered. "So he can either spend the night, or you can take him home, but I will need him here around nine thirty tomorrow for a CAT scan."

"What will the CAT scan detect?" Laura asked.

"It will outline any kidney cysts or growths," Gray replied.

Laura gave out a big sigh and lowered her head in her hands.

Nicholas put his arm around her and said, "It's okay, Mommy, whatever is wrong with me, Dr. West is going to make it better."

"Thanks, buddy," Gray replied. "He's right Laura, were going to make him one-hundred percent again."

Philip had his arm around Laura, and his hand on Nicholas's shoulder as he said. "He's quite a guy. There isn't anything that's going to stop him from getting well."

"I know," Laura said. "It's just getting there that's rigorous."

chapter xxv

VALLEYFIELD, INDIANA
2nd WEEK of AUGUST 1995

It was now into the second week of August. Gray had the final results of Nicholas's tests, and they weren't good.

At noon that day, Philip was having lunch with Laura at her house. Nicholas was lying on the sofa. The phone rang, and then again, and once more. Laura stood sort of in a daze, and stared at it, having the intuition that the news at the other end wasn't good news.

"Would you like me to get it, hon?" Philip asked.

"Yes," she replied, "would you?"

Philip picked up the receiver and said, "Hello, oh hi, buddy," it was Gray. "Yes, we're all here having some lunch. Nick's resting on the sofa."

"Would you mind staying with Nick?" Gray asked. "I want Laura and Nick's father to come to my office."

"I'd be glad to," Philip replied. "Here's Laura."

"It's Gray, honey," as he handed her the receiver, and rubbed the back of her neck and shoulders.

"Hi, Gray," Laura said. "I've been expecting your call."

"Hello, Laura," Gray said. "Now, I don't want you to get upset. I worked on Nicholas's tests until late last night and again all morning. What I'd like you to do is call Gord, and the both of you meet me at my office about two thirty. I'll explain the diagnosis to you, and what we have to do."

She agreed, and as she hung up the receiver she started crying. Philip comforted her and assured her that everything was going to be okay. He also assured her that Nicholas had the best doctor in the country.

Laura said, "Thanks," as she wrapped her arms around his waist and rested her head on his shoulder. "I don't know what I'd do, I don't think I could go through this alone."

"You'll never be alone," Philip said. "We're all here for you and Nick—Ryan and Lucy, my kids, Pedro and Juanita. We'll never let you be alone."

Laura looked at him, smiled, and said, "I love you, you know that?"

"Yeah, I know, and you know that I love you," Philip replied.

"I better phone Gord," she said. "He has to drive down from Fort Wayne." She dialed his place of business where he's an accountant for a firm.

By two thirty, Laura and Gord entered Dr. West's office, and were greeted by his kind and friendly secretary, Valerie. Valerie buzzed her boss's office and announced that Laura and Gord had arrived. At once Gray came out to greet them, and directed them back to his office, telling Valerie to hold all calls.

He had just gotten back from the operating room, and was dressed in green scrubs with a white smock, and a stethoscope hanging out of his pocket.

As they sat down Laura said, "I hope and pray you're not going to tell us that something serious is wrong with him."

Gray stood up, came around in front of his desk and pulled up another chair so as to be facing Laura and Gord. He then took Laura's hand in his, and placed his other hand on Gord's arm, and looked at both of them and answered her statement by saying, "Remember last week when I told you that we were going to make him well again?"

"Yes, you did say that," Laura replied.

"And remember when Nick put his arm around your waist and said, 'It's okay, Mommy, whatever is wrong with me, Dr.

West is going to make it better?'" Gray continued.

"Yes, how could I ever forget that moment?" Laura answered.

"That was the nicest statement that a patient has ever said to me, and I shall never forget it," Gray said. "And, that's exactly what were going to do," Gray continued. "So, no matter what I tell you both today, I will not let him or you down, okay. This little guy trusts me one hundred percent."

"We couldn't ask for more assurance than that," Gord said.

"Thanks, Gord," Gray replied.

"Now," Gray said, as he looked them straight in the face. Laura's hand tightened on Gord's hand. "We do have a problem. I was hoping the diet would subside it, but it didn't."

Gord took a deep breath and asked, "What is it that he has?"

"He has uremia, and it's gone to the terminal stage of chronic nephritis," Gray replied.

Laura's face dropped as tears clouded her eyes and said, "That sounds so serious, what does it mean?" she asked.

"Inflammation of the kidney, redness, swelling, and pain goes with it as well," Gray explained.

"So, what can be done about it?" Gord asked.

"The only cure may be through a kidney transplant," Gray replied, "which means dialysis, the use of an 'artificial kidney', until a donor kidney is available," he continued.

"Oh my God! My God, what's happened to our little boy? What did he do to deserve this?" Laura cried, as she broke down with her face in her hands.

Gord put his hand on the back of her neck and slightly massaged it and said, "We will get through this. We will have him well again, won't we Gray?" he asked.

"Yes, we will," Gray replied, "we just have a bit of a tough go to get there, but I promise, we will get there."

"Let me explain and refresh you on how dialysis works," Gray continued. "The artificial kidney acts as a kidney. It sends a liquid through the veins and filters the blood while it takes toxins out of the body."

"How long will it be before he will need the artificial kidney?" Laura asked.

"Laura, Gord, he now has most of the symptoms," Gray explained. "His temperature is high, he has blood, pus, and bacteria in his urine, there is some tenderness over the kidney area. You said yourself he's nauseous, vomiting, and his appetite is lacking. So I would say within a week."

Gord was shaking his head in wonderment, and Laura was wiping her eyes with a tissue.

"I know all this sounds serious, and believe me it is," Gray said. "I also believe in explaining everything, all the procedures."

He put his hand on Laura's and asked. "Are you okay. Would you like a coffee?"

"I think I would," Laura replied.

"How about you, Gord?" Gray asked as he called Valerie to bring in a pot.

"No, I'm fine thanks," Gord said.

Seconds later Valerie carried in a tray with a pot of coffee and three cups along with sugar and cream, and placed it on a small table that looked as if it were for a tray. As she was backing toward the door, she looked at Laura and asked, "Laura is there anything else I can get for you?"

Laura gave a small smile in appreciation to her and replied, "Thanks Valerie, I'm fine."

Valerie left the office and closed the door.

Gord poured a cup of coffee for Laura, something she very seldom drank, and then sat down.

"Now," Gray continued, "I'd like to explain how transplantation is done. I have a diagram showing where Nick's kidney is situated. We're going to put the donor's kidney lower in the abdomen, which will create a shorter ureter, which will be less likely to deteriorate. However, difficulties following transplantation of a kidney often ensure when the rejection reaction sets in, and this could occur anytime from a few weeks to a few months after the operation has been performed. This means that he will be on medication for the rest of his life, but he will still have a normal life."

"That rejection reaction sounds pretty scary," Laura said.

"I know," Gray replied. "It doesn't happen that often, but I like to be thorough. I'm also going to explain all this to Nick, one-on-one."

"I think he will appreciate that," Gord said.

"He's a brave little gringo. I haven't seen anyone like him." Gray laughed. "He does everything I tell him."

"Well, he has changed since you and Philip have come into his life," Laura said.

"How successful are kidney transplants?" Gord asked.

"The patient survival rate for kidneys is ninety-seven point nine percent. Pretty good," Gray answered.

"Have you done many kidney transplants?" Laura asked.

"I've done forty-two, twenty-eight children, and fourteen adults between this hospital and Chicago General in the last three years, and I'm happy to say that they're all very healthy and living a normal life. One is a twenty-eight year old NHL hockey player, who plays for the Chicago Black Hawks. The medication that they take everyday becomes a way of life."

"Would you have any idea," and before Laura finished, Gray cut in and finished her question, "when there will be a kidney available?"

"Laura, I don't want to discourage you," Gray said, "but the number of registrants on waiting lists for kidneys in the U.S. alone is approximately thirty-nine thousand. Organ transplant recipients are selected on the basis of medical urgency, and that's what Nick's will be, a medical urgency, because he has only one kidney, and it's damaged."

"So, what we have is people aren't signing donor cards," Gord suggested.

"Right, Gord," Gray said. "In this country, as in others, we have a great shortage of donors. If more people would specify in their wills, or sign that little section of their driver's license, it wouldn't be as bad as it is."

"I'll bet there's a lot of donors that are missed," Gord remarked, "because their families don't know of their loved one's wishes."

"Exactly," Gray replied. "That is one critical reason for the shortage of organ donors. I suppose we doctors see it more than anyone, but misconceptions also play a role in the shortage of organs."

"Many people may not realize that the cost of the medical procedure involved in organ donation is covered by the healthcare system. There is no cost to the donor's family."

"I never knew that," Laura said.

"So Nick will go on a waiting list. The transplant has to succeed by matching of the donor and recipient when the tissue typing occurs," Gray explained.

"Getting back to what you said about the transplanted kidney being rejected," Gord asked, "what causes it to die?"

"It's like this," Gray explained, "all people have antibodies, whose function is to protect against invading foreign bodies. Tissue cells from other animals or humans are judged by the host to be foreign body, and the normal protective mechanisms of the host are mobilized to destroy them. So a transplanted kidney will be attacked by the white blood cells of the host, which will cause the grafted organ to die."

"Is there going to be a waiting period," Laura asked, "where we're going to be on pins and needles?"

"No," Gray replied, "there are many measures that can be taken to tide the host over the period when the rejection reaction is at its height. Various drugs can be given to slow down or entirely stop the host from producing the antibodies that will kill the transplant."

"When will we know, or when will it be time to bring him to the hospital?" Gord asked.

"By the end of next week," Gray replied. "In the meantime he and I are going to have a little 'doctor patient' talk, and I promise you we'll make him as comfortable as possible, and of course you can be with him anytime, day or night. We have a special room that I'm sure he'll like. We call it *The Railroad Room*."

The Railroad Room is a special room in the children's wing of the hospital that Philip and Gray donated. It has three complete model trains and the tracks circle the entire room with tunnels, bridges, and a small mining town with all the buildings. It also has a TV, video games, and a table-hockey game. Everything can be operated without the child getting out of his bed. The room is large enough to accommodate two beds and any equipment, like a dialysis machine.

The room is for seriously ill children who will have a long hospital stay. Any child is welcome with the discretion of Dr. West who will make the decision, and if a family isn't covered by insurance, Philip's company takes care of the cost. Philip, Gray, and Theresa are the only ones that know of this benefit, and that's the way Philip wants it.

There is also a room being constructed for little girls. It will be called "Sarah's Room."

They both left the hospital and returned to Laura's house, where they explained the situation to Philip, who again assured them that his best friend would pull Nick through this emegency.

chapter XXVI

FOUR HOURS OUT OF HONOLULU

Crossing over the international date line, Philip was awakened by a sudden drop of the aircraft. A condition of the atmosphere that is called an "air pocket." There was a little turbulence, so the flight attendant made an announcement for the passengers to make sure that their seat belts were fastened, until the captain gave notice when they'd be through the storm.

Ten minutes later the seat belt sign was turned off, so Philip decided to use the washroom. Before returning to his seat, he decided to walk the aisle a couple of times to exercise his legs.

When he returned, Lisa was standing by his seat and asked, "Would you like a snack, Mr. Mariano?"

"I think I would, Lisa," Philip replied, "and maybe a cup of tea."

"How about tuna on rye bread?" she asked.

"That would be nice," he answered as he sat down.

A few minutes later she returned with the tuna sandwich, pickles and olives on the side, and a cup of tea.

"Thank you," Philip said, "it looks great," as he bit into the sandwich. "Tastes great, too."

"I hope you enjoy it." Lisa remarked.

"Say, why don't you join me?" he suggested. "Flight attendants must get hungry too, and I could use the company, if you're not too busy, that is."

"I appreciate the offer," Lisa replied, "but Quantas take a dim view of socializing with individual passengers, at least on the aircraft."

"Oh, I understand," Philip said. "My thoughts have been miles away lately," he continued.

"I know," Lisa whispered. "You talk in your sleep," she remarked with a smile.

Philip placed his sandwich on the plate, looked up at her with a surprised look and asked, "Are you serious?"

"Well," Lisa smiled, "you were really kind of murmuring."

"I hope I didn't disturb anyone," Philip said.

"No," Lisa replied, "I was the only one who heard you. She must be very special to you," she stated.

Philip tightened his lips, and shook his head a little, took a breath, and wandered how much he had unconsciously said, and then with a half smile he replied, "they both are."

Lisa was now very concerned about bringing up the subject, as she looked mystified and asked, "Are you okay?"

"Yes, I'm fine, Lisa," Philip answered, "but thanks for your concern. I'll tell you what," he continued with a smile. "You have my permission to give me a kick if I do any more talking in my sleep."

"Oh, I wouldn't do that," Lisa answered, "but you looked so calm and comfortable, I didn't want to disturb you."

Then she disappeared to the galley to help the preparation of the breakfast.

Philip finished off his sandwich, picked up a magazine and started flipping the pages. It wasn't too long before he found himself relaxed again, and his mind wandering back to three memorable weeks in the fall of ninety-five, where he had the pleasure of meeting and spending time with a brave and warmhearted little boy who shared the *Railroad Room* with Nick.

It was now nearing the end of September. The flowers were in their full bloom, and the numerous deciduous trees were becoming bare from losing their leaves. Most kids were now settled with their classes in school. Philip spent a great deal of time at the hospital with Nick, but only when Laura wasn't present.

She knew he was visiting him, and felt maybe it was better for Nicholas' recovery that they should be still in contact with each other, but sooner or later she would have to end that alliance, not knowing that Philip would do that for her.

One Wednesday afternoon, Philip, Gray, and Ryan were having a drink after eighteen holes of golf at the Valleyfield Golf and Country Club. During the conversation Gray suggested, "I'm thinking of moving a little eight-year-old boy in the *Railroad Room* with Nick. His name is David. We all call him Davey; he prefers that."

"Good idea," Philip commented, "he would be great company for Nick. He could use it."

"Yeah," Ryan said, "Nick will have some competition with that hockey game, instead of beating me all the time. They will also have two of the trains running at the same time."

"Don't worry Ryan, they'll still let you play," Gray said jokingly.

"You still have your race car set at home, don't you?" Philip asked.

"You guys are really funny," Ryan replied, as they all laughed.

"I've known Davey and his parents for over three years. He's been in and out of the hospital, mostly in, for all of that time," Gray said. "He has leukemia, and there's not a damn thing that I can do for him."

"My God," Philip said, "his parents must be emotionally exhausted. Didn't we see them in your office about a month ago?" he asked.

"Yes, that was a very depressing visit," Gray said sadly. "That's the most difficult part of my job."

"He seemed so cheerful," Philip said. "He introduced himself to Nick and gave Laura and me the high sign."

"That's our Davey," Gray said. "The little guy knows what he has, and is prepared for what's ahead. I'm moving him in tomorrow, so the next time you visit Nick, he'll be there. I'm also going to fill Nick in on Davey's condition, and tell Laura as well."

The next day Philip entered the hospital and went directly to the *Railroad Room*. Laura had left about a half hour before he arrived, after seeing Nicholas through his lunch and meeting Davey. As he entered the room, he saw Gray sitting on a chair watching two young boys, Nick and Davey, playing table hockey.

Davey looked his way and said, "Hi, you must be Phil."

"Yes, I am," Philip replied, "and you must be Davey."

"I'm glad to meet you," Davey said, as he kept on playing. "I hope you don't mind if I don't shake your hand right away, I'm trying to beat Nick. He's one goal up on me."

Philip looked at this pale-skinned little guy who was perhaps about thirty pounds lighter than a boy his age should be. He was wearing an L.A. Kings hockey cap with the peak turned sideways on his little bald head. For a boy his age, he had an air of distinction.

"No, that's all right Davey, we can't interrupt a hockey player while he's playing."

Davey laughed and very frankly said, "Nick and Gray told me all about you, and I liked you before I met you."

"Thank you, Davey, that's very nice of you to say so." Philip said. "You know that's a coincidence because when Gray told me about you, I couldn't wait to meet you."

Philip went over and patted Nicholas on the shoulder just as they ended the game, and then he shook Davey's hand.

Nicholas said, "I'm really glad that Gray moved Davey in here with me. He's a lot of fun, and he makes me laugh."

The two boys grinned at each other and hit each other's fist.

Philip and Gray gave each other a look of satisfaction that this was a great decision.

"You must know that I have cancer," Davey said."It's leukemia, and I'm not going to get better."

Nicholas looked at him with a sad look. Gray surprisingly looked at Davey and then turned to Philip who took a deep breath, and with a lump growing in his throat said, "Yes, Davey, I know you have leukemia, but only God knows about you getting better or not."

"Oh, that's okay, Phil. You don't mind me calling you Phil, do you?" Davey asked.

"No, not at all, I like it," Philip replied.

"Well, I talk to God," Davey continued, "and I know that he has a very important job for me when I reach Heaven. I believe my duties will be to help Him make young people, who are really sick, get better again."

"I guess that's one of the most important duties," Philip replied as he gave Davey a hug, and looked over at Gray with wonderment about this brave and outspoken little guy.

Gray remarked, "That's our Davey."

Davey looked at him with a crooked smile, and then took a shot at Nick's goal keeper and added, "I know God knows everything, but I'm going to mention to him about all the nice people that I know."

"*All* the people you know?" Nick inquired.

"Yes," Davey replied, "and even people I don't know, just because they are nice, and they do things for others who need help, like Wayne Gretzsky. He's my favorite."

"You're right, Davey," Philip remarked, "he is a nice man, and of course a great hockey player."

"Philip knows him and has met him," Nick cried out. "He's my favorite too."

"Have you really met him?" Davey asked with excitement.

"Yes," Philip replied. "I was at a fundraising dinner in Indianapolis where he was a guest."

"He also has his autograph, and I saw it," Nick said.

"Wow, that's awesome," Davey replied.

Almost at once Gray and Philip looked at each other with an expression that said, "I wonder if we can swing it."

Davey then changed the subject as he looked at Philip and very casually asked, "You and Nick's mommy love each other, don't you?"

The question caught Philip by surprise as he answered him with a question, "Hey, you know quite a lot about me, don't you?"

Davey laughed and said, "I asked Nick's mommy the same question."

"You're right, Davey," Philip replied, "but we're having a little rest from each other until Nick gets better."

"Nick will get better soon," Davey said with assurance.

Nick was staring over the game table at his new friend who was so "free in speech", and said with a big smile, "Thanks, Davey, I hope you're right," as they both started a new game.

Gray then turned to Philip and asked, "Did I mention about the new irons I bought?"

"No, you didn't, why?" Philip asked, knowing it was an excuse to talk in private.

"I picked them up last night," Gray continued. "They're in my office."

"Well, let's take a look at them," Philip remarked.

They excused themselves to the kids, saying that they'd be right back.

When they reached the office Philip searched through his day-timer. He had the number of Gretzsky's agency in L.A. from the fund raising dinner that he attended for a crippled children's campaign. He found it and dialed the number, reaching the secretary of the agency. He identified himself and explained the purpose of his call.

The secretary told him that the team would be playing in Chicago the following Saturday night, and she would have Mr. Gretzsky's personal agent call him the next day.

Philip hung up the phone after thanking her for her time, and turned to Gray, banged his fist on his, and said with a satisfying smile, "The wheels are in motion. I'm sure we'll receive a couple of autograph cards for two happy kids from the 'Great One'."

"Hey, that's excellent," Gray commented. "You never know unless you try."

The next day Philip was in his office working out a deal of a large shipment of soybeans to be exported to Peru. Theresa was by his desk when the phone buzzer sounded. She picked up the receiver and took the message. She then turned to Philip and asked, "Why should I be surprised that Mr. Gretzsky's agency in L.A. wants to speak to you?"

Philip looked at her and nonchalantly said, "It's a guy thing," as he took the receiver and pressed line one.

"Hello, this is Philip Mariano."

The voice responded with expression, "Hello, Philip, this is Wayne, I remembered you from the Fundraising Dinner in Indianapolis last fall."

"Well, this is an unexpected pleasure. How are you?" Philip asked.

"Good," Wayne replied, "and you?"

"Very well, thanks," Philip said. "I'm a little surprised, I have to admit. I know you must have a busy schedule, especially this time of year. I was expecting perhaps your secretary, but this is certainly an honor."

"Well," Wayne said, "when my agent told me about your call, and the nature of it, I decided to take this one on myself. We're flying to Chicago on Friday for a game with the Hawks on Saturday night," Wayne continued," so we made arrangements for me to fly to Fort Wayne, I like that name, after our nine o'clock practice on Saturday morning. I should arrive in Fort Wayne by noon."

"That's great, and I use that word 'Great' literally," Philip replied. "I'll be there to pick you up. It's only a twenty-minute drive to Valleyfield. Your visit is going to make two little boys very happy," Philip continued.

"I guess that's the least we can do," Wayne replied, "so I'll see you at noon on Saturday."

"I'll be there," Philip said, "and thanks again from all of us, especially from Davey's parents."

Davey went through chemotherapy on Friday morning, which of course made him very weak. By Saturday he was still pretty frail. Gray was in early to observe his recovery. His parents had been with him the entire night, and were still there at twelve thirty when Philip walked into the room.

Five minutes before, Lucy and Ryan had dropped in to see Nicholas, and were still there.

Gray was taking Davey's pulse, and asked him, "Do you feel a little better today Davey?"

"I don't feel good right now, Dr. West," Davey replied, "but I'll be okay in a little while."

He looked over and saw Philip and said, "Hi, Phil, what's it like outside today?"

"It's pretty gloomy out, Davey," Philip replied, "you wouldn't enjoy it."

Davey very silently, and slowly said, "Every day is beautiful to me, Phil."

The room suddenly became very quiet. Davey's parents were hiding away tears, as was Lucy, when Philip said, "You're absolutely right Davey, we all should enjoy every day. You know, you're a pretty brave guy, and we're all delighted to be your friends."

"Oh, I almost forgot," he continued as he looked at Davey's parents and winked, "there's someone here to see you two guys. The nurse thought that there were too many visitors in here already, so she told him that he'd have to wait, but Dr. West is like the boss, so he told her that it was all right."

"Who is it?" Nicholas asked.

"Well, we'll let you see for yourself," Gray answered, as he opened the door and asked, "Would you like to come in, sir?"

As the man entered the room, with his wide smile, he asked, "Has anyone seen my number '99'? I seem to have misplaced it, and I need it for tonight's game. Oh, there it is, at the end of your bed," as he pointed to Davey's bed.

Nick's eyes lit up like two shining marbles in the sunlight as he whispered out loud, "Wayne Gretzsky."

Ryan and Lucy looked at each other and thought, "How the hell did Philip swing this?"

At that moment, as sick and weak as he was, Davey sat up in his bed. You could literally see the color come back to his tiny little face, as he said, "It's really you."

His parents looked on at this hockey hero with tears glistening in their eyes, and knew, then and there, that someone was surely looking down at their son.

"Hi, guys," Wayne said, "I hear there's a couple of my favorite hockey fans in here."

"We sure are," Davey replied.

"Yeah, we sure are," Nick repeated, as they held out their hands to meet with Wayne's.

Wayne presented them each with an autographed hockey stick, and spent the next hour talking to them about hockey and other sports. He even played a game of table hockey with them, where they both beat him, but they knew in their hearts that he didn't play his best.

Everyone there could see that Davey was his old self again.

Before he left Davey said, "I'm pretty sure Nick and I know whose idea it was for you to visit us," as they both looked at Gray and Philip, "and we're very happy about it, but if it's possible, could you do me one more favor?"

Davey's father said, "Davey, Mr. Gretzsky's a very busy man."

"That's all right, Mr. Powers," Wayne replied, "Davey is going through a bit of a hardship right now, and if I can do something that will make him well again, then I will because I want him on my team."

"The favor is," Davey continued," if I sign my name to this hockey stick that you gave me, will you use it in tonight's game?"

Without hesitation, Wayne said, "I'd be honored to, and my next two goals I will dedicate to my two best fans, and now I can say, friends."

Mr. and Mrs. Powers couldn't be more thankful. Mrs. Powers told Wayne that he would forever be in their prayers.

Wayne came over and embraced her and shook Mr. Powers hand, and with a straight face said, "You must be as proud of

Davey as my father is of me. He is a priceless little guy, and I will remember to carry this moment with me, in my prayers."

He shook hands with the two boys, and everyone in the room, and then left.

Driving out of the hospital parking lot Wayne said, "You know Philip, most of us don't realize how fortunate we really are. I complained this morning because I wasn't satisfied about how my skates were sharpened. When I get back I'm going to apologize to that guy."

"I appreciate what you did today, Wayne," Philip said. "When you entered the room, I saw a little boy who was next to death, sit up in his bed and the color came back to his face, like all he had was the common cold. Like I said before, I know how busy your schedule must be."

"Sometimes the busy schedules have to be put on hold, and this was one of those times," Wayne replied.

Two eight-year-old boys were now looking forward to the evening to watch their hockey hero, who they met in person earlier that day.

Laura, Lucy, and Carol spent a couple of hours at the hospital in the afternoon. Carol and Laura are still friends, and still keep in touch, desspite their differences about Carol's father. Carol respected Laura's decision because she knew that she and her father were both still in love, and in time, Laura would comprehend the fact that her judgment about Philip was wrong.

Nicholas told his mother all about Wayne Gretzsky, and also asked her if she wouldn't mind not coming in tonight because it was going to be "boys night out" and they were all going to watch the game on TV.

She agreed and thought it was a good idea as long as he didn't get too excited. He assured her that Dr. West had said the same thing and was going to watch that they didn't.

All arrangements were made, everyone was contacted, so at game time, seven o'clock, Philip, Pedro, Michael, Ryan, Jack, Davey's father Del, Nick's friend Bobby, and Gray all found space in the *Railroad Room.*

It was Nick and Davey's wish that all the guys share the evening with them, and watch the L.A. Kings and Chicago Black Hawks on Saturday Night Hockey. The evening went well, everyone enjoyed themselves. Some were rooting for the Hawks, and some for the Kings. Needless to say, we know who two guys were rooting for.

At the end of the third period, the score was Kings-4, Hawks-1. Two of the goals were scored by, "The Great One."

When he was interviewed the commentator asked, "Wayne, the last five games, no goals, no assists. I know everyone experiences a bit of a slump, and then they bounce right back again, but you came back tonight on fire. You fired in two goals and assisted on the other two. Were you making up for lost time?" he asked.

Wayne sat with his stick in one hand, and a towel in the other, and showed his usual contented smile. He lifted the towel to his face, wiping the sweat that the heat from the strong lights had caused, and said, "You're right, Joe, most athletes go through a slump many times in their careers, and most of the time we survive it. I owe tonight to two eight year old boys that I had a visit with earlier today in a hospital in Valleyfield, Indiana. They filled my system with courage that I never knew I had."

"One of the boys, Nick, follows me everywhere I go, even keeps a scrapbook. Anyway, Nick is waiting for a kidney transplant. He is frequently on dialysis. The other boy is Davey." Wayne put his head down for a second to gather a breath. "Davey has leukemia, and he said to me, 'Mr. Gretzsky, I can't do too much anymore, honest, I'm not complaining, but I talk to God a lot, and I always tell him about you, is that okay?'" He hesitated again to wipe the sweat mixed with some tears and to swallow a lump in his throat.

At that time, the commentator was getting signals from his producer that it was time for a commercial, but Wayne kept on talking. Nobody cuts Wayne Gretzsky off.

Wayne continued, "I gave the boys autographed hockey sticks, and as I was about to leave Davey asked me to do him a favor. He signed his name to his stick and asked me if I would use it in tonight's game" as he held it up.

"So, Nick and Davey, the two goals are for you! Get well. I will be back your way again, and I will also talk to God about you."

Then the commentator said with a broken voice, as he looked at this superstar, "Thank you, Wayne, it's always a pleasure."

Nick and Davey hit it off like two lost brothers. In the three weeks that they spent together in the *Railroad Room*, they had become very close.

Davey knew the outcome of his disease, and he tried to explain it to Nick, as did Dr. West, but it was difficult for Nick to accept. He couldn't comprehend the feeling of anything drastic happening to his new friend. Couldn't they find a cure? Davey's too young. All these thoughts were preying on his mind, and yet his little friend lived every moment without expressing feelings of dissatisfaction.

It was October the 6th two o'clock in the morning. Nick woke up from a light sleep, because there was a great deal of commotion in the *Railroad Room*. Dr. West and two nurses were over with Davey. Tubes and wires were being taken from his little body, and then they wheeled him out.

When they passed by Nick's bed, Davey said, in a low broken voice, "See ya, Nick, look after my cap."

Nick replied with, "Yeah, okay, Davey, see ya."

A few minutes went by, and then it hit him. Everything that Davey and Dr. West had explained to him was now going through his mind at a rapid speed. Nick started to cry. He was afraid to be alone. At once, he grabbed the cell phone that Philip had given him to call anytime, day or night, and dialed Philip's number.

It rang twice. Philip reached to his night table, flicked on the light, noticed the clock read 2:10 a.m. and picked up the receiver and said, "Hello." No one answered. He said hello again, and then he could hear some sniffling and sobbing at the other end.

"Nick, is that you?" he asked.

"Yes,"Nick replied, and then he broke down and let the tears pour out.

He was without doubt very perturbed.

"What's wrong, buddy?" Philip asked.

With a grief stricken voice, Nick answered, "They took Davey out."

"Now look," Philip suggested, "I know it's hard, but you try and relax, and I'll be right down. Try and think of the fun things you both had, and how he used to make us laugh. I'll see you in thirty minutes."

"Hurry," Nick said. "I need you. I don't want to be alone."

"Okay, buddy, I'm on my way," Philip replied.

Philip was about to phone Gray, but then he thought that Gray would in all likelihood, be with Davey.

Thirty minutes later Philip was with Nick, trying to comfort him. In a little while, he was composed, and they were talking about the great times they had, and how Davey could make you forget about the physical pain just by his good humor.

The door opened and Gray entered. They could tell by the drawn look, and the saddened eyes that he had been through an ordeal that he could have done without.

He said, "I just came in to see if you're all right. Oh, hi Phil, when did you get here?"

"About twenty minutes ago," Philip replied. "Nick phoned me."

"I guess you were upset," Gray said to Nick. "I wanted to be with you, but I think Davey needed me more."

"I think he did too," Nick agreed.

Then Gray said to Philip, "Would you give me a hand for a minute?" as he opened the door.

Nick spoke up and said, "It's all right if you say it to me. I'm okay now. Davey died, didn't he?"

Gray came to his bedside and said, "I'm sorry Nick, you're right. I should be able to talk with you too. Yes," he continued,

"Davey left us, but he left us with some beautiful memories."

"Are his mommy and daddy here?" Nick asked.

"Yes," Gray answered, "they've been here since yesterday, but they left. They said that they would like to come in tomorrow to see you."

"I'd like that," Nick replied, "wouldn't you, Philip?"

"Yes, I would like to see them," Philip answered.

Gray slowly left the room.

Philip and Nick knew that he was hurting, so Nick said, "I think Gray needs someone, right now, don't you?"

"Yes, Nick, I think you're right," Philip replied, "thanks, I'll be back soon."

Philip figured that Gray would be in his office, so he rapped and opened the door to find Gray sitting at his desk with his head resting in his hands.

He looked up and shook his head back and forth and said with a half crying voice, "Phil, I couldn't do a goddamn thing. I stood there; his parents were holding his little hand. We tried oxygen, and then took it away. His heart just couldn't handle it. Then his eyes opened a little and he looked up at me, and a smile came to his face and he whispered—Gray stopped for a second and sniffled back a tear—"Thanks, Doc."

"He had humor right to the end," Philip said.

Then Gray continued, "After he said that, his tiny eyes looked at his mom and dad and smiled again, and Phil, as God is my witness, his eyes closed and his smile broadened, he breathed in, and very softly he said, 'Ahh, it's beautiful,' then he left us."

That's when Gray let it out, as he looked at his friend and said, "Phil, I've seen a lot, I've been with death many times, and it's always very traumatic, especially when their loved ones are present, but I've never been so close to heaven as I was tonight, with that little boy. I know that you practice your religion more than I, but I swear to you the angels were there to take him."

Philip stared him in the eye, and said, "Davey shared his moment with you. I'm glad to be your friend."

chapter XXVII

THREE HOURS TO SYDNEY

Looking through the aircraft window, it was visible that dawn was beginning to unfold. In approximately three hours they would be landing in Sydney. The long tiring flight reminded him of his return trip from Brussels, which brought back memories that he would like to forget.

Fulfilling the conditions with the sale of combines to be imported from Belgium was very gratifying. Everyone would benefit. The Belgians would gross $7,500,000, the Americans would see their profit by the end of the season, and Philip's Import/Export company would receive a large commission.

All that didn't seem to matter, because after he landed in Fort Wayne, the world might as well have caved in on him. The plans and dreams that they had made were now shattered by an ugly rumor by someone who hated him, for reasons he didn't even know.

The hatred had started when Philip was a child. Vince Tedesco's father was very vindictive towards Philip's father, who was a miller. He entered the field of milling when he was a young man, just a year after emigrating from Italy.

Many Italians immigrated around the same time. In fact Vince's father came from the same town in Italy as Philip's father, and came over on the same ship. He worked on the railroad, and lived in one of the company houses. He also bootlegged.

Bootlegging was against the law, then, as it is now. But in those days it wasn't frowned upon, unless you went into it in a big way, (e.g. Capone) and was very rarely brought to court, quite presumably because most of the police, and the police chief frequented the bootleggers often.

Times were tough in those days, and nobody really got hurt, and there wasn't a lot of profit made from it. So on a Sunday afternoon the Tedesco house was quite a familiar spot. Therefore it was likely because Philip's father became successful without breaking the law, that Vince's father resented him for it, and the jealousy rubbed off on Vince.

Philip hadn't seen or heard from Vince for years, and this wasn't the first time he tried to meddle with him. When they were kids Vince was always trying to cause trouble. Most of the time Philip ignored him, which made him all the uglier, so Willy, who was never as patient as Gray or Philip, used to beat him up for some of the half-witted things he would say or do. So now, he must be in his glory, most likely out partying with his loser friends, and bragging about messing up Philip's life with Laura.

Almost three months had passed since that incident, but Philip would never forget the hurt look on Laura's face when she told him that her decision was not to see him any more.

It was around twelve-thirty Friday afternoon when Lucy dropped him off at his office. She pulled into an empty car space, placed the gear shift in "PARK," and turned off the engine.

She then turned to Philip and said, "Philip, in the short time that Ryan and I have known you, we have become very good friends. We don't want to lose that friendship, and we also don't believe what that asshole Vince said about you, and it wouldn't have mattered anyway, but I can't vouch for Laura. She's going through some difficult times right now, and God knows this is when I think that she would really need you. Being her best friend," she continued, "I won't judge her, but I know the love that you two and Nicholas have for one another, and I'm sure that she will come around to herself again."

"Thanks Lucy," Philip replied, "I've never doubted you two for a moment. You and Ryan have always been nice to me and I treasure your friendship. If I didn't before, I can see now why you are Laura's friend."

"So, you will keep in touch with us?" Lucy asked.

"Of course I will," Philip answered. "I have a golf game with Ryan and Gray this coming Wednesday, and I'll be seeing Nick in the hospital most every day."

Then he reached over and touched the back of Lucy's hand, that was resting on the console and said, "You know, Lucy, I feel I can say this to you in confidence, and I'm not one for sharing my sorrow, but I'm angry. I can't ever explain about my past, I don't think I should have to. I have some great friends, (as he squeezed her hand, and she looked at him with a comforting smile) and I was very fortunate to fall in love with two beautiful women. My wife Sarah I lost to a greater spiritual power, that I had no control over, and now I'm losing Laura to an ugly rumor that she heard at her office."

Lucy looked at him sorrowfully for what he had just told her and said, "She will come around, I'm sure of it, just give her a little time."

He turned to her and replied, "Yes, you're right, she does need the time. I'll wait. Thanks again Lucy, you seem to ease the pain."

"Anytime," she said, "I'm an old comfort kitty."

"Ryan is one lucky guy," Philip said.

"Tell him that," Lucy joked.

They smiled, and as Philip was opening the door to get out, he said, "I'll see you and thanks again, you guys are the greatest."

Lucy smiled and waved her hand and replied, "You too."

Lucy pushed the trunk button and watched as Philip retrieved his luggage and entered his office, and then she slowly left the parking area.

All the staff except Theresa had left for the weekend. Philip was just as glad; he wasn't really in the mood for conversation.

The office always closes at noon on Fridays from the middle of June to the middle of September.

He plunked his luggage down and said "Hi" to Theresa, and then lazily sat on the sofa.

Theresa looked at him fixedly and asked, "What, did something go wrong with the closer in Brussels?"

"No," Philip answered as he stared out the window, while rubbing his jaw as if he were feeling his whiskers. "Everything went great. The deal is now closed."

"Then what's wrong?" Theresa asked. "I know that look. Is it Nick?" She asked again with concern.

Philip shook his head and replied, "No, I haven't been to see him yet." And then he told her what had happened at Laura's office.

She listened with intensity, like a mother would listen to her child, and then said, "I'll make a cup of tea. You stretch out on the sofa. You must be exhausted."

A few minutes later Theresa came back with two cups of tea.

"Vince is a very cruel man," Theresa said. "He will, one day, have to answer to his pitiless ways."

"I guess so," Philip replied. "You know, Theresa, it's like someone hit me with a sledgehammer. I feel so numb. Did I go wrong somewhere?" He asked.

"No you didn't," Theresa answered, "don't sell yourself short. Like you said, Laura has a plateful, and the memory of her brother brings more pain. Talk to her, and go slowly."

Shortly after Theresa left, Philip sat in his office, debating to call Laura, or just drop by.

He decided to call.

chapter XXVIII

VALLEYFIELD, INDIANA
AUGUST 20, 2:00 p.m.

She didn't hear the phone ring because of the sound of the vacuum cleaner. When the house cleaning was finished, she decided to take a shower and get herself ready to go to the hospital to be with Nicholas, who was now on dialysis three days a week.

When Laura was about to leave the house, she noticed the light on her answering machine was on. There was a message. Someone must have called, she thought, when she was in the shower, or doing the vacuuming.

Rewinding the tape, and playing it back, she heard:

"Hi, Laura, it's me Philip. I'm at the office, and I will be here for a while. Lucy and Ryan filled me in on what happened at your office. I'm sorry that you're hurt. Please call me, I'd like to meet with you so we could talk."

Laura looked at her watch. It was one forty-five. It had to be done sometime, she thought, to meet with him, to hear his side.

Her intentions weren't to judge him, but that seems to be what she was doing. Her mind was already decided. Sorrowful memories of losing her brother through drugs, and now the man that she is in love with was involved with narcotics about the same time as her brother's death.

The phone at the reception desk rang once.

Philip picked it up and said, "Hello."

The voice at the other end said, "Hello, Philip."

"Laura, oh Laura," Philip said, with a distressful voice. "What's happening?" he asked.

"I don't really know," she replied with sorrow in her voice. "There is so much hurt in my life right now," she added, "I can't even think straight."

"Honey, can we meet somewhere? I must see you," Philip appealed.

"I'm on my way to the hospital," Laura replied.

"Then I will meet you there," Philip suggested. "We must talk. It hurts me to see you like this," he continued.

"All right," Laura said, "I'll meet you there, but not for long."

"Not for long," were the words that went through Philip's mind as he thought how sure she must be about not wanting to see me.

The Valley Hospital was about ten minutes from Philip's office, and the same from Laura's house. On the way he was trying to rehearse what he would say to her, but then he thought that it's up to her to make the decision whether to believe someone else's unverified story or the truth.

He remembers many meetings that he had to attend with customers, where he and Theresa had spent a considerable amount of time writing speeches that he never used. The words he used were off the cuff. He always found that the truth was the truth. It wasn't to be treated as a commodity, to be bargained or traded with. It's so easy to lie when you're trusted explicitly. His motto was that if he treated his employees right and was honest, then they would treat his customers with the same respect.

Laura was already with Nicholas when Philip arrived. He had been on the dialysis machine, which left him very weak. When Philip entered the room, Nick's eyes lit up and so did his smile.

Laura could see that it wasn't going to be easy to explain to Nicholas that she was going to break off with Philip.

"How are you buddy?" Philip asked, as he held a small replica of a combine in his hand.

"Okay, I guess," Nicholas replied. "Dr. West is with me a lot, and he tells me stories about you and Willy, when you were kids."

"He does, eh? I'll have to have a talk with him," Philip said.

"Willy sounds like he's lots of fun. Is he?" Nicholas asked.

"He is really a fun guy," Philip answered. "There's never a dull moment when Willy's around."

"We will meet him sometime, won't we, Philip?" Nicholas asked.

"You darn right we will," Philip replied as he looked Laura's way; she just bowed her head.

"Did you have a good time in Brussels?" Nicholas asked.

"Nicholas," Laura cut in, "you need your rest right now. I think that's enough talking for a while."

"Your mother's right Nick," Philip said. "We'll have lots of time to talk later, but your answer is yes. I had a very successful trip, everything went well, but I missed you two like crazy," as he looked at Laura, and she returned the look with sadness.

"Then why aren't you hugging Mommy like you always do?" Nicholas asked.

Laura looked at Philip and then to her son, sort of mystified, like he knew something was different, and he could tell.

At the same time Philip, who was usually fast with an answer, spoke up and said, "Hey, this is your moment, you're the most important guy here, so we're saving our hugs for you."

Laura, again, looked at Philip and smiled, and under her breath said, "Thank you."

A few minutes later Philip excused himself, saying that he had to see Gray, but told Nicholas that he'd be back shortly.

Gray was sitting at his desk talking on the phone, when Philip stuck his head through the open door. Gray motioned with his hand for him to come in, and pointed to a chair for Philip to sit down. Philip complied, and in a few seconds Gray was off the phone, and said as he held out his hand to shake Philip's

"Welcome back. How are all those Belgians?"

"They're all rich," Philip replied, "and when they aren't making money, they're partying. My hangovers could tell you stories."

"You look kind of down. What is it, change of time, not enough sleep?" Gray inquired.

"Yeah, that's part of it," Philip replied, and then he told him what had happened at Laura's office, and how Laura was handling it.

"That asshole, he never gives up, does he?" was Gray's remark.

"That's what Lucy called him to his face. Laura and I haven't discussed it yet, but I have a feeling that she doesn't want me to be part of their lives."

"That's crazy," Gray remarked. "You three are nuts over each other. Do you want me to talk to her?" he asked.

"No," Philip replied. "Don't say anything. We'll straighten it out, I hope. I'd like to borrow your office for a while, so we can talk."

"Sure, I'm going to do my rounds in a few minutes, that will probably take me half an hour," Gray said. "So be my guest and good luck."

"What about Nick?" Philip asked. "What's your diagnosis?"

"He's very weak. I want him to stay here." Gray replied. "He definitely needs a kidney, so he'll be on and off dialysis until we can find a match."

"It's come down to that, has it?" as Philip shook his head in sorrow.

"I'm afraid so," Gray said. "I'm going to move him into the *Railroad Room* tomorrow," he continued.

"That'll be great, he'll love it," Philip remarked.

"So," Philip continued, "what about a kidney donor? It's too bad that someone has to die to find a proper match, that's if their donor card is signed."

"And, there's a waiting list," Gray added.

"I want you to know," Philip stressed, "that you have full control of my check book, and I don't think I have to say anything more on that subject, do I?"

"I here you," Gray replied.

Gray stood up and said, "I'm leaving now, to make my rounds, and listen, buddy, everything will work out, you'll see."

Back in Nicholas' room, Philip told them all about the *Railroad Room*, and they were both delighted. It was getting close to four o'clock. Dinner would be at five, and Laura was always there to help Nicholas.

Nicholas, who was still groggy from the dialysis, said, "I feel like sleeping for a little while. Why don't you two go to the cafeteria and come back when my dinner comes."

"Are you sure you'll be all right?" his mother asked.

"Yeah, I'll be fine," Nicholas answered, as he turned his head and closed his eyes. Out of the room, Philip told Laura that Gray was making his rounds and they could use his office, saying that it would be more private than talking in the cafeteria. He didn't mention that he told Gray about their situation, and she didn't ask.

Valerie was on vacation, so there wasn't anyone in the office when Laura and Philip entered. He pulled a chair up to Valerie's desk for Laura, and used Valerie's for himself.

"Would you like a cup of tea?" Philip asked.

"No thanks, I'm fine," she answered.

"Would you rather not discuss this now?" he asked. "I know you have enough on your mind, and this can always wait."

She looked down, and took a deep breath, and then lifted her head, looked at him and said, "We can talk."

He looked at her with sadness, for he knew that her son was her first priority, and nothing was going to stand in her way. It would be so easy for him to walk away, but that wasn't to be because he also had a special bond with the little guy, and was deeply in love with Laura.

"I know what you heard at your office on Monday from Vince Tedesco," Philip explained. "Lucy and Ryan filled me in, but I want you to know, that we grew up and went to school with Vince, and he's always been a very cruel person towards my friends and me."

"I didn't know that he worked out of your office," Philip continued, "and it wouldn't have mattered anyway. I had heard that he was in real estate, but it never concerned me to know where."

"That really doesn't matter," Laura cut in, "I know that my brother died eleven years ago from drugs, and I also know that was the approximate time when they had that drug bust. I researched the newspaper, and read all about it, names and charges. Lenny would be alive today, if there weren't people out there selling drugs," she stressed.

"You went to great lengths when all you had to do was ask me," Philip said. "Laura, I'm really sorry about your brother. I too, wish he were here. I might have been able to help him."

"How, with money? It doesn't buy everything," she asked, and then thought to herself that wasn't a fair thing to say, especially to Philip.

Before she could apologize for making that statement, Philip answered with, "You're right, Laura, anything that I've loved, was never bought."

"So, tell me," Laura asked, looking him straight in the eyes, like she was reading his mind, "were you involved with that drug ring?"

"Do you think I could be involved in anything like that? Would my answer, yes or no, make a difference of the outcome? I have a feeling that you've already made up your mind."

"Then, I'm sorry Philip," Laura replied. "I can't see how we can be together with this on our minds. Nothing would be the same as it was."

"How would you feel about me," she continued, "if the shoe were on the other foot?"

"That's quite simple," Philip answered. "I didn't know you then, I only know you now. Your past life is part of all the things that make you what you are today, and that's why I love you."

She looked at him as though she were surprised at his answer, which she was, but knew that he was honest about what he said.

He continued, "Laura, don't do this. I know you love me as much as I do you, and what about Nick? Are you going to suggest I don't see him?" he asked.

"I think it would be better that you don't," she replied.

"I understand that you're upset," he continued. "You have plenty on your mind. You don't need anymore, but I'd like to see you through all this, even if it's just to see Nick well again. He and I have created a special relationship with each other, and it would be difficult, especially for him if I should be away from him, you should know that."

Philip leaned forward in his chair, looked at her seriously and said, "I'll make you a promise. When he's well again I'll leave, and I will keep out of your way in the meantime."

"I don't think that would work. There are some things I can't let go," Laura said.

"You mean, you won't let go," Philip replied in haste.

"I'm sorry Philip, my mind is made up."

Philip cut in and said, "I'm sorry too. I'm sorry that you let others make up your mind and I'm sorry that you have these derogatory opinions of me, but it seems that there's nothing I can say to convince you. I wish you could throw away that doubt you have about me."

Laura looked at him with sorrow, her eyes sparkling with tears, as she rose from her chair to leave.

Philip came around the desk, and before he opened the door for her, he said, "Laura, you will always have my love, if you wish to keep it."

She looked at him, smiled, and with a loud whisper said, "I know I will Philip."

They left the office and as they were walking down the corridor towards Nicholas's room, Philip said, "I'd like to say good-bye to Nick."

"I was wrong," Laura blurted out, "maybe you should continue to see him for a while, if you wish to."

"Thanks, honey," Philip replied. "It means a lot to me, and

him too, I'm sure."

Philip said good-bye to Nicholas, and told him that he'd be in tomorrow, and then turned to Laura and nodded, as he said, "Good-bye Laura.

At that moment Nicholas looked at his mother, noticing her sad look as she said good-bye to Philip without a kiss, and then to Philip as he was leaving the room, put two and two together and knew that there was something wrong.

Laura stayed with her son, and saw him through what dinner he was able to eat and then left for home.

Philip was on his way to Millcreek. He never remembered the drive to the Hills of Caledon. He was angry. Is being in love a fool's road? he thought. It only ends with tears.

chapter XXIX

MILLCREEK
AUGUST 20, 1995 7:00 p.m.

Pedro and Juanita had just finished dinner, and were sitting on their back porch, enjoying the fresh country air while sipping on a cup of tea. Without warning, they heard this thundering sound of hoof beats heading towards the back bush.

"That can only be one person," Pedro said as he stood up and looked out toward the back fifty.

"Who?" Juanita asked. "Philip," as she answered her own question. "We didn't hear him drive in," she continued.

"I guess you were making dinner and I was in the basement, fixing the pipe," Pedro suggested. "There's only one other time that I know of that he galloped that horse that hard," he continued. "That was the day after Sarah died."

"You better go see to him," Juanita said.

"Yes, my love, you're right," as he put on his boots and headed for the stable to saddle up Buck.

When he was saddled, Pedro mounted the horse and rode with a trot to the large sugar bush at the south end of Millcreek. There he saw Philip with his big stallion, Phantom. Philip was standing in front of his big black Arabian steed, patting his jaw and apologizing to him for riding him so hard.

Pedro pulled up Buck and dismounted, leaving the reins hanging down on each side of Buck's head.

Pedro said, "Hello, amigo, good night for a ride," as he patted Phantom on his sweaty rump.

Philip lifted his head toward him, while Pedro was still looking over Phantom and said, "You have a special sense to know my mood my friend."

"I have no idea what you're saying, comrade," Pedro replied, "but I do know that I have a bottle of Dos Dedos Tequila at the house that will ease most any discomfort if you wish to drop by and share it."

Philip pulled in his bottom lip between his teeth, nodded his head and replied, "Sounds like a good idea."

They rode back to the stable. Not a word was spoken. They stripped their mounts of their saddles and bridle, groomed down Phantom, and turned them loose in the field.

As they entered the house, Philip gave Juanita a kiss on the cheek, as he usually did, as she said, "You look hungry, and I have a large pot of pasta with your favorite meatballs simmering on the stove."

"I still don't know what hungry looks like," Philip remarked, "but as usual you are right. Airline food is impartial. It's so nice to come home to this." He still had his arm on her shoulder. He continued, "You always know how to get to me, don't you?"

"How do they say in America?" Juanita asked. "To get to a man's heart, you must first go through his mouth."

Philip smiled and said, "Something like that."

Pedro poured him a tall shot of tequila, with salt and a wedge of lime.

After a large plate of spaghetti and meatballs, and on a second ounce of tequila, Philip started to tell them what had happened.

When he had it all out, Pedro poured another drink for both of them. As he was a man of few words, unless they were important words, he just sat by his wife, looked at her, knowing that she would have the answer, and said, "I think you know what to say, my love."

She smiled at her husband, and said as she looked at Philip, who sat by the table circling the rim of his glass, "It was very cruel of that man to say what he said about you. He has hurt many people by his rumor. Laura is a lovely, kind woman; you chose well. There is too much love between you. You both still have an endless amount of feelings for each other and little Nick as well, and it will overcome the sadness. Go slow Meester Philip, and keep a distance for awhile, and you will find that crossroad again."

Philip looked at her, thought for a few seconds of how beautifully she put that, touched the back of her hand, and said, "You know Juanita, a man in trouble always feels better when there's a woman around, and you are usually always that woman."

Then he turned to Pedro and said, "You chose well, my friend."

"He knows that," Juanita replied, as she kissed him on the cheek.

Pedro returned the kiss and said, "Yes I do."

After finishing their drinks, Philip said, "I must leave and get some sleep. It's been a long day, and thanks my friends, because of you I will sleep well."

"Come by in the morning for flapjacks, sausages, and hot coffee," Juanita proposed.

"Sounds good, I'll be here," Philip replied.

chapter xxx

VALLEYFIELD, INDIANA
SEPTEMBER 5, 1995

It was a bright September morning; the leaves were beginning to change color. A slight breeze in the air was assisting them to drop and flutter to the ground. Autumn was slowly approaching.

There were more children milling about the street that morning, and meeting at one specific spot. They were waiting for the school bus that would transport them to the Valleyfield Elementary School.

One child would be missing on that bus... Nicholas.

Eight-fifteen, Laura was ironing a blouse for her to wear to work where she would put in a couple of hours before going to the hospital, when she heard a knock on the door and then the door bell rang. She put the iron down, tightened the belt of her nightgown and went to open the door.

Young Bobby O'Neil, Nicholas's friend, was standing there with his knapsack attached to his back and a baseball mitt in his hand, and said, "Good morning Mrs. Manning, how are you today?"

"I'm fine, and how are you Bobby?" She asked.

"I'm fine too," Bobby replied.

"It's nice to see you," Laura said, "and I see you're ready for your first day at school."

"Yes, I'm waiting for the bus," he responded. "I just wanted to tell you that I'll bring any homework back for Nick. We probably won't have any today, but I know we will later in the week, and if you don't mind, maybe I could go to the hospital with you a couple of days a week, and maybe one day on the weekend, and help Nick with his school work."

Laura could feel her eyes clouding up as she said, "Bobby, you are a true friend. I'm sure Nicholas will appreciate it, and so do I."

"Nicholas is now in a room they call the *Railroad Room*," she continued. "It's a room with all kinds of games in it, so I know he'll look forward to seeing you."

"Hey, that sounds neat," Bobby excitedly replied.

"I'm going to talk to your mother today," Laura suggested, "and maybe we can make out a little schedule for you to tutor Nicholas."

"How is he?" Bobby asked.

"Well, he's going through some hard times right now," Laura replied, "but when he hears you're coming to see him, I'm sure he will spruce right up, and hopefully he'll soon be playing road hockey with you."

"Thanks, Mrs. Manning, I feel better now," Bobby said.

"You've made me feel a lot better too, thanks Bobby," Laura said. "Oh, I see your bus coming."

Bobby ran down the steps, and then turned around and waved. Laura waved back, and thought, "What a kind and well-mannered young man."

After putting away the iron and ironing board, Laura cleaned up a few dishes that were in the sink, got herself dressed and left for the office. As she was scanning the computer to keep up to date on new listings (because for the most part of the last week was spent in the hospital with Nicholas), many of the agents and office personnel showed their compassion by asking about Nicholas. She thanked them and assured them that her little boy was in good hands, namely Dr. West.

While she was using the copying machine, Madge came over

to her (looking very serious as if she was about to cry) and said, "Laura, I'm sorry your little boy is ill, and I hope that he will get well soon."

"Thank you, Madge. I'm sure he will," Laura replied. "It's a bit of an uphill battle, but we're going to make it."

"I know you are," Madge said, then she added, "Laura I don't know if you are a religious person, but I have a St. Christopher's medal that my little girl Christina gave me for you to give to your Nicholas."

Laura looked at her with a smile. She could see that she was going through some despair and said, "Why thank you Madge, this is very nice of you and your little girl. I will give it to Nicholas; I'm going to see him in an hour. Thank Christina, for me and Nicholas."

Madge was about to leave, and then she turned and looked at Laura with an almost appealing look, and asked, "Laura, could I talk to you for a moment?"

Laura sensed from the beginning that Madge had something else that she wanted to get off her mind, as she said, "Of course you can, Madge. Let's go into my office."

They entered her office and Laura closed the door. She put her papers on her desk, and pulled up a chair for Madge and asked her if she would like a coffee.

Madge declined and then said, "Laura, you've always been very nice to me, even when others weren't. I've been given the cold shoulder from most of the girls, and I know your good friend Lucy hates me as well, and I don't really blame them, but you've never judged me or listened to the rumors, and this is why I'm confiding in you. I know you're going through some trying times with Nicholas, and I suppose I shouldn't bring out my problems to you, but I don't have a friend I can talk to."

By this time Madge was in tears as Laura handed her a tissue, put her hand on Madge's left shoulder, and said, "That's okay Madge, go right ahead, I'd be glad to listen."

Madge began, "I think I have lost my husband, and my little

girl. I haven't been a loyal wife or a good mother for almost a year. I've let men with power in this industry use me so that I could get ahead financially, and now I'm so ashamed of myself, not only for what I've done to my own family but also to the wives of some of those men. I know if Connie ever found out she'd be very upset. It's hard for me to walk in here and face my working colleagues. That's why I'm asking your advice."

"Wow!" Laura let out. "Well to start with, I can see that you're sincere about patching things up. I don't think my friend Lucy hates you, she just hates the lifestyle that you just explained to me. Do you think your husband still loves you?" Laura asked.

"Yes, I think so, and it's in his character to forgive. You see, Gary and I got married very young. I was twenty and he was twenty-two. We had Christina a year later, so for the first two years I was home with her, and he was still an apprentice in carpentry. There wasn't much money coming in, but when I look back, we were happy and in love. Then I took a real-estate course, and you know what this industry is like, weekends, evenings, trying to get housework done, ironing your clothes at ten in the evening for the next day, and raising a child. Gary was marvelous through it all."

"Maybe that's why I started running around. He permitted me to have so much free time, thinking of course, that it was all business."

"I can remember the first time I cheated on him. I came home that night and cried my eyes out. I felt like committing suicide. I couldn't face him. He asked me why I was crying, and I told him it was just the pressure of the job, then he cuddled me and said not to worry, that everything was going to be okay, and it was. I had more listings, and was making more money, because I was sleeping with the boss, and others."

"Now he's doing well, has his own company, and I wish to God that he'd forgive me and take me back. I've never stopped loving him," as tears formed again in her eyes.

"What are you willing to give up?" Laura asked, "other than

the running around."

Madge started to answer, when Laura put her hand on hers and said, "Let me finish. You could go to him, ask for his forgiveness, let him know that you'd give up your career to have him and Christina back in your life again. If he's the kind and forgiving man that you explained, then I think things will work out."

"You're a smart girl. I've seen some of your listings and how you handle them, of course I mean the ones you found yourself. You could sell somewhere else, like in Fort Wayne or any of the small towns. There's a lot of development going on, and where there are new homes, there have to be resales."

Madge looked at her and smiled, and said, "I wish I had you for a friend a few years ago."

"Well, I don't know if I've been any help to you, but I'm glad we had this talk. I never knew this part of you, and I like it," Laura said with sincerity.

"You've helped me tremendously," Madge said. "I'm going to call Gary today to have lunch with me. I've been wanting to for some time now, but I guess I needed someone to confide in. Thank you Laura for listening," as she touched the back of her hand. "I won't forget this moment."

As Madge was leaving Laura's office Laura said, "I'll give Nicholas the medal."

Laura never let anyone know about the little talk she had with Madge. Not even Lucy.

Two weeks later, Laura and Lucy were talking in their office while Laura was opening her mail. There was a thank-you card, with a note enclosed; she read it silently to herself.

Everything is great. We both are like newlyweds again. I thank you for leading me in the right direction, and being a friend when I needed one. I will never forget you. Christina and I pray together every night, and we always include Nicholas. I hope we can have lunch sometime soon, and if it's

possible, we'd like to visit Nicholas. I will call you."
Madge…Addressed………Anderson, Indiana.

Lucy asked, "Who is that from?"
"Oh, just a thank-you note from a client," Laura replied.

chapter XXXI

SYDNEY INTERNATIONAL AIRPORT
NOVEMBER 19th 1:00 p.m.

The Boeing 747 was gliding out of the stacked up traffic pattern, while making its final approach to Sydney International Airport. It had been a long and tedious flight, and Philip was exhausted, mainly because his mind was so preoccupied on memories of most of his life. He was glad to be here in Australia, the feeling of contentment would be good for him, at least for awhile.

As the huge plane was taxiing to the finger of the Quantas terminal, Lisa, who was occupying the seat beside Philip for the landing segment of the flight, turned to him and said, "I have to phone my sister to pick me up, and it usually takes her about thirty minutes, so if your friends aren't here to meet you yet, I'll buy you a coffee. I feel I owe you for being such a perfect passenger."

Philip smiled and said, "I would be honored, but if I know my friends, they were most likely here all morning, but if they're not, then I will look forward to it. Maybe next time I'll keep you busy, and then you won't think I'm so perfect." Then he continued by saying, "May I ask, do you have a boyfriend?"

"I did," she answered, "two weeks before I left here."

"I'm sorry," Philip said, "I shouldn't have been so inquisitive."

"Oh, that's okay," Lisa remarked. "It was inevitable. He wanted to control my life, even do my thinking for me, so I decided that he wasn't the man that I wanted to spend my life with."

"You likely made the perfect decision, and the wisest," Philip suggested. "You are a lovely and attractive young lady. The man that you choose will treasure you forever, and he will be the happiest man alive."

She looked at him with passion, and her eyes were lustrous as she asked, "Why are all the good ones so far out of range?"

"They're not, Lisa," Philip replied. "Just keep being yourself and his path will cross with yours."

"Thank you, you are such a nice man," she looked at him with a smile. "I wish you the best."

"You do, don't you?" He looked at her with delight.

The plane came to a stop, and the captain came over the intercom saying, "Welcome ladies and gentlemen to Australia, and thank you for selecting Quantas."

Lisa was up helping the first-class passengers retrieve their carry-ons. As she reached up above Philip's seat to open the overhead compartment Philip said, "Thanks Lisa, I have it here."

"See what I mean," Lisa joked, and then added, "I'll always remember the kindest man with the kindest words, thank you."

"Anytime, Lisa," Philip replied.

Jim and Sylvia Cameron, Philip's good friends, were at the arrivals when Philip came walking up the ramp. Philip had sent them a fax when he was at Willy and Susan's place in Sacramento, stating the day and the approximate time that he would be arriving.

His intentions were, when he arrived in Sydney, to take a Quantas shuttle the two-hundred miles up to Coff's Harbor, and have Jim meet him there; but Jim and Sylvia had a Cattleman's Convention to attend in Sydney with the Consolidated Meat Group where they are members of the board.

Consolidated Meat Group is an Australian owned company operating from rural base. They combine pastoral interests with modern processing techniques to provide quality products. They also have a strong relationship with pastoral companies, grazers and feedlotters throughout Queensland, New South Wales, and the Northern Territory, who supply premium quality stock all year round. So, although Jim and Sylvia's station is one of the largest distributors of beef, they had now ventured in to the management end of a large meat industry, as spokespeople.

Their meeting ended the evening before Philip's arrival, so they stayed over the extra night in order to meet Philip when he arrived.

He had very little luggage, one large suitcase and a carry-on. After he was ushered through customs, he noticed his friends standing by the rail. Sylvia rushed over and embraced him, as he did to her with a kiss on the cheek. Her husband, Jim followed, shook his hand and tapped him on the shoulder, and said, "G'day mate, have a good trip?" then he motioned to the porter to follow him to the car. Sylvia had her two arms gripped around Philip's as they followed Jim and the porter out of the terminal and to their car that was parked illegally by the curb.

An airport official was about to plunk a ticket on it as they showed up.

"Another minute mate," the official said, "I'da had her towed."

"Have a g'day mate," Jim replied, as he patted him on the back, and then opened the trunk for the porter to place the luggage in. Philip tipped the porter generously, and then they entered the car for a three and a half hour trip to Jim and Sylvia's two thousand acre station, where they raise Black Angus cattle.

Sylvia was not what you'd call "a woman of beauty," but there was an attractive feature about her that stimulated men to turn their heads for a second look. She was a woman of average height, blond, short hair, her skin was soft, and well tanned, there was a special prominence about her figure that was attractive.

She was wearing a jean skirt with a white blouse with two top buttons unfastened reveal a noticeable cleavage between firm breasts. She was also wearing white high-heeled sandals.

Jim was tall, about six-three, two hundred and forty pounds. He and Sylvia were around the same age, pushing sixty. His face showed the effects of the harsh Australian sun, and a lifetime of outdoor work. He was wearing khaki shorts with a light short-sleeved plaid shirt and a Tilley hat.

His smile seemed to tell it all—happy, healthy—a very successful stockman. He and Philip had been doing business for the past fifteen years. Philip had researched the beef industry in Australia, and it was his decision to select Jim and Sylvia's herd to be imported to a major restaurant chain in the U.S.

Their station is called "Cameron's Station," located near Coramba, New South Wales, where the Orara River flows through the beautiful hinterland, twenty miles west of Coff's Harbor. The small inland town of Coramba nestles in a gentle landscape, but further inland the country becomes wilder, shadowed by hoop-pine and ironbark.

As they left the airport and connected with coastal highway One, and after the small talk about the flight, Philip, who was sitting in the back said, "This is nice of you two to have me stay with you for awhile."

"Our pleasure, mate." Jim replied.

"It's about time." Sylvia said. "You know it's been seven years since you were here last, and by you coming, it's like a vacation for us."

"Last time we talked you had taken up writing a novel," Jim expressed. "How is it coming along?"

"I haven't been working on it for over two years," Philip replied, "but I hope to spend time on it while I'm here and hopefully finish it, even to satisfy myself. Like you said, I started it over seven years ago. It's about time to complete it."

"A hobby is great," Jim said, "but don't give up your day job."

"That's for sure," Philip agreed.

Sylvia had an intuition that Philip was not here just for a vacation, but that he was running away from something, perhaps a woman. She wasn't about to ask him. He would tell them in time, his time.

Jim and Sylvia were giving him the grand tour along the two-hundred mile trip, that seemed to cut down the time, because they were finally in sight of Cameron's Station.

The drive to their house was still another mile from the highway, crossing over the Orara River that moves steadily and smoothly through their property on its way to the South Pacific. After crossing the bridge over the Orara, they came upon hundreds of cattle grazing in the flatlands, and if you looked beyond the flatlands you could see the hill rise up to hundreds of acres of bushland that seemed to reach the sky.

From a distance you could see out-sheds, and a windmill, still operational, and then they reached their house they had built four years ago. It was a colonial in blue and white weatherboard in classic vernacular style of the early homestead, with stilts to create a breezeway, and deep verandas.

Philip's comment was, "It's beautiful. It's absolutely gorgeous. How did you ever come up with such a classy design?" he asked, as they stepped out of the car.

"Well," Jim replied, "we knew what we wanted, and what it should look like, so we hired a quality architect to put it together for us."

"I've had my share of traveling," Philip said, "and I've seen some beautiful homes, but I've never seen anything like this. You must be the envy of all your neighbors." as he directed that statement to Sylvia.

"Our neighbors are one hour away," Sylvia replied, "but yes, I am very happy when I get the chance to entertain. Now lets go inside, and we'll give you the twenty-five cent tour."

After the tour, they sat out on the veranda and had drinks and talked.

Philip asked, "Do you still have that little apartment above one of your sheds?"

"You mean the loft?" Jim replied.

"Yes, that's it," Philip responded.

"Would you rather stay there?" Sylvia asked.

"If it's no trouble," Philip replied. "I'd love to. I can relax and get to my novel, and maybe finish it."

"Okay," Jim suggested, "stay here tonight, and we'll move you over tomorrow."

"I also want to help with the farming," Philip said. "I've been waiting for years to get the opportunity to be on a big ranch station in this country."

"Great," Jim replied, "tomorrow we'll saddle-up and take a ride. We usually use the four-by-four, but the horses need exercising."

"Hey, I like that even better," Philip said as he looked at Sylvia with a pleasing smile.

Sylvia has a housekeeper who also cooks their dinner on occasion. So after a few drinks, and some conversation, dinner was being served. This was the beginning of a long stay that a couple of months ago wasn't even thought of.

chapter XXXII

SUNDAY JANUARY 30, 1996
VALLEYFIELD, INDIANA

Weeks turned into months. Christmas came and went. So far the winter was amiable, the consistent cold north winds that swept down from Wisconsin in the past had not struck Valleyfield yet.

During the last week in January, Laura, Lucy, and Nicholas left the shopping mall and were on their way to Lucy's house. Nicholas was showing the size and weight of a normal eight year old boy. His recovery has been fantastic, even Dr. West couldn't get over his fast restoration, but still kept a close eye on him to be sure he took his medication that stopped the host from producing the antibodies that could kill the transplant. Nicolas caught up with his classes at school, thanks to the efforts of his friend Bobby, who tutored him. Laura was so happy and grateful that she had her healthy son back again.

Everyone around him noticed that he wasn't happy. He seemed to be distant, kept to himself. Something was definitely missing in his life, and they knew what—Philip.

He knew now why Philip went away. He never ever believed that he would desert him, but he remembered Philip telling him the day that they had a discussion in the park, he said, "Nick, I love your mother very much, but if you don't want to be my friend, then I will leave. I'll go away." So he believed that's what happened, only it was his mother that didn't want him to be her friend anymore.

As they were nearing Lucy's house, where Laura and Nicholas were staying for dinner, they were waiting at a traffic light, when Nicholas, pointing towards the car beside them asked, "Mommy, what's that hanging on that lady's mirror?"

His mother said, "Don't point Nicholas, that's rude."

"Well, what is it?" he asked again.

"They're called rosary beads," she answered. "Catholics use them. The rosary is a series of prayers, and rosary beads are for keeping count of these prayers."

Nicholas didn't say anything for a few minutes and then he commented, "Philip is a Catholic."

"Yes, I know," Laura replied.

"He has rosary beads," he said again.

Lucy looked over at Laura, who returned the look and raised her brow, and asked, "Oh, did he show them to you?"

"No," Nicholas replied. "When you and Lucy were in Seattle, Philip stayed with me all night. I woke up. It was still very dark outside. Philip was sitting in that armchair and didn't know I was awake, and I didn't know if he was awake either until I saw him reach in his jacket pocket and take out these beads. He went like that" as he touched his head and then his chest and then each shoulder.

"That's called the sign of the cross," Lucy said. "They say 'the father, the son, and the holy spirit'," then she looked at Laura, shrugged, and said, "I went to St. Joseph's High School."

"Then he kissed the cross that's at the end of the beads," he continued.

"That's called the crucifix," Lucy explained. "There's a small statue of Jesus on the cross."

"I learned that at Bible class," Lucy continued as she glanced at Laura, whose eyes were now clouding with tears, and thinking about this man who would stay with her son all night and pray for him.

Nicholas, unaware of his mother's reaction continued to say,

"After a while he kissed the cross again, and then put the beads back in his pocket."

"A lot of people pray for someone who is sick," Lucy said. "Ryan and I prayed, your mommy and daddy prayed, Dr. West and Betty, Juanita and Pedro, we all prayed that you'd get well."

"I know, and that was nice," Nicholas replied. "I believe that Davey must have helped some way too, but Philip also whispered out loud, when he was finished with the beads… 'Lord', that's God isn't it?" he asked.

"Yes," Lucy answered.

"Well," Nicholas continued, "he said, 'Lord, please don't take this little boy from his mother,' and the next day I was better," as he smiled and sat back in his seat.

At this time the tears were overflowing from Laura's eyes, and she was biting her bottom lip to keep her from bursting out, and having difficulty concentrating on her driving. Lucy, who was also in tears, put her hand on her friend's shoulder and told her to pull over to the donut shop that was to their right.

Nicholas asked, "What's wrong, Mommy, why are you crying? Is it what I said that makes you cry? I'm sorry."

"It's okay," she replied, as she reached over the back and gave him a hug.

Then Lucy said, "I'll go in and buy a dozen donuts. Ryan would like that, wouldn't he?"

Nicholas answered, "We all would."

Later on, when Lucy and Laura were cleaning up the dinner table, and Ryan and Nicholas were playing with the racing car set, Lucy said, "I have something to show you, something that Nicholas gave me to send to Philip," as she reached in a drawer of her buffet and picked up a letter.

"He said that I would know where to send it. Here's what it says,"

Dear Philip, this is Nick. I don't spell or write very good, so I hope you will be able to read what I say.

You told me that you were going away on business for a while, it's been a long while, but I know now why you went away, and I know it's okay to tell a little white lie so someone won't be sad, like you didn't want me to be. I wish that you would come back. I am well now; I don't get sick anymore and no more needles. Thanks for staying with me until I got better. I don't get chosen last to play road hockey anymore because I can go faster and I don't get out of breath like I used to. I am good on left wing. Next year Mommy said that she would join me up on a little league team so I will be playing on ice. I want you to see me play.

I really miss you and I know that Mommy does too. I hear her crying some nights and one time I got up and went into her room. I asked her why she was crying and she said because she was so happy that I wasn't sick anymore. So I said to her, Mommy, you always said to me to be honest and never tell a lie, and she said that's right, so I asked her if she missed you like I did, she said that she did. I know that you love Mommy and me and we love you, so why won't you come home to us? I know Mommy thought you did something a long time ago, but I don't think she believes it now. I don't believe you did anything bad, and I don't even care, so please give us another chance.

I want you here with us.

Nick X X O O

"You're not going to send it are you?" Laura asked.

"Yes I am," Lucy replied. "I see you tearing yourself to pieces over this, and there's no need for it. I've said this before, he adores you both very much and if you don't want to show your affection because of your unreasonable obstinance, then at least Nicholas can let him know that he still cares."

"I'm sorry," Laura stressed. "I keep thinking about Lenny; being by his side when he died of an overdose of those drugs."

Lucy and Laura were sitting by the dinning room table and

Lucy took both of Laura's hands in hers and said, "Laura, we love you, you know that, and maybe I shouldn't say this, but......what you've told me about Lenny, I think he was the author of his own misfortune."

Laura looked at her as if to say, "How dare you, you didn't even know him" but instead she said, "I am so confused, I don't know what to think, maybe the time away from him will let me get some of the bitterness out of me."

"Maybe you're right," Lucy replied. "I'm sorry for pressuring you."

"We'll talk again, okay?" Laura suggested.

"Okay," Lucy said as she squeezed her hands.

chapter XXXIII

TUESDAY, FEBRUARY 8, 1996
VALLEYFIELD, INDIANA 1:00 p.m.

Lucy arrived home after spending the morning at the office, parked her car in the garage, and lowered the door with the automatic door switch and entered the house. Before taking off her coat, she opened the front door to check for mail. Sorting through the many pieces of advertising and brochures that agents usually receive, she came across a letter post marked "Australia," and addressed to Mr. and Mrs. Ryan Dawson. Very excitiedly, she opened it even before removing her coat. She knew who it was from by the hand writing, very similar to a Christmas card that they received from Philip.

It started…

Hi, Lucy and Ryan,

Hope you are both well. I'm fine, been working quite steadily on my novel. My concentration hasn't been that great, but I manage. I have this little loft. It's like a studio above one of their outbuildings. It's ideal, very quiet, except for some of the animal noises.

Jim and Sylvia are two great people. We get along fantastically. Quite often I help them on their 2000-acre station, that's what they call a ranch over here, or is it "under here." It's big, but there are some to the north much bigger. They are doing well. Their home is gorgeous, custom built;

the style is "old colonial" in blue and white weatherboard. (A great commission to sell one of these.)

I received Nick's letter. Thanks, Lucy, for finding its way to me. You are special. Made me choke-up a little, but a real pleasure to hear from him. He says "my spelling isn't that good," wait until my proofreader and editor get to see my novel, if you think spelling and grammar are inadequate.

He is a precious little guy, and I am so privileged that I was a part of his life for a little while. I'll bet he's out on the driveway trying his slap shots.

Lucy, I have no idea when I will return. It won't be for a while. I think the time away from Valleyfield will disclose the true character in our relationship. Whoever said, "out of sight-out of mind" is a liar. Maybe when I find the "out of mind," which I'm not looking forward to, then I will come home, and Nick and I can resume our friendship again.

Tell him for me that I think of him all the time, and I will write to him soon and if he's allowed to, Gray will take him to Millcreek; Juanita and Pedro would love to see him, or any of you.

Pedro will be training Silverdollar this spring; it would be nice if Nick were there.

Although we are five thousand miles apart, let's not let a little geography get in our way from keeping our friendship alive.

There's an old African proverb that says, "Hold a true friend with both hands."

Ryan, I miss beating you at golf...

Keep well and safe…….. I'm thinking of you all….

Philip….

Lucy, I just couldn't finish this note without letting you know, well I think you know what I'd love to say…

chapter XXXIV

MONDAY MARCH 4, 1996
VALLEYFIELD, INDIANA

Pedro leaned over and gave his wife a kiss, got out of the pickup truck, went around and opened the door for her and said, "I'll pick you up in an hour my love," as Juanita entered the mall.

He was on his way to scrape away the slush that had gathered up in the parking area of the import/export office. The snow scraper that is attached to the front of the pickup truck is the handiest and most practical way of removing snow. Pedro should know. He has pushed enough of it over the past seventeen years that he's been employed by Philip's company.

Most of the stores in the mall were having clearance sales to get rid of all the winter stock, and to make room for the spring fashions. Juanita was taking advantage on some of the great buys. Her husband spent a great deal of time outdoors, even in the winter, so she would benefit by stocking up on heavy socks and shirts.

After going through the discounts, she decided to treat herself to something nice. So off to the perfume department. She always loved the aroma that Sarah used, which was called "Tre`sor." Although it was very costly, it was worth it, and it made her feel good, and it also had an effect on her husband, a sexual desire. Pedro and Juanita are very passionate with each other, even though they are both in their late sixties.

So two ounces of "Tre`sor Eau de Parfum" at $150.00 passed through the cashier and into Juanita's handbag. As she was leaving the cash counter, a familiar voice said, "Hello, Juanita." Juanita turned and had her breath taken away as she saw Laura leaving from the other cashier.

She said, "Laura, oh, how nice to see you. How are you, and Nicholas, how is he?" as she noticed that Laura looked a little different. She still had that full smile that showed off beautiful white teeth, but Juanita noticed something else. She had tired looking eyes, as if they had their share of crying, not that happy lady that used to visit Millcreek with Philip.

"I'm fine," Laura replied. "I'm finally back to my work full time, and Nicholas, he's in school right now, and he couldn't be better. I can hardly keep him down, but I love it. Do you have time for a cup of tea?" she asked.

"I would love to. Pedro won't be here for at least an hour, and he will come in and get me. He's at the office plowing snow."

They walked out in the mall where there was a coffee shop, ordered two teas and sat at a table and chatted for at least half an hour about what went on with everyone all winter, and then Laura asked what was on both their minds, "Do you hear from Philip?"

Juanita was glad that Laura broke the silence about him, and answered, "Yes, but not too often. We receive a card from him, and he writes a short note on it. He isn't the letter writing type, although I believe he's finished his book that he's been working on for a few years. I here from his friends Jim and Sylvia more than I do from him."

"How is he?" Laura whispered as she looked at Juanita with a frown.

"According to what Sylvia says," Juanita replied, "and that was over three weeks ago, he keeps himself busy working with her husband Jim, but she also said he was getting itchy feet, and as she put it, he said he wanted to explore the continent. Any sorrows that I've known him to have, he's handled with the belief that time will heal. He's a survivor." She added.

"There isn't a day goes by that Nicholas doesn't talk about him," Laura said, "for one reason or another. He says his prayers every night and he asks God to keep Philip safe."

"Dr. West sees him at least once a week, and he's quite satisfied with the results. He says you would never know, unless you'd seen the scar, that Nicholas ever had a transplant. His new kidney is working as well as any healthy kidney."

"He is a little angel," Juanita remarked. "Someone is sure watching over him."

Laura leaned forward with her elbows on the table, and both her hands together propping up her head, looked straight at Juanita and said, "Juanita, tell me about him, tell me what I don't know. How did you and Pedro get to know him? I've always believed that when a door closes, God will open another."

"This door hasn't closed on me, I know that without a doubt."

Juanita took a sip of her tea, and then put her head down, and then raised it, looked Laura in the eyes and replied by saying, "Laura, if you're asking about any wrong doing about him, you're asking the wrong person."

Then she continued, "My husband and I and our son Alex lived on the outskirts of a small town called Santa Rosa in New Mexico, about ninety miles east of Albuquerque. Pedro worked at a large ranch along the Pecos River. As you know, he is a professional horseman."

"It was in the middle of July 1983, Philip was down in Santa Rosa on business, that's the only reason anyone would visit there. He was following up on some farm equipment."

"After finishing dinner at a local restaurant, he decided to take a walk. It was around eight thirty, about twilight time, and the temperature was in the nineties."

"There were some men standing outside a bar smoking and talking as Philip walked by. Three of them started to follow him, unnoticed by Philip. When they were away from the buildings in a dim area, they came up behind him and demanded his wallet. One of them had a knife. There were two twenty year olds and an eighteen year old. The eighteen year old was our son Alex."

"Alex, Dr. Alex" Laura asked astonishingly, "that kind, good-looking young man?"

"Yes," Juanita continued. "Alex is very bright. He never had a problem with his grades in school. His marks were always in the 90s, an honor student. He graduated from high school that previous May. He has always wanted to be a doctor."

"Earlier that evening, at the dinner table, he and his father had an argument. His father asked him what he wanted to do about college or university. Alex knew that it was going to cost a lot of money, and he also knew that we didn't have too much, and Pedro was about to lose his job because the ranch was sold, and they couldn't guarantee his position. He told him that he would put a small mortgage on the house that at least would get him one or two years of tuition. He wanted his son to have the best education. Alex got into a huff, and left the table saying he was going to meet his friends. Pedro knew one of the boys that Alex was hanging with, and he also knew that he was never up to anything good. He was in trouble with the police a few times before. So my husband decided to follow him. He was afraid that he might get into trouble."

"Well, getting back to Philip," Juanita continued, "being held up. He was reaching for his billfold, when out of nowhere Pedro runs up and stands in front of him saying, 'No, don't give these punks anything.'

"The guy with the knife yells, 'Get the hell out of the way, old man, or I'll carve you up.'

"Then Alex said, 'Pop, what are you doing here?'

"Again, the guy with the knife, points it within two inches of my husband's face and says, 'If this is your old man, tell him to move on or he will get it.'

"'No,' Pedro yells back, 'give the knife to my son,' pointing to Alex, 'let him kill me. If you're going to be a killer, why not start with your father?'

"At that moment Alex punched the one with the knife, in the face, the knife dropped, and Alex put his foot on it. The third guy ran away, and Alex told the other one to get lost or he'd bust him up again.

"He left, holding his hand on his jaw, and with a mumbled voice he yelled back, 'I'll get you for this and kill your whole family, I know where you live.' Then he used a few curse words.

"Alex put his arms around his father and said, 'I'm sorry, Pop, I don't know why I went along with them. You must be ashamed of me, I'm really sorry.'

"'I will never be ashamed of you my son, I was surprised,' he said as he hugged him back.

"All this was going on and Philip was looking from one to the other, and then said 'I didn't think there was this much excitement in such a small town.'

"Alex apologized to Philip, and Pedro took a deep breath, looked at his son, and then to Philip and said, 'I am sorry too, mister. You have all the right to call the authorities and report what happened here tonight. We will go with you.'

"'No, no,' Philip answered. 'It was very brave of you to step in, and I thank you for it, but it was only money they wanted. It wasn't worth getting killed or injured for.'

"'I hear you, sir,' Pedro replied, 'and you are right, but this is our son, my wife's and my only child, and I would rather be dead than see him go into a life of crime."

"'What is your name?' Philip asked.

"'My name is Pedro Lopez and this is my son Alex," Pedro replied.

"As Philip stretched out his arm to shake hands, he said, "My name is Philip Mariano, you are a fine man Pedro, I can see by the way you stand by your son."

"Then he shook hands with Alex and said, 'You are a fortunate young man, and I accept your apology.'

"'Our home is only a ten minute walk from here,' Pedro said, 'and I have a bottle of the best tequila. Would you join me for a drink?"

"I think we need one," Philip replied. "I would be honored."

"'Thank you, Mr. Mariano, I'm glad you accepted,' Alex said. 'You will meet my mother. She is an exceptional lady.'

"'I am looking forward to it,' Philip replied, 'and Alex, just call me Philip.'

"'Yes," Pedro said, 'my son is right, she is charming. Her name is Juanita.'

"'That's a lovely name.' Philip remarked.

"'Like all Mexican girls, she has other names,' Pedro said, 'but she prefers Juanita.'

"As they got closer to our house, Philip asked Alex, 'Are you still in school Alex?'

"'I graduated from grade twelve last May,' Alex replied.

"'Do you have any plans to continue your education?' Philip asked again.

"Alex hesitated for a few seconds, as he thought about the argument that he and his father had at the dinner table, then he looked at his father and said, 'I would like to go to university, but the closest is in Albuquerque, about a hundred miles away. I'd like to study medicine for research, but that's just another dream.'

"'That dream will come true, my son, you will see,' Pedro said, as he patted him on the shoulder.

"'Your father's right, Alex," Philip said, "if you want it badly enough, it will come true.'

"When they entered our home," Juanita continued, "Alex wrapped his arms around me, and sobbingly, he said, 'I'm sorry Momma, I got into some trouble that almost got Pop hurt, and I put our lives in danger,' then I started crying, walked over to Pedro, wrapped my arms around his waist, looked up into his face and asked, 'Are you all right, my husband?' Then I turned to Alex and said, 'It's okay, my son, we will work it out.'

"Philip was still standing by the door while all this forgiving was going on, and then I asked, 'What has he done? Is this a policeman?'

"'No my love,' Pedro replied, as he set down a bottle of tequila and two small glasses on the table. 'This is the man that

Alex and the two thugs tried to rob.'

"Then I started to sob again and said, 'I'm sorry, sir, won't you sit down?'

"'It's all right, Mrs. Lopez,' Philip said, 'I believe Alex was in the wrong place at the wrong time. I also believe that some things happen for a reason.'

"'He was right, because of what happened that hot evening in July, there have been a thousand rights.'"

"My God," Laura expressed, "what an experience."

"That's not all," Juanita continued, "Philip said, 'You know, you can't stay here, that guy that threatened you will certainly come by, and you never know what he'll do.'

"'I think Alex scared him away,' Pedro replied.

"'No, Pop,' Alex said, 'I think Mr. Mariano…I mean Philip, is right. I know of things that he has done, and he will take revenge.'

"'What can we do?' I asked. Then I looked at Pedro and said, 'You know, you're going to be out of work soon. Maybe we could move further north toward Colorado. You could find work there'

"Then Philip cut in and said, 'Please excuse me, Juanita, what type of work do you do Pedro?'

"Pedro replied, 'I am a skilled horseman. I manage horses at a large ranch, but the ranch has changed ownership, and in less than two weeks, I will be out of work. I am also handy with woodworking and most of the trades.'

"Philip shook his head and laughed, and said, 'How would you feel about living in Indiana?'

"'We looked at each other and replied, 'I don't think we've ever put much thought to it. We've always lived down here.'

"'We get winter up there, stuff we call snow. You don't have to make a decision right now, and this is the truth, but I'm looking for someone who loves horses and is handy with tools.'

"He explained what business he was in, and told us about Millcreek, his horses, and about the work that he wanted done, like fixing up the old mill. Then he talked about Sarah, and when he finished, I knew that I wanted to go.

"Alex said, 'Pop, this sounds great.'

"Pedro could see in my eyes what my decision was.

"'We won't except charity,' he said.

"'It won't be charity,' Philip replied. 'I need someone, you need work. I've known you folks less than an hour, and yet I feel I've known you for years.'

"'Alex,' he continued, 'I have a very good friend. His name is Graham West. He is a doctor at the Valley hospital, chief of staff. I know he would assist you in getting accepted to the University of Chicago, and also work with him at the hospital.'

"'Really?' Alex said with surprise. 'Did you here that, Momma, Pop? What do you think?'

"Pedro always thinks for a few seconds before answering a question, and his answer is always secure, as he did here when he replied, 'I think I should drive Philip back to his hotel.'

"'Pop can't we think about it?' Alex sorrowfully asked.

"'Let me finish,' Pedro said, 'to pick up his belongings and stay with us tonight.'

"Alex then gave his father a huge embrace, and then he kissed me on the cheek, shook hands with Philip, and said, 'Thank you, sir.'

"We all thought that this sounded to good to be true, but Philip assured us that he needed us. He stayed with us for the next three days. We tidied up our affairs. Pedro received a small severance package from the ranch, put the house up for sale and moved to Millcreek. All within four days and we haven't regretted one minute of it.

"The thug with the knife was locked up for auto theft the day after he tried to rob Philip."

"That's beautiful." Laura said, "and about Sarah. What was she like?" she asked.

Juanita leaned back in her chair, and was about to say, "You," but changed her mind and said, "Sarah and I became instant friends. She insisted that I call her 'Sarah' not 'Miss Sarah' which I started to call her."

"You really liked her, didn't you?" Laura asked.

"Yes, I loved her," Juanita replied, "We spent a great deal of time together. We'd shop at the mall, go to an afternoon movie, or just sit and have tea together, like you and I are doing, as she raised her dark eyebrows toward Laura and smiled. When I worked at her house, she worked with me," she continued.

Laura returned a satisfied smile as if to say, "It's because you are so comfortable to be with."

"When I was a young girl, living in Mexico, I had a friend, her name was Maria. She was killed by a drunk driver. God bless her.

"Oh, I'm so sorry," Laura said.

"We were always seen together." Juanita went on. "People used to think we were sisters. When she died, part of me died with her, and how crazy it may sound, I felt that when I met Sarah, my friend Maria came back to me." With tears glistening in her deep brown eyes, she continued, "And when at first, I was acquainted with you I feel part of my other two friends are with me again."

Laura reached over the table and clutched Juanita's hands with hers and said, "Thank you, it's because you are such an honest and loving person that people want to be with you. I feel the same, and I really want it to stay that way."

Juanita smiled and said, "I am glad, we are glad, Pedro and I."

"I still love Philip very much," Laura insisted. "I always have, and I think I always will. I know now that I was wrong about him. I went through a confusing time last summer, anything and everything ticked me off, and I seemed to have taken my frustration out on the people that were the closest to me. It's a wonder that my friend Lucy didn't desert me, and then Philip who meant so much to my little boy. I chased him out of our lives. I hope, one day, if it isn't too late that he will forgive me. Juanita, how could I have been so cruel?" she asked.

"I know him well enough," Juanita said, "that he hasn't held you at fault for anything. You are still in his heart. For your friend Lucy, that is why she is your friend, to see you through your bad times as well as your good."

"You and Pedro are extraordinary. You make someone feel so content," Laura said. "Is there anything that you can't solve?" she asked.

Juanita looked up as if she were thinking of something, and then looked at Laura and replied, "I don't think so." They both broke out laughing.

Gray has asked Nicholas and I, and Ryan and Lucy over to his house for dinner on Saturday night," Laura said.

"That's nice," Juanita replied, "I hope you will go."

"He is a remarkable man. My husband and I are very thankful for what he and Philip have done for our son Alex. They are forever in our prayers."

"I have told him that Nicholas and I are going to fly to Australia to see Philip. Do you think I should?" Laura asked.

"Yes, absolutely," Juanita replied. "You won't be disappointed," as she put her hand on Laura's.

Just then, Pedro came in view, and Juanita waved him over.

He said, "Hello, Laura, it's nice to see you, and it's also nice to see you both so happy," as he gave his wife a peck on the cheek, and then took Laura's hand in both of his.

"The good news is that Laura and Nicholas are going to Australia," Juanita said.

"That is the best news," Pedro answered, as he looked at Juanita. That makes us very happy, doesn't it, my love?"

"So very much," Juanita replied.

"When you return, I want young Nick to help me train Silverdollar," Pedro said.

"He's looking forward to it," Laura replied. "That's all he's been talking about all winter," she continued.

After a few minutes Laura gave them both a hug, and told them that she would call them before they left . She also said to

Juanita, "Thank you for being here for me. These moments with you I will never forget."
    They then parted.

chapter XXXV

SATURDAY, MARCH 9, 1996
VALLEYFIELD, INDIANA

The little sign by the driveway read *The Wests'*. Ryan parked the car in the driveway, got out and opened the back door for Nicholas, as Lucy did for Laura. Gray and Betty have a stunning bungalow on a fabulous mature lot, set against a back drop of large trees, professionally landscaped. As they were walking towards the front door, both Gray and Betty were there to greet them with, "Hi, come on in out of the cold." Laura and Lucy gave them a hug, while Ryan shook Gray's hand and Gray rubbed Nicholas on his head and said, "How's my favorite patient?"

"I'm fine," Nicholas replied, "how's my favorite doctor?" he added.

They laughed, as Betty took their coats and handed them to Gray who hung them in the closet.

"Let's sit in the family room," Betty suggested.

In the corner there was a gas fireplace that gave off a wavering light that offset the hardwood floor partially covered with a beautiful Indian scatter rug.

"What would you ladies like to drink?" Gray asked, as he fixed a Scotch on-the-rocks for Ryan, knowing that was his drink.

"Khalua with a little milk for us ladies," Betty suggested. "Right girls?"

"That's good for me," Laura replied.

"Me too," Lucy added.

"I'll bet Nick wants iced tea," Gray guessed.

"Yes, please," Nicholas replied.

"There's a few bottles in the fridge," Gray said. "Would you like to help yourself Nick?" he asked.

Nicholas agreed.

Lucy and Laura had the same thoughts on their minds. If you could read them they would say, "Philip has very good taste in friends." Gray and Betty are very dedicated to being great people. They're kind, down to earth, and seem to make you feel so comfortable.

After conversing for half an hour, they sat down in the dinning room and had dinner that Lucy and Laura helped Betty serve.

Later on as they were enjoying dessert and tea, Gray announced, "Laura and Nicholas have some news that they would like to share with us."

Lucy looked at her friend as if to say, "I wonder why she kept it from me."

Laura said, "Yes we do, would you like to tell them?" she asked Nicholas.

Nicholas belted out, "We're going to Australia to see Philip."

"Really, that's great," Lucy said as she reached out and touched Laura's hand. "We are so happy for you."

"What a relief," Ryan said.

"You know how happy that makes us feel. Isn't that right Gray?" Betty asked.

Gray said, "Yes, I couldn't be happier."

But there was something in his voice that made Betty say, "What, what is it Gray?"

"Well, you see we don't know exactly where Philip is," he replied.

"What do you mean?" Betty asked. "Is he not at Jim and Sylvia's?"

"No, he hasn't been there for four or five weeks," Gray

answered. "I received a letter from Sylvia a few days ago. I have it here, I'll read it to you." he continued.

Hello Gray,
We hear so many nice things about you and Betty we feel we've known you both forever. I'm writing you now because, well I'm not overly worried, but Philip hasn't been his usual self. He hasn't been eating or sleeping well, but what I'm concerned about is that I don't think he's been taking his medication that you prescribed.

Laura cut in and asked, "What medication? I didn't know of him taking any."
"I'll get to that later," Gray answered, as he continued the letter.

About a month ago, he left saying that, as he put it, he wanted to explorer the "outback". A week before he left he was talking to some truckers at a pub in Coff's Harbour about the Northern Territory Region, and the Kimberly Outback. He wanted to see and experience how the Aboriginal people lived.
There is still a small proportion of the Aboriginal population living in Northern Regions, where it is still possible to pursue a relatively traditional lifestyle. So he flew to Alice Springs. That's about the center of the continent. I heard from one of the truckers who come to our station that he hitched a ride on a mail plane to a place in the Western Region called Hall's Creek. He really couldn't find a more outback than The Kimberly.
The other day I was cleaning the loft, that's a little "flat" that we built and furnished on the upper part of one of our out buildings. Philip found it to be a great spot to concentrate on his novel.
Anyway, I was emptying the wastebasket in a bag when

this wrinkled up letter fell to the floor. I know it was something he would prefer private, and it <u>was</u> in the waste, and believe me I thought twice before sending it to you, hoping that you will understand that my reasons are a matter of concern for our friend.

He must have written it when he was at the beach at Coff's Harbor, and then decided not to send it.

This is the letter…

Gray then looked to Laura and said, "Laura, this note is directed to you. Would you feel more comfortable if I just handed it to you or read it?" he asked.

"Go ahead and read it Gray. I think you all have a right."

"All right, if you wish," he said.

Dear Laura,

I have no idea why I'm writing this note to you, because I have no intention of sending it; but I feel that if it's worth thinking about then it should be on paper. It eases my thoughts.

It's sunset and quiet here by the ocean, except of course for the incessant plaintive calls of the sea birds, who have belonged here for all time, the gulls, lotus birds, and even the little corellas that travel in flocks of thousands.

You can see every star so plainly, hear the splashing of the white caps as they turn themselves under each wave that laps the beach. I feel more at peace with myself now; I've found the ending to my novel. I guess that's what I've been searching for. Although you're thousands of miles away, I feel closer to you now then I have for a long time. I suppose it's because I've come to the realization that the sun has gone down for us, and never to rise. No matter how important it is that we must be apart, when I'm alone from you, the reasons don't matter, but I promised you when Nick was well again that I would leave.

I love you, Laura. I think I always will. The thought of

losing you has taken its toll. Loving you is wishing you every happiness, and I say that with all sincerity, and I pray that the pains that you've endured have now ended. I wish I could say goodnight to you under the evening star, but I can't, your ears have been silenced to my voice. Maybe it's time to say good-bye to yesterday.

Betty and Lucy were holding back tears. Laura had her head in her hands as she cried, "We have to find him. I can't let him go on without telling him I'm sorry."

Gray continued Sylvia's letter.

Whoever she is; she is still a very special person to him. Hope to hear from you soon…
Jim and Sylvia.

Gray turned to Laura and said, "Thanks for sharing this with us," as he handed her the letter.

Nicholas looked at his mother and asked, "Mommy, are we still going to find him?"

Laura wiped her eyes and replied, "Yes, but I'm going to need a lot of help."

"I'll call Jim and Sylvia tomorrow," Gray suggested, then he hesitated and said, "No, I better call tonight. It's already their tomorrow. First, I should call Willy," he continued, "I was talking to him the other day about us both flying down, and he agreed."

"Jim and Sylvia will have everything arranged after you reach Sydney," he commented.

"That's a relief," Laura sighed, "we'd be completely lost as to where to go or how to get there."

"It's a big continent," Ryan said, "and by the sound of it, you two are going to be covering about half of it."

"Are you sure you should go there alone?" Lucy asked with concern.

Before Laura answered, Betty said, "Jim will have an

experienced guide hired to be with you, and they're very skillful and have great knowledge of the country, especially the outback."

Betty stood up and suggested, "Let's go to the family room, it's more comfortable. I'll bring in a fresh pot of tea."

As they got comfortable, Gray handed a small shot of brandy to Ryan, as he had one for himself, sat down, and said, as he looked at Laura and Nicholas, "We couldn't be happier that you two are going to meet with Phil, and I know that he'll be head-over- heels to see you. But there are some things I want to tell you both."

"Other than Betty and Jason, Phil and Willy are the most important people in my life. I'm perhaps closer to Phil," he added, "and this is why I'd like you to know him as I do."

"I don't think that's possible," Betty commented.

Gray smiled and continued, "You see, I can't remember when I didn't know him. There's only two months difference in our ages. Willy fits in there as well. The three of us went through grade school together. We lived just outside of Valleyfield. My father was a pharmacist, Phil's was a miller, and Willy's father was a farmer. Their farm was about half a mile from us."

"Anyway," he continued, "I hope I won't bore you all, but there was this time, the first or second week in March, we were in grade eight. We made plans to play hockey after school one afternoon on Mullet Creek. Phil had a dentist appointment and Willy had chores to do at the farm, so I said that I'd go ahead and shovel the snow off the playing area and meet them around four fifteen."

"I got there at four o'clock. A couple of girls were just leaving; I guess they didn't feel like shoveling. Up on the embankment Vince Tedesco and a couple of his loser friends were throwing snowballs and shouting obscenities at the girls. When the girls were out of sight, they started tossing at me."

"I had my skates on by then and was scraping the snow when suddenly the ice gave way under me and I was in the cold water. At that certain section of the pond the water was about six or seven feet deep. That's where we used to swim in the summer. So here I was splashing around, and every time I'd grab hold of the ice it would break. Never try to swim with skates on. I hollered at Vince and his friends to help me, but they turned and ran up the hill."

"That bastard," Lucy scolded.

"Right," Ryan agreed.

"As they reached the top," Gray continued, "Phil was coming the other way pulling a toboggan with the goal pads on it. Vince hollered, 'You better go save your buddy, he's drowning in the creek,' then I heard them laugh."

"When Phil saw me, he ran down the hill, kicked one of the two-by-ten dasher-boards to loosen it, then he picked it up and jumped in the water right beside me. I grabbed the board with one arm but couldn't lift the other, I didn't have any strength left. Phil pushed us to the edge and then let go of the board and boosted me up on the ice surface, got up himself, rolled me on the toboggan and pulled me to his house. How he managed to do that, I don't know, because I was always a couple of inches taller and twenty pounds heavier than Phil and Willy."

"By the time we reached Phil's house, I was like a block of ice, I couldn't move. I heard Phil call for his dad and within seconds he appeared at the door. Without asking any questions about what happened, he told Phil to run the bath with warm water and then to strip down. He was pulling me in the house and taking off my clothes at the same time. He grabbed a bath towel off the top of the dryer and started rubbing me down. By this time I could feel a little circulation coming back in my body, and could smell the aroma of food spices heating on the stove. Mr. Mariano was preparing spaghetti for Phil and himself. I'm sure you know that Phil's mother passed away when Phil was ten years old."

"Yes, he told me," Laura replied. "How sad."

"He then pulled me into the bathroom, with the help of Phil, who was in a bathrobe with a towel wrapped around his head, felt the water to be sure it wasn't too hot, and then put me in it.

"It wasn't too long after that my strength came back, so I got out and wiped myself dry and put on one of Phil's father's bathrobes. He had thrown our wet clothes in the wash; they stunk of the creek water. Phil mentioned to him that we had fallen through the ice, as if he didn't know, but I couldn't hold it back, I told him what really happened. He looked at his son with a warm smile, and you could see that he didn't have to say, 'I'm proud of you.' You just knew it. Then I said, as I was still wiping my hair with the towel, 'I better phone my parents.' He said, 'It's okay, Gray, I'll call your dad,' and then he dialed our number. My father answered the phone, because I heard him say, 'How are you, Henry?' I whispered to Phil, 'Christ, he's going to be quite upset and worried, which I didn't want.' Phil just shook his hand back and forth and said, 'Don't worry.'

"Mr. Mariano carried on a conversation for a few minutes, and then we heard him say, 'Oh, by the way, we're just about to have dinner, and Gray would like to stay. My father must have asked, 'Are you sure he's not putting you out?' or something like that, and he said, 'No, not at all, he's always welcome. They're just washing up and I'll drive him home right after.'

"From that day on, I had always thought that no matter how great your father is, you would always like one like Phil's. At that moment there was a knock at the door. Mr. Mariano answered it and said, 'Hello Willy, come in.'

"'Hi, Mr. M., I can smell your spaghetti a block away.'

"'Is that what drew you here?' Mr. Mariano asked, jokingly, as they walked into the kitchen.

"'Not really,' Willy replied. He saw us in our pajamas and a grin came over his face. 'I came to see if my two friends were going to play hockey, but I see they're having a pajama party, and what's with the goal pads spread over the hills?'

"That is when I told him what had happened.'

"'Holy shit,' he uttered. 'Are you both okay?'

"'We are now,' I answered, 'but no thanks to Vince and his jerk friends.'

"'That little shit, he gives me the creeps,' Willy remarked.

"Willy had a way with adults that Phil or I didn't. Other than in front of his own father, he got away with swearing any time or anywhere. Phil's dad and mine used to just shake their head and smile, meaning no one is going to change this guy.

"'Willy,' Mr. Mariano asked, 'you're going to have a plate of spaghetti with us, aren't you?'

"'The way you make it Mr. M I'd be nuts to refuse it, but I have to leave right after.'

"'That's okay, Willy,' he replied, 'we're glad to have you.'

"'We didn't know, and he didn't tell us why he had to leave so soon, but we found out the next day at school when Vince showed up with a shiner and when we passed the principal's office, we saw Willy in there, *again*. He looked our way, and with a grin on his face, he winked. I hope I'm not boring you all?" Gray commented.

"No," Nicholas replied, "that was a good story."

They laughed, and Betty said, "You never told me about that."

"Up until now," Gray said, "I didn't think it was necessary, and you know my feelings towards those two guys."

"Yes, you're right, honey," Betty agreed.

"Do you have any more stories, Dr. West?" Nicholas asked.

Gray smiled and replied, "Yes, Nick, but this is an adult story."

"Should I leave the room?" Nicholas asked.

"No, no," Gray replied, "it's okay if you hear it," Gray continued.

"We had graduated from high school; Willy knew exactly what he wanted to do. As sure as I wanted to be a doctor, he wanted to be an electrician. The last couple of years of high school when he wasn't helping his father on the farm, he worked with one of the local electricians here in Valleyfield.

"Phil was interested in business and finance. Through high school he was working at Stefaniacs import/export company. So they both attended the same college in Fort Wayne. They commuted every day, taking turns driving.

"I went the opposite way, to the University of Indiana in Indianapolis. I shared an apartment near the university with a guy from Fort Wayne. So for the first time in possibly seventeen years, we were split.

"A couple of years later Willy finished with some kind of degree, but still had to put in an apprenticeship. Phil had another year to go and then returned full time at the import/export company.

"To make a long story even longer I could go on, but to make it shorter, Willy finished his apprenticeship, moved to California, met and married a beautiful woman, Susan, have a child named Peter, and started his own electrical contracting business that Peter now runs.

"You know what Phil does—bought out Stefaniac and more than tripled the company into one of the largest in the country.

"As for me, my two buddies were well into their business, and doing very well while I was in my third year of medical school. No regrets, we knew it would be a long time coming. My father had died the year before, and it took most of his savings for my schooling and to keep my mother living comfortably. My love, Betty and I were engaged. One day I was having lunch with Phil, and I asked him to give me a job. I told him that I decided to take a year off to make a few bucks to get me through my last year.

"He said, 'Gray you can't lose a year, you're doing great, you're first in your class, I've been checking on you.'

"'What's one year?' I shrugged. 'It'll go by fast.'

"'One year is a year later that you graduate,' he said. 'Why don't you and Betty come over for dinner tonight? I'll call Sarah to put out another couple of hamburgers.'

"I laughed and said, 'Okay, but I still want that job.'

"We showed up around six, and you know what, we really did have hamburgers. After dinner, we were having coffee when Phil very casually said to Sarah, 'Gray wants a job. He wants to come and work with us.'

"'Doing what, Gray?' she asked.

"I replied, 'I don't know, what ever it takes to help get me through my last year. With what I can make and Betty's help, I'll be all right.'

"Sarah looked at me and said, very seriously, 'You and Willy have been Philip's friend all your lives. Nothing or nobody will ever change that, and I know that each of you would do anything for one another, so we want you to accept our help. We are doing very well and can afford to.'

"'Well," Philip said, 'you heard it from the boss.'

"Then I said, 'Come on you guys, that's the reason we're great friends. With money between us you never know what might happen.'

"'No Gray,' Philip stressed, 'that will never happen. You've wanted to be a doctor as long as Willy and I have known you, and we've bragged to our friends and colleagues about you, so don't let us down. If Willy were here, he'd say the same thing.'

"'Are you sure?' I asked seriously.

"'We couldn't be any more sure as we are right now, right honey?' Philip said.

"'Absolutely,' Sarah replied.

"Then I looked at him and asked with a kind of grin, 'Do you and Willy really brag about me?'

"'Don't let it go to your head,' Philip commented.

"'Here's the way we'll do it,' Philip suggested. 'You and Betty figure out what you need, tuition, books, and resident fees, anything you can think of, and don't go cheap on us. Betty will need her car, so you will have one of our company cars to use. Drop by the office in the morning, I'll be there around ten, and we'll arrange everything. Theresa will prepare the paper work in confidence. She likes to be meticulous. When you become the best doctor in the world, that's when you can pay it back,' he added.

"I looked at Betty, who was not only surprised, but overjoyed as I was, and said, 'I'm speechless, what should I say?'

"Betty's words were, 'Well, you could start with thanks and give Sarah a big hug.'

"So, that's how I got my degree," Gray said. "Sure," he added,

"I would have got it without their help, but it would have been at least two years later."

"At least," Betty agreed.

"When the time came that I could pay back the loan, he suggested that we put the money towards a room in the hospital where a child could enjoy his stay more comfortably."

"*The Railroad Room*," Ryan guessed.

"Right," Gray answered. "He also furnished it with all the toys, and we almost have one completed for girls. It will be called *Sarah's Room*."

"I never knew any of that," Laura said. "He never mentioned anything."

"He never will," Gray stated. "His motto is, *You do what has to be done*."

"Laura, there's something else I'd like to say, something that you won't hear from Philip," Gray stressed. "As I sit here in front of you all, and as God as my witness, Phil and Michael were never involved in any drug dealings in any way. What you read in the newspaper about Phil's arrest was wrong. The press went wild. The reporters swarmed his house and office. They hounded his employees. This was big news, and they created a big story. To this day he never uses that paper for advertising. In fact, he doesn't even read it. Three weeks later they wrote a retraction, ten words, on the seventh page that wasn't even noticeable.

"So when you meet him, don't come upon him with these stories on your mind, because they are really my stories and my memories, I only wanted you to know how I feel about my friend. If you still have any doubts, it would be better if you didn't go, because he will see it, but he will also see your love, if it's in your heart."

"Thanks, Gray," Laura said as she hesitated to take a breath, "I know it wasn't easy for you to open up to us about something that is very private between the two of you, but I assure you that I don't have any doubts about him. I was wrong, very wrong. Lucy and Nicholas have been trying to tell me that for months. I know now that I must find him and apologize. Do you think he could forgive me?" she asked.

"He never blamed you for anything," Gray replied.

A few minutes went by, Betty and Lucy brought in some desserts from the kitchen, and then Laura asked, "In Sylvia's letter, she mentioned about some medication that you had prescribed. Is it something you can discuss? Does he have diabetes?"

"No, no," Gray replied, "it's not that serious. You see, a month before he left for Australia, he had an operation. I performed it." Ryan sensed where he was going with this, so he put his arm around Lucy's shoulder and pulled her towards him. "And the reason he's on medication is so he won't get an infection, especially in a foreign country, and furthermore, in the wilderness of a foreign country."

"Why didn't he tell us?" Nicholas asked. "I was looking for him when I woke up from my operation. He was with me when you operated. I would have understood if he had told me."

"You see, Nick," Gray replied as he looked at Laura, "he promised your mommy that he'd stay until you were better, and then he would leave, and I've never known him to go back on his word. Never until then," he added.

"What do you mean, until then?" Laura asked, "and why did he have an operation?"

As Gray put his hand on Nicholas's head, his eyes glossy with tears, his wife Betty and Lucy looking at him with a kind of sorrow on their faces, and Laura anxiously waiting for an answer, he said very slowly, "Nick, Laura, he *was* there when you awoke from your surgery. He was on the third floor recuperating from his surgery. You see, the night before I removed a kidney from him."

As Ryan hugged his wife, who was now in tears, and Betty, who knew nothing about it until now, stood up, looked at her husband with pride, shook her head and said, "I love you," and then kissed him.

Laura was hugging her son, and with tears flowing over her face, she grasped what Gray was telling them, as she said, "My

God, you mean….," and before she could finish, Gray replied, "Yes, Laura, Nick has his kidney."

Nicholas hollered out as he clutched his fist, and shook his arm up and down, "All right."

Laura broke down as she hugged Nicholas again, and Lucy, who came over to console her said, "I'm glad these are tears of joy."

"They are," Laura replied, "but I can't help thinking about what I've done to this man, after what he did for me."

"No, Laura," Lucy replied, "he did it for Nicholas. He left you his heart."

Gray then took Laura's hand and said, "Laura, it's a perfect match. It was like he was carrying it for him. I've done many transplants and never have I seen one to be as perfect as this one. It was like Phil was Nick's twin, whose organs are usually identical."

"I thought the kidney came from an accident victim," Laura inquired. "Didn't you say, when you called us in Seattle that there was a fatality?" she asked.

"Yes, I did, and there was, but the autopsy showed too much damage," Gray replied.

"I guess little Davey was right," Ryan said, "when he said he'd be looking after you."

"That's right, he did didn't he?" Nicholas answered.

"I gave him my word that I would keep this from you," Gray explained, "but sometimes things have to be brought out," he added.

"Who all knew about this?" Lucy asked.

Pedro and Juanita, and their son Alex, who he sent for to assist me with the transplant, no one else knew. I told his kids the other day, Dianna cried some happy tears and Michael said, "That's my dad who would say, 'You do what you have to do.' I love him."

"When did you do the operation?" Ryan asked.

"Friday the thirteenth of October, ten-thirty in the evening."

Gray replied. "We were finished at three Saturday morning."

"But, Gray," Ryan asked, "the age difference, that's okay?"

"Yes, Ryan," Gray replied, "it's not the age of an organ, but the condition it's in. Most people are unaware that there's no firm age limit for organ and tissue donation. It is the health of an organ, not its age, which is one of the determining factors."

As he directed his attention to Laura and Lucy he said, "The day that you two left for Seattle, Wednesday wasn't it?"

Lucy answered, "Yes, Wednesday afternoon."

"Philip spent most of the evening with Nick, and he was in several times on Thursday and all of Thursday night he sat by him. The machine was working overtime. He left Friday morning; I made him go home for some rest. He called me that afternoon, I told him the news about the accident victim that you called me about, whose kidneys were both damaged. Two weeks before, he left me a signed checkbook, telling me that if there were a way I would know. We tested about twenty tissue samples, none matched."

"You mean to say," Ryan inquired. "That there are people that will sell their organs."

"Isn't this the land-of-opportunity?" Gray commented. "There are people that will sell anything."

"Anyway, that Friday evening about five o'clock, we were with Nick, you two were fogged in, remember?"

"Yes," Laura replied. "It was a nightmare."

"Well, I was adjusting the dialysis machine and they were carrying on a conversation, when out of the blue Nick asked him what Heaven was like." Phil was kind of stunned for a few seconds. He didn't want to tell him it was like Disneyland, or he'd want to go right then. So he told him, "If all the beautiful things on earth were put together, it wouldn't be a fraction of how beautiful Heaven is. It's a place where people and animals are always friendly, there's no fighting, only love."

He was really getting carried away on the subject. Then he said, "When you touch the hand of God, like I believe Davey did, then you will know, but I've never been there, I'm only going by what the great leaders of our churches say. Why do you ask?"

Nick said, "The other day Dr. McAllister came in for a visit, and when he left he met Mommy in the hall. I guess he didn't know that he left the door open a little because I heard them talking and he said that I was getting weaker, and he hoped that they'd find a donor soon."

"'Now don't you go worrying,' Phil told him, 'you're going to be okay, and soon, I promise.'

"That's when I left the room, but I was standing by the door talking to a nurse who was about to come in and change his sheets. I heard Phil say that he'd be back in a few minutes that he was going to have a coffee with me.

"As he was coming out the door, I heard Nick said, 'Philip,' Phil turned around and replied, 'Yes buddy.'

"Nick said, 'If I do die, and go to Heaven, I'm going to ask God if He will let you and mommy get back together again.'

"Phil, very quickly rushed over to the bed. I motioned to the nurse not to go in at this moment. We both heard Phil say, as he put both his hands on Nick's shoulders, 'Now you listen to me young man, you're not going to die, you're going to get well, don't talk like that again,' as he pulled him close to him.

"Tears were flowing down Nick's cheeks, he was in hysteria, as he cried, 'I just want someone to look after my mommy, my daddy doesn't want her.'

"By this time Phil's eyes were sparkling as he hugged him again and said, 'Don't you worry, if anything ever happened to you, which it won't, then I would look after your mommy, I promise.'

"Nick looked at him and asked, 'What will you do if she won't let you in the house?'

"'Then I will sit on her doorstep,' Phil replied.

"'What will you eat?' Nick asked.

"'I'll go to McDonalds,' Phil replied.

"'What will you do if it rains or snows?' he asked.

"'I guess I will dress warmly and ask your mommy for an umbrella and a blanket, and maybe she will cuddle up to me like this,' Phil answered as he cuddled him.

"By this time they were both laughing, and Nick said, 'You're funny. I love you Philip.'

"'And I love you too, buddy,' Phil replied. 'Now can I go out and have a sandwich with Gray?' he asked.

"'Long as you come back,' Nick replied.

"We went to the cafeteria, and as we were sitting having a coffee he took a deep breath and very casually said, 'I think I should have a physical.'

"'You just had one six months ago,' I reminded him. 'You're as healthy as a horse. Burning the candle at both ends can be very exhausting,' I added.

"'Maybe that's what's wrong,' he said, 'but I think I'll have one to be sure.'

"Then I asked him if he was having a problem that he hadn't told me about.

"He said, 'I don't know, I'll explain after the physical.'

"'Well, that's a hell of a way to put it,' I replied, "you usually tell your doctor your problem ahead of time, then we go from there.'

"'When can you do it?' he asked.

"'Right now,' I replied. 'We're already in the hospital, and everything is here—testing equipment, lab, everything we need.'

"So he slipped back to Nick's room, and found him asleep, then he returned, and I gave him his medical.

"An hour later I said, 'We're done, you have me puzzled, as far as I can see you're in perfect health, so what's your problem?' I asked.

"'Are all my organs in good shape?' he asked.

"'Yes,' I replied, 'they're like a twenty-two year olds, why?'

"'How about my kidneys?' he asked.

"I said, 'Perfect.' Then I thought for a couple of seconds and said as I shook my head, 'Oh, no. No, Phil you're fifty-two years old.'

"'Yeah,' he replied, 'but my kidneys are only twenty-two, you said so yourself. I want you to do a match with Nick's.'

"'Phil, even if there is a match, this could be harder on you,' I explained.

"'I've had hard times before,' he said, 'I'll survive.'

"So, I said okay, and we started testing. I was glad there was still a technician in the lab. We did blood tests, and the tissue typing, and after an hour I came to him. He was with Nick, who was still asleep. We went to my office, I told him to sit down, he looked at me like I was about to give him some bad news and then he said, 'Well, no good, eh?'

"I sat down and I looked at him, square in the eye. I guess in one way I looked a little disappointed, and yet I was happy and also surprised, so was he when I replied, 'Perfect, a perfect match, I can't believe that it's so close.'

"'No shit,' he said, 'let's do it. I don't know why I didn't think of this before. I guess I just figured I was too old.'

"'Phil,' I said, 'your recovery time won't be as fast as his. The healing will be slower. You may be here for a week to ten days, maybe longer.'

"'That's okay,' he said. 'I'm not going anywhere. Don't try to talk me out of it Gray.'

"I remember when I was in medical school, he lent me money, I told him I didn't know how to thank him, and he said, 'Don't, just be the best doctor in the world and one day I might ask you to do me a favor.' I know now that this was it.

"It was around seven-thirty when Phil said, 'Why don't you go in and tell Nick that you found a donor, but don't tell him who it is. I don't want anyone to know except Pedro and Juanita and their son Alex, who I want you to phone to tell him to catch the next plane out of Chicago to assist you. He'll do anything for you,' he added.

"Then he said he needed two hours to let Pedro and Juanita know, so they could look after his affairs, and for Juanita to bring him in some of her homemade soup, while he was recovering."

Laura said, "Juanita knew all the time, and yet she kept his secret, no matter how much it hurt her."

"At nine forty-five, Phil walked into Nick's room, and before he could say 'hi, buddy' Nick all excitedly said, 'Guess what? Dr. West was here and told me that I was getting a new kidney. One that's really going to work.'

"'I know, buddy,' Phil replied. 'He told me too. That's great, and he's going to operate tonight. Are you going to stay with me during the operation?' he asked.

"'I'll be as close as the doctor will allow me, I promise,' Phil replied.

"'Dr. West is going to call Mommy,' Nicholas said.

"'He was just talking to her when I came in,' Phil told him.

"'I heard two nurses talking about an accident where a little boy was killed, that's really sad,' Nicholas told him. 'Do you think that I will be getting his kidney?' he asked.

"That is sad," Phil replied. "I don't really know."

"As you know, that was earlier in the afternoon, and his kidneys were damaged, but nobody asked and we didn't say."

"By ten-thirty everything was ready. Alex and I were washed up, two anesthesiologists and a staff of nurses were waiting (none of who knew Phil). Nick was wheeled in the operating room. Phil was with him but had to be hurried out when Nick was administered anesthetic."

"Phil, too, who was already in a hospital gown, was put on an operating table close to Nick, as Alex and I did what we do best. Three o'clock Saturday morning the operations were competed, with success. Nick was wheeled to the intensive care unit on the second floor, and Phil to the intensive care on the third floor."

"Is the transplanted kidney always placed in the position where the diseased one was situated?" Ryan asked.

"No, it's transplanted lower in the abdomen. There's a greater chance for it to function satisfactorily, and the ureter will be much shorter, therefore it will be less likely to deteriorate."

"It's amazing what the medical profession is capable of doing," Ryan added.

"That's Dr. Alex Lopez's field. Research."

"I stayed for a couple of hours, and then went home. Alex left with his parents who were at the hospital the entire time, then he left the next morning for Chicago."

"That's it. I met you and Lucy when Nick woke up."

"Yes, I won't forget that day," Laura remembered, "we hadn't any sleep the night before, knowing that Nicholas was being operated on and we couldn't be with him, because of being fogged in a thousand miles away."

"I'm glad we were there when he woke," Lucy said, "along with his father Gord who had just flown in from England that morning."

"Do you recall what Nicholas said when he woke up?" Laura asked.

"Yes," Lucy replied, "he was pretty groggy when he said, 'Hi mommy, hi daddy, hi Lucy,' and then he looked the other way, opened his eyes a little wider and asked, 'Where's Philip?'"

"That's when I told him," Gray explained, "that he had to leave on an emergency. He didn't think you'd wake up so soon."

"Then his eyes started closing," Lucy said, "as he muttered out, 'Thanks Dr. West.'"

"Meanwhile on the third floor," Gray said, "my other patient was waking up. His two guests were Pedro and Juanita, who he asked to visit Nick and fill him in on his condition. Eight days later, in his housecoat, he stood looking out the window, as he saw you and Lucy and an orderly helping Nicholas in your car."

chapter XXXVI

CAMERON'S STATION
THURSDAY, MARCH 14, 1996

Laura and Nicholas were exhausted when Jim and Sylvia met them at the small airport in Armidale, about thirty minutes from their station. Their fourteen-hour flight from Los Angeles, and another hour by commuter, plus the time change had been exhausting.

Jim and Sylvia greeted them with wholehearted friendliness, and drove them to their home. Nicholas hit it off with Jim right away, when he asked him why the people in Australia talked so funny. Jim laughed and told him that he thought people in America talked funny. Then he sat with him and told him some of their sayings that you don't hear in Valleyfield, such as: G'day for hello, mate for friend, ta for thank you, tucker for food, station for ranch.

He also explained to him about the seasons in Australia. He told him when it's spring in America, it's autumn in Australia, when it's summer in America it's winter in Australia, only our winters are never really cold, it's just cool, he explained. Nicholas also learned that water swirls down the sink or toilet the opposite way than it does in America. He thought that was pretty amazing.

Laura didn't have to spend much time with Jim and Sylvia to see why they were great friends with Philip. She found that they were an exceptional couple, who treated her and Nicholas like they've known them for years.

Sylvia also could see why Philip was in love with Laura. She bore such a resemblance to Sarah with her personality and charm, although she never told her so.

The remainder of the day was spent with how and where they would meet up with Philip. Jim and Sylvia had made up the itinerary.

Jim said, "Tomorrow at noon, you and Nick will fly out of Armidale, back to Sydney. Connect with Regional Air at one-thirty that will take you to Alice Springs. As he explained their route, he also showed them by a map exactly where they were going. From Alice Springs at four-thirty you will board an Outback mail plane to Lake Argyle, which is a tourist village. There you will spend the night and the next day, to back-of-beyond."

"Any questions so far?" Sylvia asked.

"Well," Laura uncertainty asked, "When we reach these 'outback' places should we run into any kind of danger?"

"Oh, no," Sylvia answered, "you'll always be around people. There are a few villages in the outback where there's only maybe ten or twelve people. Usually they belong to the same family, but they're safe and mostly friendly."

"How about you, Nick?" Jim asked. "You haven't said anything."

"It sounds like fun," Nicholas replied, "like a camping trip, we get to go a way, way out in the country, but what's back-of-beyond mean?" he asked.

Jim answered, "You said it yourself Nick, it's a long, long, long, way."

They laughed, and Sylvia continued with the itinerary, "The next morning around eight you'll meet with a professional tour guide; her name is Olga. You'll have breakfast with her. She's been informed on the nature of you being here, so it won't exactly be a sightseeing tour. From there, Olga will drive you to Hall's Creek, and be with you at all times."

"That makes me feel a lot safer," Laura stressed.

"You two must be pretty tired," Jim said, "and you both have a long day ahead of you."

"You're right," Laura replied.

"I'm not tired, Mommy," Nicholas said, anxious to hear and see more.

"Jim's right, Nicholas," his mother replied. "We better get some sleep, we have a busy day tomorrow."

"Okay," Nicholas slightly pouted.

"When you all come back," Jim said, "we want you to stay for a while, and then I can show you our big station."

"Oh, good, did you hear that, Mommy?" Nicholas asked.

"Yes, I think we'd like that very much."

"By the way," Sylvia said, "the flights, the lodging, and the tour guide are all looked after. We want you two to focus on finding and reconciling with Philip, plus it's not a good idea to carry a lot of money with you."

"Jim, Sylvia, you are so kind," Laura stressed. "We're paying you for all of this. We are so grateful to you both for being so nice to us."

"When you come back," Jim said, "we will talk about it."

Sylvia showed them to their room, and wished them a good nights sleep.

As she was leaving the room, she said, "Tomorrow morning we'll have breakfast on the veranda."

chapter XXXVII

LAKE ARGYLE, NORTHERN TERRITORY
7:00 p.m.

In the vast middle of nowhere, the sun begins to rest, as she remembered an enjoyable evening at Jim and Sylvia's', and an early morning breakfast of orange juice, waffles, fruit, and tea, with the sound of the breeze wafting through the eucalyptus and pine trees, as brightly colored lorikeets and cockatoos flitted above.

Laura and Nicholas were now two thousand miles away from the lovely couple that were so nice and helpful to them.

After checking into the lodge, having a shower, and changing their clothes, Laura and Nicholas decided to take a walk around the village and have dinner at a lakeside restaurant.

The village was busy with tourists, mostly well to do people from the southern cities who want to get away from the cool weather. The temperature was about eighty-five degrees, fifteen degrees higher than Sydney, and tomorrow it would be higher once they start their trip down to Hall's Creek.

After dinner and back at the lodge Laura was tucking her son into bed while explaining to him not to get his hopes built up too high about finding Philip. She explained that it might be impossible. He could be in an area that even our escort might not be able to find, or maybe he won't want to be found.

"Why wouldn't he want us to find him, and why wouldn't he

want to come home with us, Mommy?" Nicholas asked.

"I don't know honey," Laura replied, "but I do know that I hurt him and sent him away for no reason. I failed to believe him, and I know now that I have to tell him that I'm sorry even if he won't come back . Now lets get some sleep."

The next morning about eight o'clock, Laura and Nicholas were in the lobby of the lodge with their luggage. There were a few tourists milling about, waiting for a tour bus to take them to some attractions in the outback.

Coming through the door was a full-figured lady about forty-five years old, with khaki knee-length shorts, blue blouse, white socks, hiking boots, and a bush-trader hat. She just *had* to be their guide. She was pleasant looking, but seemed to know how to look after a situation if one should arise.

Laura watched her approach the front desk and then saw the clerk point towards where they were sitting. When she came over, she introduced herself by saying, "Good morning, I'm Olga, and you must be Mrs. Manning, and I'll bet this is Nicholas, right."

Laura looked at her smile and knew right away that she and Nicholas were going to be very comfortable with her.

"Yes," Laura answered, "but you can call me Laura."

They shook hands and Olga said, "I was talking to Mrs. Cameron by phone the other day, and she filled me in on what you're here for."

"That's right," Laura replied, "we're here to find our friend, his name is Philip Mariano. We believe he's most likely at an Aboriginal village or camp somewhere near Hall's Creek."

"That's what Mrs. Cameron told me," Olga agreed, "and that could be possible. Why don't we have a nice breakfast, and then we will leave before it gets too hot. I hope you both have hats," she continued.

"Yes, we do," Laura replied.

They left the lodge for a restaurant down the street. Olga suggested placing their luggage in her truck.

Nicholas said, "Hey, that's neat," as he jumped on the running board of this rugged looking vehicle.

Olga laughed and said, "Nicholas this is called an *Oka*. It's a Japanese word meaning 'hill,' and that's what we will be crossing a lot of. It's going to be a winding hilly route, so we need a four-wheel drive vehicle. We will also be crossing numerous creeks with water reaching the floorboards, but don't worry," she continued, "with this rig we can travel through four feet of water without a problem. We also have a two-way *flying-doctor* emergency radio."

"Wow," Nicholas said, "it has everything."

As they settled in the restaurant, and after ordering their food, Laura turned to Olga and said, "Olga, when I mentioned that our friend could be at a village or camp near Hall's Creek you seemed to be a little skeptical about it. Is there a logical reason why he wouldn't be there?" She asked.

"Well, by all means," Olga replied, "we will cover the villages surrounding Hall's Creek, but I understood that he wanted to experience Aboriginal life in the Outback, and Hall's Creek is on two main highways, so most of the natives surrounding that town live very modern lives."

"That makes sense, should we bypass it?" Laura suggested.

"Oh, no," Olga replied, "we'll spend today and a few hours tomorrow looking and seeking out any information we can."

The Oka was filled with fuel plus a couple of extra cans, two containers of water, and an "esky" (cooler) full of food and cold drinks.

They were on their way.

The trip would take them an hour and a half to two hours along the Great Northern Highway.

Nicholas was full of questions. He wanted to know about wild life, if they would see any kangaroos, and where kids went to school if they lived in the Outback. Olga had all the answers. She's had the experience of big city life, traveling all over the world as a tour guide for one of Australia's largest tour companies, and also working in the Outback, which she now prefers. They stopped periodically to use the *dunny* (outside lavatory), and to have a snack.

At twelve thirty they reached Hall's Creek, which is situated on the corner of the Great Northern and the Buchanan highways. It's often referred to as the "Oasis of Kimberly" and it sits on the edge of the Great Sandy Desert.

Back in 1885 there were rumors of a gold find at the Elvire River, and by the end of the year there were twenty-five hundred miners living in sheds and calico tents around old Hall's Creek making it Western Australia's first gold mining town.

The balance of the afternoon was spent visiting merchants and pubs, to see if anyone had seen or heard of Philip. No one had. That evening was spent at a motel and the next morning with their food and water packed in the Oka, they left to visit a few local villages.

Some of the camps were house trailers, and others were stone and stucco huts, but nobody had seen or heard of Philip Mariano. After covering over a hundred miles, and visiting five camp sites, they returned to their motel and had dinner.

As they were going over their itinerary Olga said, "The camps that we visited so far are too modern. As I mentioned before, if Philip was interested in experiencing first hand about Aboriginal life as it was years ago, then he would likely be in the East Kimberly, a region called *The Bungle Bungles*."

Laura looked at Nicholas, who was laughing about the word Bungle Bungles, then turned to Olga with a smile and asked, "Where is that?"

"It's east of the base of Lake Argyle," Olga replied, as she showed them on the map.

"We were there," Nicholas pointed out.

"No, we were at the top of Lake Argyle, at the tourist village," his mother said.

Olga continued, "We'll leave first thing in the morning, take the Buchanan highway to the Duncan highway north and in less then two hours we'll be there—Lake Argyle that is. There's a small resort, so we can have lunch, and if it isn't too hot we'll head for the Bungle Bungles."

"Is there anything there?" Nicholas asked.

"It's actually called the Purnululu National Park," Olga replied. "There are a few attractions, like gorges and chasms, and the famous beehive formations."

The trip north on the Duncan highway was quite interesting, especially for Nicholas who saw his share of kangaroos, wallabies, and wombats, as he sat on the elevated aircraft-like seats in the part truck, part bus Oka.

When they reached the lake, they rented one of the string of cabins that were bordering the shore, changed into their cozzies (bathing suits), and went for a fresh water dip in the lake, more or less to wash off the red dust that had caked their bodies from the open-air ride in the heat.

After a quick lunch, and refilling their water containers, they then left for the one hour trip across a rugged, desolate road to the Bungle Bungles. There wasn't much to write home about. A large cottage type building that was the general store, a small bar, a couple of tables with chairs, a washroom and living quarters for the owner. I guess a roadhouse pub would identify it. There were five small cabins, two on one side and three on the other side of the general store.

An older Aboriginal man was making quick sweeping motions across the floor with a long handled corn-broom, while a younger woman, possibly in her forties and in all probability the old man's daughter, was stocking a shelf with tobacco products. The camp is solar-powered with electric lights, and a hot shower, but its main purpose is supplying the nearby native communities with supplies. Olga introduced herself and asked to speak to the manager.

Pointing to the older man, the woman said, "The manager is my father, but I will speak for him. What would you like to know?" she asked.

"We'd like to rent two of your cabins," Olga said, "probably on a daily basis, because we don't know how long we are staying. We're looking for a friend of these two people. He is an American and we think he is in these parts, somewhere, possibly living with some Aboriginal people."

The woman looked Laura's attractive body up and down, and then to Nicholas, who was holding his mother's hand, and said, "Ain't nothin' here mate, 'sept a lot of roos and empty space. Some of our people come here for supplies, maybe three or four times a week, mostly for fresh water that we have trucked in."

"Where are the nearest camps?" Olga asked.

"There are four established communities ten to fifteen miles from here, mostly to the north and east," the woman replied. "Your mate could be at any one of them. I don't know why, the temperature rises to 115°, and rain is nonexistent. No place for a white man."

As they were speaking, another lady came in, who had been cleaning the cabins after a group of Asian nature-watchers had left the previous night. Before they were settled in their cabins, they asked directions to a couple of communities that they would visit the next day.

chapter XXXVIII

WEDNESDAY MARCH 20, 1996
BUNGLE BUNGLES 3:30 p.m.

The air was so calm you could hear the termites building their tombstones; the sky was a solid blue. The beehive domes were as unbelievable as the boomerang that won't come back.

Laura and Olga were having a glass of lemonade in Laura's cabin while going over the last three days of searching and inquiring about the whereabouts of Philip. Nicholas was on the porch playing with his game-boy, and swatting at the flies that were roosting on his sandwich, when surprisingly he saw a large truck pull up to the general store. He got up from the chair, while still playing his game, opened the door of the cabin and said, "Mommy, there's a big truck at the general store."

"That's okay Nicholas," his mother replied. "He's most probably delivering goods."

A few minutes later Olga suggested, "Maybe it would be a good idea for us to go over to the store and ask the driver if he has seen or heard of anyone fitting Philip's description."

Sitting, and slouching over the small bar, with cigarette smoke swirling around his bushman's hat and guzzling down his fourth can of *bitters*, he turned on his stool when Laura, Olga and Nicholas entered the room.

His garb was typical for a trucker in the Australian desert;

tight shorts, and an open-to-the-naval blue denim shirt, and leatherwork boots.

"Well, well, what have we here?" as he focused his bloodshot eyes on the two women.

"You may be able to help us," Olga suggested. "We are looking for a friend, and since you cover a great part of the territory, you might have come across him." Then she described Philip to him.

His eyes were still undressing Laura as he said, "No ma'am, I've seen no one who looks like that, and a white man would surely stand out in these parts, but if you two ladies wish to have a couple of coldies with me, I'm sure we could become mates."

"Ta, we'll pass," Olga replied.

They turned and walked towards the door, then suddenly stopped when they heard him growl out, "If he doesn't want to be found, you won't find him. These people won't talk, (referring to the Aborigines) but you may come across him at the Corroboree tonight."

"Is it at the park?" Olga asked, as she and Laura faced him again.

"Yes, Purnululu," he replied, "you'll see the fire."

"Well, ta again mate, have a g'day," Olga said.

"No worries," he said back.

As they were leaving Laura asked, "What is a corroboree?"

"It's a ceremony that the natives celebrate to commemorate their ancestors, and to reflect the *Dreamtime*," Olga replied. "It's being held at the Purnululu Park that we came through to get here."

"Are we allowed to go?" Nicholas asked.

"Yes, but we can't join in, not that we'd want to. We just watch." Olga replied.

"Good," Nicholas said. "Maybe Philip will be there."

"That's what we're hoping," his mother wished.

At three in the afternoon, they drove back to Lake Argyle where there were hot showers to freshen up, and a nice roadside restaurant by the Duncan highway.

There was plenty of time before the festivities of songs and symbolic dances, and it was only a forty-minute drive from the restaurant, so they enjoyed a full dinner, which wasn't available for them at the Bungle Bungles.

It wouldn't be dark for about three hours, but Olga suggested that they should be at the park while it was still daylight so they could park their vehicle in an area where they could see any other vehicles that would enter.

"If Philip was at a nearby native community, he would have a four-wheel drive vehicle, wouldn't he?" Laura asked.

"I would imagine so," Olga stated. "He had to get here some how."

"Do you think maybe he rented one from Hall's Creek, or Lake Argyle?" Laura inquired.

"That crossed my mind too," Olga replied, "so that's the first thing I checked at Lake Argyle and again at Hall's Creek."

They finished dinner, topped the fuel tank in the Oka and left for Purnululu National Park. On the way Nicholas asked, "Are there going to be places to play games and buy things at the park?"

"Oh no, Nicholas," Olga replied. "This is a ceremony for these natives to remember their ancestors. They have a large fire, and they have a tribal dance."

They reached the park shortly after seven. There was still about an hour of daylight left. Olga parked the Oka just off the road beside a huge boab tree that was blossomed with a flock of little corellas.

There were a dozen or so natives gathering and piling wood for the enormous fire, which would be a large part of the ceremony. Looking in the direction of the fire pit, they could see the Aboriginal people approaching by the tens and twenties. They were advancing from the bush in every direction. Three jeeps went by with small families in them, and it was still light enough to see that there wasn't a white person among them.

Two Okas loaded with tourists parked across from Olga's vehicle, and the people all got out with their cameras and folding chairs and moved a little closer to the action.

There's only a small portion of the Aboriginal population that live in the continent's northern regions, and it is still possible for them to pursue a relatively traditional lifestyle. So, it is a rare treat to have the opportunity to be here at a corroboree.

Perhaps this is why Philip decided to spend time with Aborigines; to learn of their *bush-tucker* (food), how they gather it, and use traditional medicines.

The setting sun lights the orange and black western wall with constantly changing colors while the fire was being lit. The natives were gathering with their bows and arrows, boomerangs, spears and clubs for their dance of the timeless spirits. Laura and Olga kept one eye on the road hoping to see a familiar face, while Nicholas was watching the fire grow into an inferno.

The natives were now well into their dance routine, conjuring an image as old as their ancestors, and donning a mask of mud. One man was sitting down, blowing on the didgeridoo to accompany the songs and dances of a 40,000 year old tradition, while six or seven men would depict their ancestors by waving their weapons in the air, and doing their tribal dance around the fire.

The corroboree lasted two hours. There was no sign of Philip. Discouraged, they returned to the camp at the Bungle Bungles, east of the National Park. It was a long tiring day for the three of them. Nicholas plunked himself on his cot. Laura and Olga sat at the table and were going over the map, and where they had gone during the past three days, covering a twenty-mile radius of the camp.

Laura, with her eyes on the map, and her elbow on the table, resting her head in her hand, asked, "What do we do now?"

Olga, looked sadly at Nicholas, and then to Laura and replied, "We've covered every little community within twenty miles of here. We've asked just about everyone we've run into, and no one has seen or heard of your friend Philip. I hate to say this, but he could have changed his mind about coming to this area. He could be a thousand miles away."

"What do you suggest we do?" Laura asked.

Olga looked over at Nicholas again, and knew how much he wanted to find him, so it was difficult for her to say, "I think it's best that we leave, go back home. We could be wandering around here for weeks and still not find him."

Nicholas spoke up and said, "No, we can't go, I know we will find him."

Laura went over to him, hugged him and said, "Honey, Olga's right, she knows this country and we could be looking for weeks and still not find him."

"We can stay at Jim and Sylvia's. They've invited us to, and he will surely contact them sooner or later. Maybe he already has," she continued.

Olga, however, knew that he hadn't. Twice a day she radioed her base to see if there were any messages.

Nicholas buried his head in his pillow, sobbing, and mumbling, "I know we will find him, I just know it."

They decided to try and get some sleep and leave in the morning.

chapter XXXIX

THURSDAY MARCH 21, 1996
BUNGLE BUNGLES 2:00 a.m.

There wasn't the slightest breeze; there was stillness in the air. Every star in the universe was visible, and they all seemed to be twinkling.

The old man was on the verandah, rocking back and forth in his squeaky rocking chair, enjoying a stogy.

Once in a while you could here the bark of a dingo.

Then he grumbled, "Where you go boy?"

That was the first time that Nicholas heard the old man speak English, as he was startled to see him.

"To the dunny," was Nicholas's reply.

"Ugh," the old man growled.

Nicholas carried on into the store and used the washroom, which wasn't why he was out of his cabin.

On his way out, he sauntered into the kitchen, saw a flashlight and put it in his bag, and then he noticed the knife rack on the counter, so he reached up and took one of the biggest butcher knives and slipped that in his knapsack as well.

After leaving the store he let the old man see him go directly to his cabin, but he slipped along the side and headed for the trail that led through the bush, not realizing the dangers that awaited him.

Laura awakened from what she thought was a light sleep.

She glanced at her watch that was on the end table. It was six thirty in the morning. The sun was still hidden behind the hills to the east so the room had very little light. She reached out her hand to wake up Nicholas, who slept on the cot beside hers, but found that he wasn't in it. She immediately got out of bed, threw on her robe, and rushed out of the cabin calling his name.

At that moment Olga was coming from her cabin and asked, "What's the matter?"

"Nicholas isn't in his bed," she cried out in alarm, and then started to call his name again.

"He's probably in the store," Olga suggested.

"Would you mind taking a look, while I get dressed?" Laura asked.

"Not at all," Olga replied.

She entered the store to the sounds of pots and pans that were being set out by the cook to prepare breakfast for a few sightseeing tourists who were waiting for their tour bus to take them to Lake Argyle to catch a mail plain back to Alice Springs.

Olga didn't see Nicholas in the store or in the washroom. She called out his name as Laura came through the door. She went immediately to the cook and asked if she had seen her little boy. She said she hadn't seen him since last night.

Laura hurried out onto the veranda and called his name several times with no reply.

Olga searched all around the cabins, also calling his name, then she saw the proprietor, the old man's daughter, so she asked, "Have you seen Nicholas. He seems to be missing?"

"No I haven't," she answered, "and I've been up for two hours, but I will ask my father."

Her father was sitting at the bar having some breakfast. He always has priority, even over the tourists. Although he does very little, he is the original owner; it's their custom.

She talked to him in their native tongue, commonly called *Pama-nyungan* which takes its name from man in two languages. He was answering her with his hand pointing one way and then the other.

She then came out to the veranda where Laura and Olga were patiently waiting and said, "My father saw him many hours ago, about two o'clock and said that he used the washroom, and then went back to the cabin, but he said he didn't see him go in the cabin."

By this time, and what they heard from the proprietor, the two women were very much alarmed. Olga went directly to her vehicle and called her office which is run out of the home of the owner. She was told that he was the only person in. All the five tour buses were on tour, but he would call the authorities to have a search plane cover the territory, and also send out a search party. That of course wouldn't be there for an hour.

Olga relayed the message to Laura, who by this time was very upset. She said, "Nicholas was quite disturbed that we decided to leave this morning."

"Yes, he was," Olga replied.

"Maybe he was kidnapped," Laura suggested.

Olga put her mind at ease by saying, "There are, without doubt, very few dishonest natives. I've never run into any, but I'm sure that they wouldn't run off with a child, especially a little white boy."

She continued, "Let's go to your cabin to see if there's anything that we can go by, any clues."

As they entered, Laura noticed that the clothes he had on the day before were not there, and his knapsack was also missing.

Olga noticed a note on his pillow that Laura failed to see earlier because of her rushing out to find him. She handed it to Laura.

The note read:

Mommy, please don't be mad at me, or worry. I know you wanted to leave in the morning, and I also know that I don't want to leave without finding Philip. He means too much to us now, and if I have to look forever I will find him, even if it's to tell him that I love him.

I can feel that he is close by. One of the natives told us yesterday that he could be at a village over the big red hill. I'm not afraid Mommy because I think that God told Davey to watch over me.

I love you, Nicholas.

As tears were clouding in her eyes, Laura said, "We have to get some people to help us find him. How about the tourists, would they help us?" she asked.

Olga tried to console her and answered, "Laura, the tourists don't know their way in these parts. The authorities should be here in about half an hour."

"How about the people that live here, couldn't they help?" Laura asked in a panic.

"There's only the old man and two women. They wouldn't be much help." Olga replied.

They entered the office that was in the store. There was a short heavyset woman sitting at a desk. She was from Hall's Creek, and came out once a week to take orders for goods that her company would supply to the camp. This day she arrived early. Olga had met her before, so she introduced Laura to her and told her about Nicholas running off.

She introduced herself as Mrs. Palmer and said, "To be honest with you there isn't too much we can do. I have a jeep that you're welcome to use, but as Olga knows there are four or five trails leading to the big red hill. Some are safe and some dangerous, and who knows, we may get stranded. It's best to wait for the rangers."

Laura was sobbing and wringing with her hands, while Mrs. Palmer and Olga were trying to ease her mind by telling her that he'd be found safe. But their thoughts of a little boy being lost in this large wilderness were something that they wouldn't discuss with Laura.

Australia has ten of the most poisonous snakes in the world.

Then there are the dingoes that hunt singly or as a family group, that will follow a prey, especially if it's wounded or alone, until it drops; and if you're near a swamp, there are crocodiles.

None of these were mentioned to Laura, but the dangers were in her mind. Olga told her that there are always hunters in the bush, and if they came across a child they would definitely bring them in.

Meanwhile, out in the bush, Nicholas was definitely lost. Nobody knew where he was or even if he was alive. For the first hour or so he headed straight for the red hill, on and off trails. He had almost run into a swamp infested with crocodiles. He ran across grassy sections where snakes were on the hunt for small rodents. At this time he was very tired and scared. He was whimpering for Davey to help him.

You could see their eyes sparkling in the night, as a family of dingoes was lingering in the bushes. They were closing in, waiting for him to drop from exhaustion. He was almost completely used up. It was terrifying, as he was now running for his life, wielding the flashlight in one hand and the large butcher knife in the other. The barking noises of the dingoes that were keeping pace with him on each side were now getting louder.

While running as fast as he could he turned his head to see if they were getting closer, and without warning he tripped as he tried to jump over a decomposed River Red gum tree lying on the ground that threw him ten feet ahead.

The flashlight went hurling through the air and smashed against a tree, and the knife flew the other way.

Nicholas's head hit another tree trunk just before he rolled into a large net that was set by a hunter to catch wild boar. The net was sprung up about eight feet off the ground with Nicholas dangling unconscious inside it.

The victorious howling dingoes were now jumping up, trying to snatch the prey that they had conquered, when amazingly, out of nowhere he appeared at the edge of the clearing.

The animals knew him, and were afraid. His eyes could

hypnotize them. People rarely saw him. Rumors spread that he was a myth. He kept himself in the bush and was only seen by the Aboriginal people, and only at night.

The dingoes started to scatter, except for one who hadn't seen him. It reached the net and was pulling on it until it was almost on the ground, and then the lone dingo made a leap for Nicholas, and at that moment the hunter became the hunted as the dingo met it's doom. The hunter grabbed the animal with his bare hand and tossed him at a force so hard that he had broken his neck, and the other dingoes fed upon it.

The hunter then picked up Nicholas from the net, checked for vital signs on his scratched and bruised little body, cradled him in his long strong arms, and then started in a fast pace, the ten miles towards the camp where he knew a white man was staying.

chapter XL

YIRRKALA VILLAGE
MARCH 21, 1996 7:00 a.m.

*M*ost Aboriginal societies have several common characteristics. They are basically egalitarian. No one in the group had notably higher standing than anyone else. Although, those with the most knowledge, most of the time the elders, obtained respect and were in command of many decisions.

When the old lady (who had to be in her nineties) was humming and mumbling about *Juwal, Juwal* (which means giant) coming to their camp, those that were awake were concerned.

They heard stories, and told stories to their children around a campfire about Juwal. He was supposed to be well over seven feet tall, and lived in the bush. Very seldom was he ever seen. Everyone, including animals, were afraid of him, but nobody knew why. It was never known that he harmed anyone, or that he never stole from the camps. He was a lone hunter.

The frantic old lady, at about 5:30 a.m awakened Frank Butler, who slept in the lodge. She was sitting on a chair by the window beside a small table, a place where she very seldom moved from. He approached her to see what she was screaming about.

Frank is not your average Aborigine. He is well educated. You see, Frank's parents had lived and worked for the Butler Station, a seven thousand acre station. His mother died when he was eight years old, so he was raised and educated by Fred and Henny Butler, who also had a son the same age as Frank. It was their decision to give Frank their last name.

Frank is fifty-five years old and has worked for the Department of Aboriginal Affairs since it was established in 1973. He is the agent for all the Northern Territory. His job consists of dealing with the Aboriginal housing, education, health and legal administration reform. He is credited for forming an "Aboriginal Rights Group" who brought to the attention of the government, excessive and unfair removal of Aboriginal children from their families, which resulted in the states and territories of Australia to revise their child welfare laws.

But Frank never forgot where he came from. His parents, before they worked for the Butler Station, and grandparents belonged to the Yirrkala group. Each year he would faithfully spend the better part of three weeks at the Yirrkala Village to keep the memories of the old ways.

This is where Philip came in....

About the third week of February, while on a flight to Alice Springs, Philip was seated next to an Aborigine man, so he decided to strike up a conversation with him, more or less to pick his brain about Aboriginal life in the Outback. As they introduced themselves, Philip could tell by his fluent English that this man was well educated. As the conversation continued, Philip found out that Frank could speak many Aboriginal languages and several dialects.

This, of course, was exactly what Philip was searching for. When they landed at Alice Springs, the two men hitched a ride on the mail plane to Hall's Creek, where they picked up supplies and a four-by-four and headed for Yirrkala Village, which is twenty miles southeast of the Bungle Bungles, the one and only camp that Olga and Laura missed.

The old lady, who they called "JoJa," which means grandmother, told Frank that Juwal was heading for their camp, seeking the white man, and then she laughed in a real cackling manner that showed what teeth she had were rotten.

How this old woman could tell, know one knew. They only knew that she could predict events before they happened. Some called her "Maparn" (which means witch) because of her foreknowledge, but they respected that knowledge, and also because she is an elder.

Frank looked at her, not knowing whether to believe her or not, but he wasn't taking any chances so he hurried over to Philip's tent, which he purchased at Hall's Creek.

As he entered, Philip instantly woke up with a jolt and asked, "What's up Frank, what's all the confusion?"

"JoJa is in a dither about Juwal on his way here in search of you," Frank replied.

"Hey, hold on Frank," Philip said, "I just woke up. You're going a little fast for me. First of all, who in hell is Juwal, and whoever he is, why is he looking for me?"

"He is a hunter," Frank replied. "I have never seen him, but he drops by the camps periodically to trade. They say he's over seven feet tall and wanders all over the Northern Territory, living only in the bush."

While Frank was talking, Philip was getting dressed, and then they left for the lodge. JoJa or Ngawuji, which means the same, was swaying back and forth on her chair, while her hands were moving up and down on each side of a short stout candle that was burning on the table before her. As she swayed, and with the movement of her hands, she was also muttering the same thing over and over.

Frank approached her and asked in their language when Juwal would arrive. Without losing her momentum, and with her eyes still focused on the candle, she pointed to the window before her.

Both Philip and Frank looked out. It was still very dark, but there was a full moon that lit up the opening towards the bush. Breaking out of the trail they could see an image advancing towards them at a fast jog.

The old woman started her cackling laugh again, as if to say,

"I told you so." As it drew near, they noticed a very tall, thin man cradling something in his arms. He was about a hundred feet from the lodge when suddenly he stopped, as if he was asking permission to come closer.

Frank said with a whisper, "That's Juwal."

They looked at each other and then Frank stepped out on the porch, with Philip right behind him. Frank loudly told him, in an Aboriginal dialect, that he was welcome to enter their camp. He must have understood what Frank said because he slowly came forward and stood by the porch.

For a few moments, both Philip and Frank stood on the porch looking at this tall figure before them. He was very dark, even for an Aborigine. He had a tight beard. His head was lowered, but you could see his eyes. They were like you've never seen, shining and sparkling, like two of the brightest stars. They seemed to soften an unpleasant fear. His pants were frayed and only came to between his knees and ankles and were tied around his thin waist with a piece of rope. A long shawl was worn over his shoulders, partially camouflaging his bow and quiver that contained his arrows.

At this moment, without moving his body, he lifted his arms even with his shoulders and took a step towards Philip and said, "Parri."

Philip didn't understand what he said, but he noticed that he was cradling a child in his arms.

Frank said, "Parri means boy."

The boy's hair and sweater were covering his face, his right arm was dangling by his side. He seemed lifeless.

Philip took him from the giant, and before he carried him in the lodge the tall man stretched out his arm and touched the child on his bruised head and lowered his own head and said something under his breath.

Philip laid the child on a cot and asked Frank to light another lantern. Frank brought two lit lanterns over to where Philip was, and then he told one of the four inquisitive people, who were staring out the window at the giant, to bring over some hot water.

Philip removed what was left of the unconscious boy's sweater, and brushed his hair from his face and said, as he was startled to see this familiar face before him, "My God, it's Nick."

He looked as if he was in some kind of accident. There were scratches and abrasions on his face, arms, and chest. The sweater Philip removed was torn to threads, and his pants were filthy with debris from the bush, and he was missing one shoe.

The next thing that went through Philip's mind was how devastated Laura must be right now. He must get word to her as soon as possible that her child is safe, but where is she? Did something outrageous happen to her? He had to know, and fast. He asked Frank to see what he could find out from Juwal.

The tall man was still standing, facing the door of the lodge, seemingly concerned about the boy. He set the large knife that Nicholas had taken from the kitchen, Nicholas' knapsack, and a shoe on the porch. He also placed a boy's cap on the railing, as he stared at it for a few seconds as if he recognized it.

Frank came out with a pitcher of cool water and a plate of fruit. He introduced himself, and asked Juwal if he wished to sit and have some tucker (food).

With his eyes staring at the treat and knowing that he was slightly exhausted from running over fifteen miles, the giant sat on the porch with his long legs stretched over the four steps and his feet resting on the ground.

First, he took the pitcher of water and guzzled it, with two swallows, and handed the empty pitcher back to Frank. Then he wolfed down four or five rings of pineapple and two oranges.

Frank then asked him his name, and where and how he found the boy. With the mumbling, the indistinct language and hand motions, Frank could put together that the big man's name is Kuminja, and he found Nicholas in one of his wild-boar nets, with howling dingos jumping up at him. He also found a large knife on the ground beneath the net.

He said that when he approached his trap, one of the dingoes had pulled part of the net to the ground and was about to attack the boy, so he broke it's neck and threw it into the bushes where the others fed on it. He then lowered the rest of the net completely to the ground and found the boy unconscious. He also told Frank that he knew there was a white man at this camp, and that's why he brought him here.

Meanwhile, Philip was bathing Nicholas's face and body and dressing his wounds, and at the same time wondering how he got here.

A few minutes later Nicholas was awakening with his arms swinging and hollering, "Davey help me, Davey help me."

Philip took a cool wet cloth and applied it to Nicholas's forehead and said, "It's okay buddy, you're safe now. Nothing is going to hurt you."

Then Nicholas's eyes opened, as he blinked for a few seconds. He thought he recognized the voice, but he had trouble focusing on the image before him.

Tears rolled down his cheeks as he whispered, "Philip, is it you, is it really you, have I found you?"

"Yes, Nick," Philip replied, "you've found me. Do you hurt anywhere?"

"Not anymore, I'm okay now," Nicholas answered with a smile.

At that time Frank came in and relayed Kuminja's story to Philip, and then said, "We better see if he can walk."

They helped Nicholas off the table. He took a few steps and then he returned and wrapped his arms around Philip's waist and said, "I knew I would find you, I knew you were close, I could feel it. You saved my life, you gave me your kidney."

"Ah," Philip replied, "I had an extra one I wasn't using."

Frank looked at his new friend, and knew that he was a generous man because of the donation he made by having a small school built at the village of his people, but donating one of his organs to a child in need made him a very special man in Frank's eyes.

"Where is your mother?" Philip asked with concern.

"Mommy and our escort are at the Bungle Bungles," Nicholas answered. "We've been there for four days searching for you. We were going to leave this morning, that's why I ran away."

"Mommy and me made up our minds weeks ago to come here and find you. Mommy wants to tell you that she's sorry for not trusting you. Just before we left we had dinner at Dr. West's house, that's when he told us about you donating your kidney. He was really worried about you, something about you not taking your medication so he and your friend Willy were going to come here until he found out that Mommy and me were coming."

"Well, we better get you back to your mother. She must be quite worried, but first there's a very tall man outside that found you in the bush and carried you fifteen miles to safety. I think he would want to know if you're all right."

Nicholas hurried outside to see this man who rescued him. Kuminja was now standing on the ground by the steps, with his head still lowered, when Nicholas came out the door. Without raising his head, his starlike eyes seemed to give off a feeling of contentment.

Nicholas said, "Holy cow!" as he admired the tallness of the man. He walked down the steps and approached him, looked up at his eyes and said, "Thank you for finding me."

Kuminja stretched out his long arm and touched Nicholas on the head and you could see that there wasn't an expression on his face, but his eyes were smiling.

By this time Frank brought up the four-by-four Jeep and parked it by the entrance and got out. Philip asked Frank to come along with them, and had him ask Kuminja to come as well. Surprisingly, he agreed.

Philip drove, Frank sat in the front passenger seat, Nicholas sat in a single seat behind Frank, and Kuminja sat at the back with his legs dangling over the tailgate. The trip back to the Bungle Bungles would take them about forty minutes to travel the twenty miles in and out of the bush, and over some rough terrain before they reached the dirt road that would take them to the small lodge.

Olga and Mrs. Palmer were doing their best to console Laura, who was pacing in and out of the building, anxiously waiting for help to arrive to search for her little boy. While Mrs. Palmer was refilling her cup with hot tea, a small bus pulled up and loaded the sightseers, and in a few moments they left for Lake Argyle.

They were no sooner out of sight, when Mrs. Palmer looked out the window and said, "There's a truck, it looks like a Jeep parked out on the road, maybe it's the Rangers."

The other two women got up to take a look at this vehicle, hoping that it was, when Olga said, "That's not the Rangers, they wear uniforms."

"Who can it be?" Mrs. Palmer asked.

"Whoever it is, maybe they can help," Laura suggested.

"Oh my God," Olga yelled, "it's him."

"Who?" Laura asked

"Juwal, that means giant," Olga answered, as they saw a tall man standing behind the truck.

"Many people have heard of him," Olga continued, "but very few have ever seen him. He is a bushman."

As they were staring out the window, another man got out of the front passenger seat. He was also an Aborigine.

Back in the Jeep, Nicholas was having a conversation with Philip, as he said, "You won't leave will you, without seeing Mommy? If you do I will come looking for you again."

"No, I will wait," Philip replied. "Now you go and give your mother a big hug. You know you put her through a lot of worry."

"I know," Nicholas said.

The women rushed out on the porch as they saw the man helping a little boy out of the back seat.

The sun was now peering over the trees, as it threw a reflection on the windshield of the truck, making it difficult to see from the lodge.

Philip remained seated behind the wheel as Nicholas started walking and then picked up his pace to running towards the lodge and yelling "Mommy, I'm back!"

At this moment Laura could see that it was her little boy as she ran to meet the open arms of her son. She dropped to her knees as they clutched each other with hugs and kisses, and at the same time she was scolding him for putting her to so much worry.

Philip looked on at this beautiful woman, who had been through so much sorrow, as she reconciled with her son who for the second time in less than a year had escaped a near tragedy.

Nicholas sadly said, "I'm sorry, Mommy, but I had to go, I know now how dangerous it was, and I really got lost, but I didn't want to leave without finding him."

Before Nicholas could finish what he started to tell her, she said, "It's okay now honey," as she kissed his forehead, "we will wait at Jim and Sylvia's place. He will contact them for sure, if he hasn't already."

"No, Mommy, he's here. I found him. He's in the truck."

Laura looked towards the truck and slowly rose to her feet still clutching Nicholas's hand, and for seconds she just stared at this man, who was now standing by the front fender of the Jeep seventy-five feet away, this man who she was still deeply in love with; this man who brought love and excitement into her life; this man who gave her the greatest gift of all, her son's life; this man who she mistakenly judged and sent away.

Now it suddenly hit her, could he ever forgive her? The absence of the past five months may have changed; he may not have the same feelings for her that she has for him. He may have lost hope that she would ever come back.

Within the next few minutes all her questions would be answered, as her son pulled on her hand and said, "Come on Mommy, let's go see him."

They walked slowly towards him, the tears that she had shed for Nicholas were dried, and new ones were falling to her cheeks, as she gazed at this man who was now walking to meet them.

Frank and Kuminja were still standing by the truck looking on at a sight they weren't familiar with. Olga and Mrs. Palmer were also staring from the porch, hoping to see a happy reconciliation.

As they came closer Philip noticed tears flowing over her cheeks, and knew at once that she had never lost her love for him.

His thoughts went back to their first meeting, when he caught himself perplexed by her beauty, and later when they had such incredulous adoration for each other and such passionate absorption in each other's bodies, that neither of them wanted to be parted. Seeing her now, he wondered how he ever got by the past few months without her. When they were within a few feet of each other, they stopped. Nicholas looked up at him with admiration, and Philip's eyes met his gaze, and they both smiled.

The smile left Philip's face, and a sort of frown took its place, as he slowly moved his head back and forth, and with his lips slightly parted, he seemed to be voiceless for something to say, and yet he couldn't wait to hold her in his arms.

Laura broke the silence as she looked directly into his eyes, her face was full of hurt for this man as she cried out, "Oh Philip, I wouldn't blame you if you never want to see me again, but please, please forgive me for judging you the way I did. I had no right, or no excuse for sending you away, I'm sorry, I'm really sorry. I never listened to anyone. Even my good friend Lucy, who never ever judged my decisions, couldn't get through to me, but now I know that they were right, even Nicholas."

As her chin was slightly quivering, and tears were flowing again, Philip took her in his arms and said, "Honey, you did nothing wrong, you have nothing to be sorry for. You had so much on your mind, and like any mother, your first concerns were for your child."

"I'm so proud of you, and now look, the three of us are together, that's if you will have me."

"Oh yes, yes," she said, as they held each other close.

"Gray said that you would act this way," she continued, "not letting me be of blame."

"Well," Philip replied, "he and I can see right through each other. We always could. He's a great friend and a hell of a doctor," as he looked at Nicholas.

Then Philip said as he stepped back, "Look at me, I must look like shit. I've been in the wilderness for the past three weeks, and haven't shaved for a week."

"No, you look beautiful, but you don't smell too well," Laura joked.

"Right," Philip answered, "I need a hot shower and a shave."

Then he continued, "I want you to meet someone," as he took Laura and Nicholas's hand and led them back to where the Jeep was parked.

"This is my friend, Frank. We met on a mail plane three weeks ago and he is my excuse for being here," as he told her about Frank.

After they extended the right hand of friendship, they walked over to where Kuminja was still standing, behind the Jeep with his head bowed and possibly wondering what these strange people were all about.

Philip said, "Laura, I would like you to meet Kuminja. Kuminja, this is my friend Laura."

Frank was there to translate the conversation, as Kuminja seemed to be looking in wonderment.

Laura put out her hand to him, as Philip said, "He saved Nick's life by rescuing him from the dingoes, and carrying him fifteen miles to our camp."

"Thank you. Our prayers will always be with you and you will always be a part of our lives."

The tall man looked down at Nicholas, put his large hand on his head, and a satisfied smile came over his somber face, as he said something in his Aboriginal language that meant "small brave wind." He then touched Laura's outstretched hand with his, turned around and started towards the bush, when Philip said, "Frank, call him back, I have something that I'd like him to have."

Frank spoke out a few words and Kuminja stopped and slowly walked back.

Philip reached in the back of the Jeep and took out a very expensive Horton crossbow with a Bushnell scope attached and a quiver full of arrows.

He walked over to him, with Frank there to interpret, and said, as he handed him the crossbow, "You are a very special man. I am honored to meet you. This gift is very small for what you have done for Nicholas, his mother, and myself. We thank you from the bottom of our hearts, and we will look forward to seeing you again."

He then put out his hand to him.

Holding the gift that Philip gave him in his right hand, he stretched out his left hand and touched Philip's and then drew it back and placed it over his heart.

He looked at Philip, then to Laura, and then he crouched down, his glittering eyes were now fixed on Nicholas as he said, "Ngapung manta purlajumkujuyu." He stood up, touched Nicholas's head, turned around, and in seconds, he disappeared into the bush.

Nicholas came over to where Philip and Laura were standing, held his mother's hand, looked up at her and said, "I know he was sent by the angels."

"Well he sure came at the right time, thank God for that," Laura replied.

"What were the meanings of those words he spoke?" Philip asked Frank.

"First of all he put out his left hand to you, because it is closest to his heart, and the words he spoke were, "May the Spirits bless you."

"The Lord moves in mysterious ways," Philip said.

"Do you think he will come back?" Nicholas asked.

"I'm afraid not Nick," Philip replied. "He has his life here, but he might if he's needed."

"Wouldn't it be neat to take him home with us?" Nicholas suggested. He could play for the Pacers and we could be his manager."

"Now that sounds like a business venture," Philip said, as they all walked hand-in-hand towards the lodge.

Laura turned to Philip and said, "Kuminja; that is a lovely name, isn't it?"

"Yes," Philip replied. "It's very suitable to his character."

Frank spoke out and said, "It is a nice name. In English it means David."

They all stopped in their tracks, looked at each other in amazement as if to say that he was someone specially sent to them. They then looked towards the bush, and in the distance they could see Kuminja with his left hand, high in the air, and then he was gone.

Nicholas looked at his mother and said, "Davey told me that he would watch over me, didn't he Philip?"

"Yes, he did, Nick, and I think he did it twice," Philip replied.

When they reached the lodge, Laura introduced Olga to Philip.

He thanked her for her compassion and guidance, for the safety of Nicholas and Laura and told her when they're back again that they would surely get in touch.

Laura said, as she hugged Olga, "Olga, this is an experience that Nicholas and I will never forget, and we will promise to write you. Thank you for being here for us."

Nicholas hugged her too, and said, "Thank you for helping my mommy and me, and you're the best truck driver in the world."

Olga gave him a kiss on the cheek and said, "I'm sure glad we met. You are both very brave and I will look forward to seeing the three of you again, maybe next year!"

"That sounds like a plan," Philip replied, and they all agreed.

Olga then left.

Philip said to Laura, "There's a few loose ends to finish up at the village. Frank and I and some of the natives are building a small school for the young children from numerous villages, that aren't bused to the school at Hall's Creek"

Frank could see how very much the three of them meant to each other, so he said, "Philip, I can look after everything out here. Most of the work is finished, and you've put enough into this project already. I'm getting a lot of help. We can open it in a week."

"Are you sure, Frank?" Philip asked.

"Absolutely," Frank replied, "but you have to come back and visit us again. Those people at the village have taken quite a liking to you," he added.

"I promise that," Philip said. "I still have to go back to say good-bye to everyone."

"Can we go with you?" Nicholas asked

"Of course you can," Philip answered. "I'm not letting you two out of my sight again."

"I hope not," Laura said, as she squeezed his arm.

"Well," Frank said with relief, "I'll take you back and then drive you to Lake Argyle to catch the afternoon mail plane to Alice Springs."

They left the lodge and got in the jeep. Frank drove, Nicholas sat in front, Philip and Laura sat in the back, with his arm around her, as her head rested on his shoulder.

She looked up at him and said, "I love you, very much, there was never a wall between our hearts."

"Never, and never will be," Philip replied, as he kissed her forehead.

"When we return to Jim and Sylvia's," Philip suggested, "we'll spend a day or so there, if that's okay with you and then home to Valleyfield, where..."

Laura finished the sentence, "Where you will meet me at Millcreek."

The end………for now…..